"Welcome to my life, lovely lady,"

he murmured as she drew up close beside him. "Play for me and bring me luck." With no note of self-protective irony, the words still didn't feel foolish on his lips. Tonight he could say anything, do anything *be* anything.

"But you don't need me to bring you luck," Caroline returned softly, her head tilted so that she could smile up into his eyes. "You've been winning without me. I know—I've been watching you."

He let his dark gaze caress her. "Strange. I haven't felt lucky. Not until now."

Neither one of them was self-conscious about occupying centre stage for their introductory exchange. They were celebrities of the night, charmed people whose purpose was to feed the imagination of those less blessed by fortune. They could speak lines that were less than inspired and bring to them the charisma of their personalities.

Dear Reader,

Spellbinders! That's what we're striving for. The editors at Silhouette are determined to capture your imagination and win your heart with every single book we publish. Each month, six Special Editions are chosen with *you* in mind.

Our authors are our inspiration. Writers such as Nora Roberts, Tracy Sinclair, Kathleen Eagle, Carole Halston and Linda Howard—to name but a few—are masters at creating endearing characters and heart-rending love stories. Their characters are everyday people—just like you and me—whose lives have been touched by love, whose dream and desire suddenly comes true!

So find a cozy, quiet place to read, and create your own special moment with a Silhouette Special Edition.

Sincerely,

Rosalind Noonan
Senior Editor
SILHOUETTE BOOKS

CAROLE HALSTON
Matched Pair

Silhouette Special Edition

Published by Silhouette Books New York

America's Publisher of Contemporary Romance

SILHOUETTE BOOKS
300 East 42nd St., New York, N.Y. 10017

ISBN: 0-373-09328-4

First Silhouette Books printing August 1986

America's Publisher of Contemporary Romance

Printed in the U.S.A.

CAROLE HALSTON

is the wife of a sea captain, and she writes while her husband is at sea. Her characters often share her own love of nature and enjoyment of active outdoor sports. Ms. Halston is an avid tennis player and a dedicated sailor.

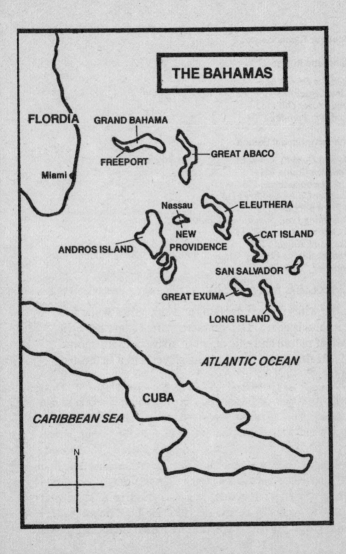

Chapter One

Nick Denton looked up from his glum perusal of the menu and knew even before he sighted his business partner headed his way that Byron had arrived. There was that familiar wave of female awareness rippling through the crowded restaurant. By now Nick had good reason to be used to the effect Byron had upon women, young and old and all ages in between. The two men had been best friends since their undergraduate years at Tulane University. This time, though, in view of particular circumstances in Nick's own personal life—circumstances Byron didn't know about yet—Byron's male charisma seemed in blatant bad taste. It was salt rubbed into a wound, not a wound gushing with blood, admittedly, but one that smarted nevertheless. Nick had been ditched by his girlfriend the night before.

To give Ginger her due, she had tried in a somewhat clumsy fashion to be gentle, to "let him down easy," claiming that her dissatisfaction with their relationship was no reflection upon Nick's character. If anything, he was too much a paragon, considerate and attentive and dependable, the kind of man any girl hoped to settle down with "one of these days." It was just that Ginger wasn't ready to settle down now. For both their sakes, she thought it better if they didn't get any more involved with each other.

"A few years from now I know I'm probably going to hate myself for letting you go," she had lamented with a heartful sigh. "But right now, you're just too nice a man for me, Nick."

Nick was too much a gentleman, too much a product of his old-fashioned Southern upbringing, to voice most of what he was thinking at that moment. He could have pointed out to Ginger that she definitely *wasn't* his ideal of the kind of woman he would want to marry, and he wasn't as heartbroken as she seemed to expect him to be over the prospect of breaking up with her. Her main attraction for him in the first place had been that she *wasn't* his type. Her idea of a home-cooked meal was to pop a frozen pizza into the oven or warm up take-out food in the microwave. Her reading consisted of women's magazines slanted toward fashion and glamour. She tried every fad diet that was published and looked upon exercise as a necessary evil to keep her body in shape, joining whatever expensive spa was popular at the moment.

Nick could have pointed out to Ginger that she wasn't plagued with most of those dull virtues she'd attributed to him. She was not considerate of other people's feelings or routinely punctual and reliable. But then, Nick hadn't been seeking those qualities when he had first asked her out or when he had become intimately involved in an affair with her. She had the kind of figure and looks that caught a man's eye. He was flattered to be seen with her, flattered that she would want to spend time in his company.

In his mind, their relationship had always been temporary. Now that the affair of several months' duration was over, there was relief mingled with emptiness and smarting pride. He could go back now to his comfortable dull routine, which he'd missed. Now that he wouldn't be keeping such late hours, he could start getting up early again and running before he went to the office. It would be nice to spend some evenings at home catching up on his reading. He was tired of eating in restaurants practically every night, too, not to mention that it got expensive. As a matter of fact, his relationship with Ginger had been damned expensive. The CPA in him had been conscious of that fact the whole time.

All these plus-factors still didn't totally ease the pain of being ditched for lacking that indefinable quality that made every woman in the restaurant follow Byron's progress to Nick's table. Feature for feature, Byron wasn't any better looking than Nick. He wasn't any more intelligent or successful, and yet he'd barely had time to sit down before the waitress appeared. Nick had been sitting there five minutes.

"Can I get you gentlemen a drink from the bar?" The smiling question was directed at the sandy-haired man with the lazy blue eyes, not at his dark-haired companion with the intense, angular features and almost black eyes.

"Club soda on the rocks with a twist for me and probably an extra-tall iced tea for my hard-drinking friend here." Byron looked over at Nick with raised eyebrows for confirmation and eyed him quizzically for several seconds after Nick had nodded briefly and the waitress had left. "Don't tell me—let me guess. All our major clients have gone bankrupt. No? Let's see.... Chase Manhattan just raised its prime five points." He smiled expansively and settled back in his chair as Nick grinned grudgingly. "Something not so serious, I see. Well, hurry up and tell me your bad news so I can tell you mine."

Nick shrugged. "Nothing serious, in your book. Ginger and I broke it off last night, that's all. Or rather *she* broke it off. On the grounds that I'm too nice a guy for her." He paused as a party of three young women in their early twenties, readily identifiable as office workers, passed the table in the wake of the hostess. Their casually assessing glances skimmed over himself and rested an infinitesimal second longer on Byron, as the latter looked up with that instinctive male appreciation it seemed no woman could resist.

"You were saying..." Byron grinned in self-deprecation when the group had passed.

Nick shook his head ruefully. "I'd like to spend just one day in your skin and find out what it feels like to have every woman in my path fall for me. Seriously, what's your secret? Just what is it that they see in you—"

He paused again as the waitress served their drinks and then took their food order. "See what I mean?" he demanded dryly when she'd whisked away. "Why should a guy drinking club soda get more attention than a guy drinking iced tea?"

Byron swirled the nonalcoholic contents of his glass and took a deep gulp. "Your problem, Nick, is that you have too much respect for women. That's what comes from growing up in the upper crust of small-town Mississippi society. Your mamma taught you too many manners." He drank another gulp of club soda and made a satisfied sound. "Seriously. A man can't do what women *say* they want him to do. He's got to do what deep down they really *want* him to do. Most of the time when they say, 'no, no,' they really mean 'yes, yes.'"

"You mean when Ginger told me I was too nice for her, I should have thrown her down on the floor and made brutal love to her to prove I *wasn't* too nice?"

Byron was so obviously entertained by his own private vision of such unlikely behavior on the part of his good friend and business partner that Nick rather self-consciously changed the subject. "So what's your bad news? Did you end up with two dates tonight instead of one?"

Byron's expression grew instantly morose. "Worse damned luck. After I lucked out and got booked on that Freeport gambling junket for next week, it looks like the Cranston audit is going to drag on, after all." He quickly raised both hands palm out to ward off the response he could read on Nick's face. "I know, I know. You warned me that it would. I was hoping my luck would hold."

"Are you positive at this point that you won't be able to finish up the audit in time to go?"

"Positive."

During Byron's elaboration of his reply, the food arrived, and both men were busy eating for several moments. Nick picked up the conversation about the canceled Bahamian trip between bites of his mushroom burger and onion rings.

"Can you still get a refund on your money? You had to pay the full amount in advance, didn't you?"

Byron let his nod and careless shrug serve as an answer until he had swallowed his mouthful of food. "Only if somebody else fills my place. It's not the money I mind. The total price on the trip was a real bargain since the Royal International Casino is sponsoring the whole thing. Naturally they hope to make up that amount and a lot more at the gambling tables and slots. I was just looking forward to getting away to the tropics for a week, making my fortune in the casino, meeting some gorgeous, sexy heiress . . ."

His sigh matched the cheerful resignation on his face, which changed to good-natured reproach as he eyed his companion's steady consumption of food. "Glad to see my bad news—and yours—haven't ruined your appetite. Of course, I wasn't really expecting sympathy from Mr. Perfect. It goes without saying that you'd never book a trip without being sure you could take off."

He stared reflectively at Nick, examining the idea that had just struck him. "Say, why don't *you* take the trip to Freeport in my place? You don't have anything really pressing next week, do you? Nothing that couldn't be put off a few days?" Byron grinned delightedly when Nick choked on his bite of food and had to gulp down several great swallows of iced tea. "You were sitting there thinking that same thing, weren't you?" he guessed shrewdly.

Not for anything was Nick going to admit that his mental processes didn't come under the category of *thinking* at all, but daydreaming. Byron had interrupted him right in the middle of an imaginary scene that would have done Walter Mitty up proud. Looking like a rakish, daredevil version of himself, Nick had been about to debark from a chartered plane in the Bahamas. It was acutely embarrassing for one who was so definitely not the Walter Mitty type to be discovered in the midst of such weakness.

"I can't just go off to the Bahamas on the spur of the moment—" As a result of the choking spell, Nick's voice was strained, robbing it of the desired dignity. He had to pause and clear his throat vigorously, while the gleam of inspiration in Byron's eyes burned stronger.

"Why not?" Byron demanded cheerfully. "Who's to keep you from it? All you have to do is make up your mind, pack a bag and climb on the plane, come Monday morning." Sprawling back comfortably in his chair, he grinned, which served as a warning to Nick. "Tell you what, I'll even do your packing for you. No oxford-cloth shirts with button-down collars, no club ties or cordovan loafers. We're going for a flashier style that's going to have all the ladies sitting up and taking notice. I'll lend you a couple of silk shirts and a gold chain. Hell, I'll even make you a present of the brand-new swimsuit I just bought for this trip." The grin on Byron's face accompanying this latter generous offer threatened to split his face in two.

"Thanks," Nick said dryly. "I happen to have some swimsuits of my own."

"So take one of them along, too." Byron waved one hand in an expansive gesture. "If it'll make you feel better, we can even tuck in a striped shirt with a button-down collar, kind of a security blanket. Take it from me, though, you won't even be tempted to put it on once you get to Freeport and slide into that decadent tropical atmosphere."

"Hey, I haven't said definitely I was going—"

"Look, man, not fifteen minutes ago you were saying you'd like to feel what it's like being in my skin. So here's your chance. Go for it. Climb on that chartered plane and have the time of your life in my place, while I'm back here in New Orleans plugging away. Just pretend you're me, and do or say whatever I'd do or say in a given situation." His grin was lewdly suggestive. "What the hell? Nobody'll ever be the wiser." He tossed his napkin on the table with a casual finality that said he wouldn't argue any further. It was up to Nick now to make up his mind.

Nick used up several seconds folding his napkin before he laid it carefully on the table and then arranged and rearranged its position. "You make it sound so easy," he said reluctantly. "But a guy can't change the way he is inside, no matter how much he might like to. Striped ties and button-down collars, that's me. Always on time. Never forget birthdays. Conscientious to a fault."

"And a hell of a nice guy to have for a friend and a partner," Byron put in quickly.

"Oh, sure, a nice guy, not to mention dull, predictable, boring." Nick was uncomfortable with the ring of bitterness in his voice. He hadn't meant the conversation to get quite so deeply personal. To cover up his embarrassment he looked around for their waitress to signal her to bring them the check and didn't see the shrewd thoughtfulness that Byron quickly screened from his expression.

"Well, it's up to you, whether you want to go on this trip or not," Byron said offhandedly. "It's not fair for me to pressure you just to save myself from dropping several hundred bucks. I should have listened to your advice and not made the reservation, in the first place."

"It's possible that somebody might turn up and want to take your place."

"Sure, it's possible," Byron agreed skeptically.

The waitress came with the check. While Nick looked it over, automatically totaling the charges, the idle conversation between Byron and the waitress intruded upon his concentration. It was the unspoken messages in their tones that he heard, not the actual words, elemental messages men and women exchange to confirm their pleasure in relating to a member of the opposite sex.

Nick felt suddenly terribly alone, excluded. He thought of the evening ahead without any plans and tried to banish a pang of emptiness with the reminder that he was not a stranger in town. He had friends, numerous contacts. If he wanted company, he could get something up, even on short notice.

Maybe he should take a few days off, go somewhere and have a complete change of scene. As Byron had pointed out, his schedule happened to be pretty light at the moment. Why not take the Bahama trip? He'd be doing Byron a favor, and the trip was a real bargain. Not that he would go along with this business of pretending to be Byron. As much as he might like to slip into Byron's shoes for a week, Nick just wasn't the silk-shirt-and-gold-chain type.

He wasn't the type to lapse into daydreams, either, but for the second time in the past hour, Nick escaped from a painful present into pleasant fantasy. As he took out his wallet and extracted from it a charge card, before his eyes flashed a rakish vision of himself. Wearing sleek dark trousers and a burgundy silk shirt open at the neck to show the luster of a gold medallion against his swarthy skin, he was a modern-day Zorro minus the mask and rapier. Gone from his dark eyes was the usual sober, penetrating expression. They gleamed with a reckless light, and a half smile of daring curved his lips as he leaned over a roulette table in a crowded casino and placed his bets. With the long-fingered, deft hands of the gambler, he coolly laid out his entire stack of chips, betting everything on a single turn of the wheel.

The wheel turned round and round. The rapid staccato clicking slowed in the vacuum of a great hush, as everyone waited with indrawn breath. The silence was broken by exclamations as it became apparent that the tall, dark gambler had won and won big. But he was paying little attention to the stacks of chips the croupier was shoving over in front of him. He had looked up and met the rapt, admiring glance of the most sophisticated, beautiful woman he had ever seen, an exquisite blonde wearing black....

Nick came to his senses to find both Byron and the waitress regarding him curiously as he sat staring at his American Express card, held firmly between thumb and forefinger.

"She'll bring it back to you, honest," Byron quipped dryly. "He's a certified public account," he explained to the waitress, as though Nick suffered from some rare and terminal disease. "They don't trust anybody where money's concerned, you know."

Nick flashed his friend a rare, spontaneous smile that completely transformed his features and brought surprised interest to the face of the waitress as she turned away. The excitement that burned in his dark eyes deepened Byron's curiosity at the unexpected change in mood.

"She'd better bring it back," Nick said, still smiling. "I'm probably going to need it next week when I'm in the Bahamas."

A huge grin broke out over Byron's face. "Hell, I doubt you'll need it. After one trip to the casino, you'll probably be paying for everything with chips!"

"Probably."

Caroline Ainsley's bedroom was large and high ceilinged with tall windows framed by lacy curtains that stirred gently with the early morning breeze. The colors in the room were all muted and feminine, soft violets and blues and pinks, brought together in the floral pattern of the satin comforter neatly folded back at the end of her antique iron-and-brass bed. The rest of the furniture was all antiques, too, graceful in design and of obvious good quality. It had that used, but well-cared-for look of good furniture that has been in a family for generations, not sought out in antique stores or bought on the block at estate sales. On the tops of the dresser and chest of drawers were scarves of fine linen with delicate stitches and handmade lace from the same bygone era as the furniture. The scarves had been in the family for years, too, more than likely the handiwork of female ancestors. Arranged atop the scarves was a feminine clutter of crystal bottles and porcelain boxes and figurines.

It was a charming room, but unrelentingly feminine, with not a single compromising masculine touch. A man pausing at the threshold would hesitate to venture inside. He would feel like an intruder, overpowered by the sheer feminine excess, the fussy ruffles, the neat profusion of fragile objects, the chaste colors. Even the young woman lying in the bed under the lace appliquéd sheet did nothing to dispel the virginal quality of her surroundings. Curled on her side with her face turned into the pillow, blond hair tousled, she did not look relaxed and softly feline in sleep, tempting a man to slide in under the sheet beside her. Her slender body, even in slumber was apparently guarded against a male attack upon her purity, here in her citadel of female virtue.

Actually Caroline wasn't asleep at all, but waging a stubborn, losing battle with her wakefulness. "Darn!" she muttered irritably, flinging back the sheet and sitting up on the edge of her bed. "Why can't you sleep, you nitwit?" she demanded of herself, eyeing in frustration the face of the exquisite little porcelain bedside clock, a Christmas present from Aunt Sarah two years before. "School is out for the summer. You don't have to get up at six-thirty and get dressed. You can sleep until noon, if you want to." She ran punishing fingers through her blond hair, shoving it back from her face. In the dignified quietness of the big old house, some desperate undertone in her voice mocked her.

With a sigh she relinquished her irritation and sat there, shoulders sagging beneath the thin lawn fabric of her nightgown, the dusky-pink color blending harmoniously with the decorating scheme. Looking around the room that had been hers for the entire twenty-eight years of her life, she found in it no pleasure or comfort. Bearing the stamp of her personality as it did, it seemed not a citadel or a haven, but a prison. And she was her own jailer, holding the keys. More so than ever now that Aunt Sarah was gone. After six months the rawness of grief had eased, leaving sadness and a void she had to decide how to fill now that she was alone.

It was silly of her to feel trapped, when really she wasn't. She was still young and not yet so set in a pattern of existence that she couldn't change. She didn't have to stay there, in that house, in the small Louisiana town, entrenched in all that was familiar and safe and dull. The whole world out there was open to her. She could move elsewhere, perhaps to a large city, which would be a complete change of lifestyle. There she could either continue her elementary schoolteacher's career or go into some other type of work.

Yes, change was entirely possible. There was no arguing with that fact. The problem was one of inertia. It was all well and good to think in general, sweeping terms about changing one's life for the better, opting for challenge and excitement. But it wasn't easy to know how to take the specific steps to bring about change, to decide the where, what, when and how. Caroline was sitting right where she was on this early June morning, faced with her own set of personal difficulties, because she had her entire life always done what was for her the "easy" thing. She had always followed the course of least resistance rather than brave the unknown. It wasn't going to be easy to break out of the mold. It might not even be possible. That was what scared her.

As a young child she had always sought approval, first from her aunt, who had reared her from infancy, and her aunt's circle of friends, most of them well-to-do spinsters like Aunt Sarah or widows. Then there had been teachers to please and mothers of girlfriends and the outside world in general. Life was just so pleasant and easy when one was being admired and liked. Tact and diplomacy came naturally; "white lies" were necessary not to hurt people's feelings and didn't come under the heading of hypocrisy. It was easier and safer to adopt and uphold accepted moral values than to question them and risk the hazards of censure and possible damage to one's person and reputation.

In her twenty-eight years, Caroline had managed with ease to avoid gossip and criticism, and only now was beginning to wonder about the price. Never an *A* student, she had always been solidly in the *B*-average category, admired but safe from hurtful envy. Because she wasn't a "goody-goody" in her attitude, everyone accepted her own impeccable moral standards, even the boys she dated in high school and later in college. She never stole, cheated, lied unless it was to spare someone's feelings, cut class, failed to keep her room neat or went "all the way" with a boyfriend. Saying no to any temptation to compromise her morals became second nature. Keeping her virginity intact wasn't even a big issue, it was just a continuation of her ingrained policy of living life according to the rules she'd been taught, her premise being: do what everybody wants, and they'll all love you.

What she hadn't foreseen and what now seemed shockingly unfair was that the sexual purity she'd guarded automatically through the years might eventually become a source of shame for her. Somehow the years had slipped by, she was twenty-eight and unmarried, and thus well on her way to small-town "old maid" status. She'd only become aware of that fact upon the death of her aunt six months before, when underneath all the sympathy and neighborhood support, she sensed an undercurrent of pity and divined its source. Everyone assumed that Caroline would follow in her aunt's footsteps, live out her life unmarried, devoted to high principles of conduct and worthwhile service to the community. She would continue to teach third grade, continue to support Aunt Sarah's favorite charitable causes, continue to attend services at the Episcopal Church, continue to be a good neighbor and never cause a breath of scandal. In short, she would continue to be the person she'd become to gain admiration and acceptance—not pity.

For the first time in her life, Caroline experienced resentment and rebellion. She didn't want anyone feeling sorry for her. It was degrading. Why, she would show them—all of them—that she wasn't stuck in a mold. She had options, lots of options, including marriage. Didn't they all realize that she could have married Arthur Potter as early as two years before, if she'd wanted to? He had become discouraged and ceased his courtship efforts, but she knew she could renew them with a phone call on some pretext or a deliberate chance encounter. It wasn't as if she was unmarried because she hadn't had any chances!

Everyone would approve the match between herself and Arthur, too, even though he was almost twenty years her senior, a widower with a son in college. He was a respected local businessman whose family history went back several generations in Covington. Certainly not fabulously wealthy, but well-to-do, he could provide Caroline with a gracious, comfortable life, and she needn't continue to teach unless she chose. He wasn't an unattractive man, either, despite the small paunch of middle age his suit jackets didn't quite hide.

Unfortunately he was as dull as he was decent and solid and likable. His idea of a big social evening was a civic-club banquet. Caroline had suffered through several of those as his date and been bored to tears. She'd also been rather bored by his kisses and caresses, all within the bounds of propriety. The thought of going to bed with Arthur was anything but exciting, but then she wasn't sure at this moment whether the problem lay with Arthur. Maybe there was something wrong with her. Surely one of the men she had dated should have had the power to awaken wild arousal. Perhaps she was one of those cold women who would never warm to a man's touch. Perhaps she was frigid and that was why it had always been easy for her to say no.

It wasn't an explanation that eased Caroline's turbulent state of mind about herself and her future, but her common sense told her that whether it was true or not true, she couldn't just sit there and brood about it. The answer wasn't there in that room. It was in the world outside somewhere, along with a lot more answers she wasn't at all sure she wanted to face. In the meantime there was the comfort of routine. She'd have her morning coffee and read the daily paper, just as she did every morning, whether school was in session or not. During the summers she was just able to take her time.

With her feet shod in wedge-heeled satin slippers and her nightgown modestly covered by a pretty ankle-length robe whose blue-gray color was a shade lighter than her eyes, Caroline stopped to comb her short blond hair into its neat, casual style before she went downstairs and through the central hallway to the front door, opening out onto a wide veranda. No one was passing on the quiet tree-shaded street as she took several steps out onto the veranda and stooped to pick up the newspaper in its cellophane envelope. If someone had been driving or walking by, that person probably would have been a neighbor, and probably would have sensed that Caroline still felt odd going out to get the paper herself, even though she'd been doing it now for a year in all, since Aunt Sarah had been bedridden the six months prior to her death. Always before, she would have been up before Caroline and sitting out in the cheery little glassed-in room off the kitchen, drinking her morning coffee and reading the newspaper when Caroline came down.

Strange how the little memories kept hurting, Caroline thought sadly as she made her way back to the kitchen. Yet it was true what people said, that time helped erase grief. She'd accepted the fact that Aunt Sarah was gone. She wouldn't have had her aunt linger any longer, not in a state of pain. Now it just remained for Caroline to get on with her life, alone.

Once she'd settled herself comfortably in one of the deep wicker chairs out on the sun porch, her coffee cup close at hand, Caroline opened up the paper and began a thorough perusal of the first section, doing her best to ignore the fact that she was deliberately taking her time, making the process of reading the paper last. After all, she had all morning. All day, for that matter. There was nothing pressing to do, and after the flurry of winding up the school year, getting all her grades turned in, cleaning up her classroom and taking care of loose ends, time hung heavy on her hands.

By the time she'd worked her way through the paper to the travel section, she'd had several cups of coffee and several brief conversations with herself over news items. It was becoming a habit to talk out loud like that, one that made her feel silly. But it served the purpose of breaking the silence of the house.

"Maybe what you need is to take a trip," she mused, not just scanning the travel pages as she usually did, but stopping to read the smaller print. It was just an idle comment, but the thought took hold as she reflected that she could easily afford any one of several very reasonably priced package trips that included airfare and hotel accommodations, as well as added perks such as sightseeing tours. Maybe what she did need was to get away, leave all her discontent and uncertainty behind her and simply enjoy herself for a week or two. Gosh, that sounded good, if she didn't allow herself to think about the fact that she would be going alone.

The trip to the Bahamas appealed to her more than the trip to Ireland or to Las Vegas. And it was incredibly inexpensive. There had to be a catch to it, she was sure, but she could call the travel agency and check, anyway. What was there to lose, but her time, and she had plenty of that. The number was toll free, and the call wouldn't cost her anything. If everything was on the up and up, she just might take the trip. There wasn't anything to prevent her other than lack of courage.

Deep down, Caroline knew that going off on some package vacation trip to a tropical island by herself was just a fantasy, but it was a pleasant, if fleeting, escape from the present. She let her mind drift and supply vague, alluring details about what such a trip would be like as she went upstairs and got dressed, waiting for the time to pass until it was late enough to expect the travel-agency offices to be open. When she made the call, the eagerness in her own voice came as something of a shock.

"I'd like some information about the trip to Grand Bahama Island advertised in this morning's *Times Picayune*," she told a woman named Mary who answered the phone for Travel Worldwide in New Orleans.

"The Freeport trip!" Mary exclaimed in a gravelly smoker's voice. "It's the greatest travel bargain available at this time. I can recommend it personally since I've recently taken the trip myself. The hotel accommodations are very nice, whether you stay at the Royal International or the Royal Tower. Both are located in easy walking distance of the casino and the International Bazaar, for shopping. I stayed at the Tower but actually spent most of my time during the day over at the pool at the Resort. It's something right out of a movie. There's this adorable man-made island of huge boulders right in the middle with waterfalls and a tunnel and a cave—it's too hard to explain with words. You'll just have to see it for yourself! And right at poolside there's an open-air restaurant, thatched roof and all, and a little open-air bar with a native band playing island music. It was just wonderful!" Mary's loud sigh underlined her genuine enthusiasm.

"At night you have the casino, of course," she went on. "It's so exciting to see people put down hundred-dollar bills like they're nothing! Then there's a great show with two performances every night. You get a free ticket for that, plus a coupon for twenty dollars' worth of coins for the slot machines or chips to gamble with. You don't have to dress formal, but lots of people do, and it just adds something to see the men in their tux and the women in their evening dresses and jewelry...." Mary heaved a sigh. "Honestly, this Freeport trip is the greatest bargain going. The only thing is—"

"I knew there had to be a catch." The regret in Caroline's voice was so real that she felt vaguely guilty for her hypocrisy. "It was just too cheap to be true."

"It's cheap because it's off-season, and the owners of the Royal International Casino, who also own the two hotels, would rather have people there to gamble than to have the whole place empty. It's worth their while to provide transportation and use of the hotel facilities for practically nothing. For one thing, people know that they've gotten such a bargain that they can justify gambling more than they ordinarily would."

"There is no catch, then." Caroline was carefully noncommittal, ready to put Mary off when she pressed Caroline for her decision.

"The only catch is that it's booked solid for the rest of the summer."

"Booked for the summer!" Caroline wailed in dismay. "Why did you tell me all about it then? Why is it being advertised in the paper?"

"I'm sorry. I should have explained sooner," Mary apologized. "The trip is still available, but only if there's a cancellation. I can put your name on my waiting list, if you like, and let you know the instant an opening comes up. Of course, you have to be able to travel on a few days' notice. Most people just aren't that flexible with their time." It was obvious to Caroline from Mary's tone that she didn't expect Caroline to want her name added to the waiting list. Mary's instincts had apparently told her that Caroline wasn't one of the flexible travelers, able to climb aboard a plane on short notice. The woman's insight irritated Caroline and raised a perverse instinct.

"I'm free all summer," she announced. "You can put my name down and let me know if there's a cancellation."

She was pleased with her daring afterward and unthreatened by the stance she had taken. If an opening should occur and the woman should happen to call back, Caroline could always say something had come up. She didn't *have* to take the trip just because she was on a standby list.

Meanwhile her spirits were much improved. Feeling quite cheerful, she went over to the town library and checked out a travel book that included the Bahamas and then circled by a local travel agency and picked up brochures. It didn't really matter that she wasn't actually going to the Bahamas. She could enjoy the pretense that she was. With the greatest fascination she read about interesting sights she wasn't likely to see and studied glossy photographs, saturating her senses with the colors and scenes that made the Bahamas seem a tropical paradise and the men and women who went there suntanned gods and goddesses. It wouldn't really be like that, she knew, but what was the harm of letting her imagination run free as a respite from everyday reality? She desperately needed a break.

In that self-indulgent state of mind, Caroline was sitting out on the veranda that afternoon, immersed in an intriguing daydream about herself off in the Bahamas when the phone rang. The elements of her daydream were rather typical fantasy for a single young woman imagining herself on a tropical vacation. There was a white beach and clear blue-green water and herself looking stunning in a daring one-piece swimsuit of shocking pink and black. All around her was a rippling of masculine interest. She was filled with leisurely anticipation, a pleasurable sense of fate and a heady feminine confidence that some attractive man was going to step forward. There was no hurry for him to materialize, though. She was content for a while to luxuriate in the sensation of being incredibly seductive, incredibly confident of her female allure. Caroline had never felt like that in real life and never reached quite this intensity of imagining what it would feel like.

She came back to the present most unwillingly to go inside and answer the phone. The caller's identity came as an awakening shock.

"This is Mary at Travel Worldwide. I have wonderful news. We have a single cancellation on the Freeport trip, departing from New Orleans on Monday and returning on Sunday. Are you still interested?"

Caroline gripped the phone tighter, unable to tell whether the wave of emotion hitting her was excitement or panic. "A cancellation," she repeated dazedly. "Could I call you in the morning and let you know..."

Mary was sympathetic, but firm. "I'm afraid you'll have to let me know one way or the other this afternoon. I have several others that called today after you did." She paused a moment, waiting and then gave her own interpretation to Caroline's agitated silence. "I know it's awfully short notice. Why don't you call again in the next day or two? Perhaps we can work out another nice trip somewhere else with reasonable rates."

The dismissal in her voice stirred Caroline to panicky speech. "No, wait! I've decided to take the trip!"

The details were settled before her heartbeat had had time to return to normal. It was one of the easiest transactions of Caroline's life, once the initial agonizing decision was made. She didn't even have to withdraw money from her bank account. She had only to give her credit-card number.

Afterward she went out to the veranda again, murmuring aloud several times, "I can't believe you're really doing this." Seated again in the swing at one end of the veranda, she closed her eyes and prepared to concentrate hard, but it wasn't necessary to expend any great effort in assembling the scattered fragments of the disrupted daydream. The scene came back with its vivid colors and its heady sensations. The man was still just out of sight in the background, and that fact still was of no concern. He was there, potentially under her spell, and would appear. What mattered was Caroline's own delicious awareness of herself, her sense of earthy freedom, her frank acknowledgment of her sexuality.

The daydream was the key to what she most longed to find in the Bahamas. Not simply a handsome man to sweep her off her feet. That was part of the romantic fantasy, but not the crucial part. She wished with all her heart to discover in herself the tantalizing woman of her imaginings and let that woman free. For a few days, at least, she'd like to step outside the mold of propriety in which she'd cast herself, drop her inhibitions and be a sexy, fascinating woman who could attract and hold the attention of a worldly man, the kind of man she'd never known before.

With that insight, Caroline was ready for her man to step out of the shadows, and when he did, she understood why she hadn't been able to see him on the beach. He was a man of the night, a gambler, tall and dark and dangerous. She shivered when his eyes met hers, burning with his desire. There in the depths was the flattering message that he had been in all the exciting places of the world, seeking pleasure and thrills, and never until now had he found a woman to challenge him as she did...

Back on the veranda in Covington, dusk was falling. The mosquitoes were out, making their pesky presence known with high-pitched humming. It seemed to Caroline fortunate that she had reached a good place to break off the daydream. Gathering up her travel book and the brochures, she went inside and gave her attention over to practical matters. There was much to be done in the next few days: shopping, packing, contacting those who needed to know of her absence. She would do well to sit down right now and make herself a checklist.

Chapter Two

Nick felt self-conscious as hell wearing the gaudy gold rope chain. The thing seemed to weigh a ton. It was like a noose around his neck. Thinking that he'd get used to the feel of it and forget about it after a while, he had put it on first thing when he was out of the shower and ready to get dressed and venture over to the casino for his first taste of gambling.

His nerve almost failed him when he reached into the closet for a shirt. It was an act of physical courage to leave the pale blue oxford cloth hanging there and take the burgundy silk instead. From the grim set of his features as he buttoned the shirt and tucked it neatly into the waistband of beltless dark trousers, Nick might have been attiring himself for some social ordeal.

Disappointingly, that was pretty much the way he felt. He knew this wasn't going to work. He was only going to feel like an awful fool, going out dressed up like a fifth-rate actor playing the rake in a Grade Z movie. But he'd never be able to go back to New Orleans and face Byron if he didn't at least give it a shot to step out of character, for once. And what was there to lose? As Byron had pointed out several times during the past week, Nick wouldn't know a soul down here. If he did make a fool of himself, who would ever be the wiser?

Earlier in the afternoon he had gone over to the casino as himself, conservative Nick Denton, and cased it out. As he wandered through the large main gaming room, familiarizing himself with the layout, he had felt like a total alien. The gaming tables with their satiny polished wood and discreet green felt surfaces had been virtually deserted at that hour, but the slot machines, all flashing lights and gleaming metal lined up one after the other like greedy little robots, had been surprisingly busy. There had been perfectly ordinary-looking men and women, dressed in comfortable shoes and slacks or shorts, plying them with coin after coin.

Strolling past them, hands thrust deep in the pockets of his tailored chino slacks, Nick had felt a blend of pity and scorn for them and for himself. They were fools, he had thought, throwing away their money in the hope of being one of the lucky ones and beating the odds. He was just as big a fool, but in a different way. The very idea of a dull, ordinary guy like himself taking on a totally different personality was preposterous. Nick's vision of himself as a Dark, Dangerous Gambler had vanished, now that he was where that alter ego could have emerged. Not that he had ever really believed in it. He knew that people were trapped in their own personalities.

Despite his pessimism, Nick would have to go through the motions of the charade anyway. If he didn't, he'd feel like a damned moral coward. Nick always did what he said he was going to do. Byron had been banking on that fact as he exacted promises from Nick the past week. *Okay, pal, if I lend*

you this chain, you're going to wear it. Right? "Okay, okay,
I've said at least a dozen times I'll wear the damned chain,"
Nick had answered in exasperation.

Nick's nerve did fail him when it came to deciding
whether he'd wear the new cream-colored jacket. He fin-
gered the silk blend fabric, thinking the damned stuff ought
to feel good. The jacket had cost enough. Reasoning that
surely he was flashy enough in the burgundy silk shirt, dark
trousers and gold chain without the added flamboyance of
a white jacket—and a jacket wasn't required in the casino—
he left it on the hanger and steeled himself to go out and
endure the evening.

He wasn't just bargaining for a few extra seconds as he
walked around the spacious hotel room and turned out all
the lights except a wall-mounted lamp between the two
queen-size beds, which he switched to its lowest beam. Even
though Nick wasn't paying the electricity bill, he didn't see
any sense in just squandering energy. It was this ingrained
thriftiness that was responsible for the rekindling of the
spirit of adventure that had died that afternoon in the
casino. As he was about to leave the room, Nick glimpsed
himself in the dresser mirror and stopped short, staring at
his reflection.

In the dimness the man he saw was a stranger, not himself. The dark hair and eyes and lean height were familiar,
but that panther sleekness wasn't anything Nick had ever
associated with himself. The heavy gold chain gleaming
softly around his neck made the kind of bold statement of
male vanity that Nick knew he would never have the courage to make. It was odd and exhilarating to see himself
transformed into this vaguely familiar stranger, even if it
was all a trick of light.

Nick grinned at himself in the mirror as though his reflection were someone he'd like to make friends with. The
reflection grinned back, and the flash of white teeth made

the image raffish and devil-may-care. When Nick murmured aloud, feeling foolish as hell but even more exhilarated, "Come on, pal, let's go to the casino," his alter ego was sardonic and amused, but plainly ready to go along with Nick and take up any challenge.

The feeling of accompanying a bolder companion persisted as Nick made his exit from the Royal International Hotel and walked the short distance over to the casino. It made him more amused than self-conscious when he attracted frequent curious glances along the way, from both men and women alike. Some of the women were quite attractive, and several had blond hair, but none of them was the stunning blonde of his fantasy. He hadn't caught a glimpse of her since his arrival in Freeport.

Her absence didn't lessen his anticipation, though, since he hadn't really come to Freeport expecting to realize his daydream. It was highly unlikely that a woman like the one conjured up by his imagination would be unattached and available, even if she was here. She'd have a rich, powerful man glued to her shoulder. And the truth was that Nick wasn't quite ready to encounter her yet anyway. The change in his identity was too new.

If he'd gone over to the casino that evening as himself, Nick would undoubtedly have eased into gambling even more cautiously than he did, probably cashing in the twenty-dollar voucher he'd been given as part of the package trip and getting coins for playing the slots, with the hope of hitting a jackpot he could use for more adventurous gambling. Instead, he took the twenty dollars in chips and bought another eighty dollars' worth with his own money. Then he ventured over to the blackjack tables and picked out one with a five-dollar minimum bet, the lowest.

He'd done his homework and knew that blackjack, or Twenty-one, was a game not just of luck but also of some judgment, since a player had the choice of taking additional cards or staying with the cards dealt him, the goal being to get a face value of twenty-one or as close as possible. Anything over twenty-one was an automatic loss to the house.

The first few hands Nick felt so conspicuously out of place perched on the high stool at the semicircular table that he had difficulty concentrating on his cards. He bet one chip at a time, winning and losing about half and half, until gradually the sense of sticking out as a rank novice faded. A camaraderie grew up among himself and the other four or five people at the table because they were all pitting themselves against the house in the person of the dealer. They weren't competing with each other.

When a waitress appeared at the table, Nick ordered a gin and tonic and drank it like it was water. Now he was betting two chips on a hand and sometimes three or four, following an instinct that grew sharper and sharper. He just *knew* whether to motion the dealer to hit him with a card or stay. His stack of chips grew into four and five and six stacks. Time melted away, and he was pleasurably aware of being the object of attention. Background comments that he was "hot" came to his ears. He ordered another gin and tonic and drank it down, but he gave no credit to the alcohol for the exhilaration that pulsed through him. It was luck, pure and simple luck. Tonight was his night. He was "hot." He could feel it. He knew the precise instant when it was time to leave the blackjack table and move on. With his winnings he could afford to try out some of the other tables. He wanted to give roulette a try.

It was at the roulette table that Caroline saw him from her place at the fringe of a crowd of watchers. Her heart began to pump madly because he might have stepped straight out of her daydream back on the front veranda of the big house in staid Covington, Louisiana. Here he was in the flesh, her man of the night, sophisticated, worldly, totally at home in this alien world of the casino, where she couldn't begin to imagine the monetary value of all the stacks of chips in different colors.

He came as even more of a shock than he would have been otherwise because of the jangled state of her nerves. Without even realizing it, Caroline was slightly inebriated. She had ordered a bottle of wine with her dinner earlier at one of the Royal International Hotel's elegant restaurants and drunk several glasses of it. Then, upon her arrival here at the casino, she had bought herself a daiquiri at the bar. She was accustomed only to an occasional glass of wine or cocktail—she didn't especially enjoy the taste of alcohol— but knew that drinking alcoholic beverages was associated with the new sophisticated image she was hoping to project. Alcohol was also generally believed to help one relax and let down his or her inhibitions. For the first time in her life Caroline wanted to let down her inhibitions.

Except for a little light-headedness that she got used to after a while, Caroline was disappointed to find that alcohol apparently didn't do its trick for her as it did for some people. She didn't feel in the least relaxed. The light from the crystal chandeliers overhead seemed brighter than it should have been, the noises of the casino loud. All her senses were too sharply on the alert rather than pleasurably soothed. Restlessly she wandered from one gaming table to another, watching, not enjoying herself but not knowing what else to do but stay there a while longer. She was certainly in no mood to go back to her room and go to sleep.

And then there he was, totally unexpected, larger than life, the man of her fantasy, seeming like some worldly apotheosis. With no thought of possibly attracting his attention, Caroline worked her way nearer to the table so that she could watch him at closer range. For the moment she'd completely forgotten the new sophisticated appearance she'd worked so hard to achieve in preparation for just such a chance occasion as this and then felt self-conscious about all evening—worrying if the eye shadow and red lipstick looked cheap, if the fashionable designer jewelry was too showy, most of all, if the deep V neckline of her black dress was indecent. This was her first time to show such a generous amount of cleavage, and she simply wasn't used to having men look at her chest with such blatant interest. She found it difficult to keep from covering herself with her hand.

Standing just a few yards away from the tall, dark man on the opposite side of the roulette table, Caroline had no feeling of self-consciousness or boldness as she quite frankly stared at him. He was too engrossed in the betting drama to be aware of her presence up on the front-row seat of this thrilling real-life theatrical performance. He was the star of the performance with the biggest part and top billing, and she was just a spellbound member of the audience. It was perfectly within the bounds of propriety for her to fix her eyes upon him, note every sensual little detail of his appearance and file each one away, the stuff for later fantasy.

He was several inches taller than anyone else at the table and very lean of build, with long arms and deft long-fingered hands that fascinated her with their utter sureness as he would pick up a stack of chips and disperse them swiftly on the numbered squares, hieroglyphs of a mysterious, decadent culture for Caroline. It fascinated her all the more that he was a prince of that culture, someone who had lived entirely beyond the pale of her ordinary, mundane life. For her, money came in the form of a printed check or sober greenbacks and was to be used judiciously in exchange for life's necessities and luxuries. This man had stacked in front of him little disks that he could trade in for more than her monthly paycheck, and they were obviously just pieces in a game of chance for him.

She watched with a mixture of admiration and horror as he recklessly scooped up stack after stack of the chips and spread them liberally over the board to the accompaniment of the croupier's bored advice, "Ladies and gentlemen, please place your bets." In front of him now was only one small stack of chips. He was betting literally hundreds of dollars on one spin of the wheel.

Caroline drew in her breath along with everyone else either playing or watching at the table. She was dizzily aware of the collective suspense as the roulette wheel turned, a movement of the cosmos, while she and the other watchers were frozen in time and place, spectators appointed to await the verdict of chance upon one much bolder than they. It seemed to her that the rays from the crystal chandelier overhead concentrated themselves solely upon the man who was the flesh and blood figment of her fantasies. The light glanced off his black hair and shimmered down over his shoulders and arms and chest to bring to life the rich dark silk of his shirt that molded itself to his body like a lustrous skin. Caroline's fingertips tingled with the dangerous urge to touch him and burn herself with the heat of that life pulsing out from him. The heavy gold chain around his neck would feel like molten gold, searing the flesh.

As the staccato clicking slowed and the tiny white ball was about to come to a rest on a lucky number, Caroline took in a deep breath to calm her excited senses and fortify herself for whatever was about to happen next. The drama had reached the point of climax. Its revelation drew her own excited voice along with those of everyone else clustered around the roulette table. The man's daring had paid off on a monumental scale. He had risked almost everything and won again. The croupier was shoving stacks of chips over in front of him.

And then the totally unexpected happened. The actor looked across the spotlights, saw his ardent fan in the front row and, wonder of wonder, beckoned her to come up on stage with him. The scene had all the elements of Caroline's daydream. Her sophisticated soldier of fortune raised his head, saw her and showed only a flicker of surprise before he carried on a swift, elemental dialogue with his dark eyes. *You're a beautiful, desirable woman. I've been looking for you all night. No, that's not true. I've been looking for you always.*

Caroline literally felt the heat of his gaze as it traveled over her and lingered on the low neckline of her dress, but her instinct now wasn't to cover her bared cleavage with her hand. Drawing in her breath, she had a pleasurable sense of her breasts swelling and the curves just barely meeting. When his eyes came back to her face, she smiled, acknowledging his male admiration and issuing a subtle compliment of her own. Just as in her daydream, she wasn't in the least intimidated by the attention of such a man, but filled with a sensuous female confidence. In response to a slight, graceful movement of his hand, she made her way around the table to him and took her place at his side.

Nick had had two cocktails earlier at the blackjack table and another since he'd moved here to the roulette table, but he didn't think what he was feeling had anything to do with the alcohol. He was high on the exhilaration of winning and being the focus of general attention. When he looked up and saw Caroline watching him, it jarred him only slightly that she had appeared, at precisely the right time, bringing to fruition the fantasy that had been born on a day when he was at his lowest masculine ebb, having just been dumped by his girlfriend for being too dull and nice. Longing that the fantasy might come true had brought him to Freeport, but he hadn't in his wildest dreams ever believed that fantasy and reality would merge with such precision, as they were doing now. Surely this was all a dream, but if it were, Nick didn't want to wake up.

"Welcome to my life, lovely lady," he murmured as she melted up close beside him. "Play for me and bring me luck." With no note of self-protective irony, the words still didn't feel foolish on his lips. Tonight he could say anything, do anything, *be* anything.

"But you don't need me to bring you luck," Caroline returned softly, her head tilted so that she could smile up into his eyes. "You've been winning without me. I know, I've been watching you."

He let his dark gaze caress her. "Strange. I haven't felt lucky. Not until now."

Neither of them was self-conscious about occupying center stage for their introductory exchange. They were celebrities of the night, charmed people whose due was to feed the imagination of those less blessed by fortune. They could speak lines that were less than inspired and bring to them the charisma of their personalities.

The croupier's final call for placing bets was like a cue for Nick. "Please. Be my guest," he invited carelessly, with an eloquent gesture toward his stacks of chips that said they were there solely for her gambling pleasure.

Caroline turned to the table so casually that no onlooker, including Nick, would ever have guessed that this was her first time ever to walk inside a casino or that her knowledge of roulette consisted of what she'd read in a leaflet provided by the Royal International Casino and gleaned from watching that night. The accountant in Nick felt a twinge as she picked up a tall stack of his chips and unhesitatingly placed the entire stack on the red number one. It was a "straight up" bet with the greatest possible odds, thirty-five to one, and thus the least likelihood of paying off. The little white ball had to come to rest on number one for Caroline to win.

Nick had accumulated his winnings with more than luck, though that was certainly involved, too. He'd balanced his straight up bets with more conservative positions offering lower odds, such as betting a whole column or row, betting "splits," where either of two numbers can pay off, or "corners," where one of four numbers spun can pay off. It might have looked to Caroline as though he was just randomly setting down chips, but that wasn't the case. He didn't guess that her daring was founded on a combination of ignorance and the assumption that the chips weren't important to him as money, but as tokens in an exciting game one played with instinct, not businesslike calculation. Taken in by what he appeared to be, a wealthy, idle jet-setter type, she also assumed that he could well afford to lose all the chips and buy more to replace them.

When the little white ball landed on twenty-one, not even in the neighborhood of number one, Caroline shrugged and smiled with charming apology up into Nick's face. "Sorry. Guess I'm not lucky tonight."

Overcoming his gut inclination to agree with her, Nick assured her smoothly that it was much too soon to tell and gestured for her to help herself to his stacks of chips for another try. The little lurch in his chest was more pronounced this time when once again she picked up a whole stack, which represented a couple of hundred bucks when turned into cold cash, and again put it down on a single number, this time the red number seven.

When the little white ball came to rest on thirty-five, Nick could only be grateful that at least it wasn't a "near win" that would have forced him to urge her to try her luck again. He concealed any regret over the loss of his money and suggested that they give lady luck a chance to recuperate while they had a drink at the bar. To his relief she readily agreed.

It wasn't just the loss of his winnings that concerned him. It was the thought that once they were gone, he'd have to dip into his pocket and buy more chips that could go just as quickly. This real-life fantasy was intoxicating stuff, but it didn't keep Nick from realizing that he wasn't in the same financial league with the men she was obviously used to encountering in casinos. At this rate, he thought, she could make some serious inroads into his bank account in an evening's time.

Caroline was complimented rather than insulted by Nick's suggestion that they leave the roulette table to have a drink. The light touch of his hand on her bare arm seared her flesh most pleasurably, and the look in his eyes and the tone of his voice were more eloquent than words. He was willing to abandon the thrill of gambling in order to have her full attention. He didn't want to share her with anyone or anything else. It was heady stuff indeed for a third-grade teacher from the conservative South over on the American mainland.

Privately neither of them really wanted another drink, but the situation called for it. A worldly attractive man and a self-assured beautiful woman meeting in a civilized den of iniquity, like a gambling casino, must have a drink and not just some ordinary beverage, either. Both felt the pressure of ordering something more sophisticated than what they'd been drinking previously.

Caroline deliberated prettily, one slender manicured hand raised to her chin in a pose of thoughtfulness. "Hmm. Perhaps a glass of white wine and Cassis. Very light on the Cassis." She told her preference to Nick, not the bartender.

Nick took note of that fact and Aunt Sarah's oversize diamond cluster ring on her middle finger. Both reinforced his impression that she was a woman used to being pampered and indulged by men of means. Under the circumstances, he simply couldn't just order the bar wine as he would have done for a date in New Orleans. He had to discuss the matter with the bartender and settle on an excellent vintage. There was no mention of price of the bottle of fine French wine deemed suitable for the lady's palate, but he knew this was going to be the most expensive white wine and Cassis he had ever bought for a date. Following this production, he couldn't order a lowly gin and tonic for himself. Instead he asked for Byron's standby and Nick's own least favorite, Scotch and soda, or rather Chivas and soda.

Caroline was thrilled to the core. To be treated in this fashion by a man such as this was every woman's dream. She felt as though she was wrapped in velvet, cosseted and adored. "Delightful," she pronounced after taking a sip of the pale amber liquid in her stemmed glass. It truly did taste wonderful and affected her like helium injected into her veins. Making note of that fact, she mentally resolved to sip very slowly and make the one glassful last and then immediately forgot that resolution as she became engrossed in the conversational exchange that was vague and sketchy only on the surface. She and Nick were able to fill in all the blank spaces for themselves, each using assumed background information about the other.

"By the way, I'm Nick Denton." In conjunction with this offhand disclosure of his identity, Nick held out his hand for hers, palm upward. The expression in his eyes made the gesture an intimate request. *Please, sweetheart. I'm dying to touch you.*

Caroline smiled into his eyes as she gracefully laid her hand on top of his, granting the request like a coy queen. "I'm Caroline Ainsley, and I'm very pleased to meet you, Nick Denton." The sound of Caroline's own voice raised a little tide of pleasure inside her. It was faintly husky and vibrated with feminine confidence, with just the right tinge of invitation and challenge.

"Caroline." Nick repeated her name, tasting each syllable, and then raised her hand to his lips.

Caroline had to suppress a shiver of anticipation as she waited, expecting the searing heat of the contact. His mouth pressed and then lingered, as though making certain that the imprint of his possession were burned into her soft skin. After he had reluctantly lowered her hand and released it, Caroline took a surreptitious glance at the place just above her knuckles, where a strong tingling sensation remained. She was vaguely surprised not to find a mark there.

"I'm surprised we haven't run into each other before," Nick remarked, managing not to grimace his distaste as he took a swallow of Scotch and soda.

"Yes, it is surprising, isn't it?" Caroline agreed in a tone of idle wonder, not needing an explanation of the basic inference underlying his remark, that since the two of them frequented all the exciting pleasure spots in the world, fate should have brought them together before now.

Nick told her with his eyes that in this particular instance fate had been cruel beyond belief. Caroline smiled her agreement and then submitted generously to another admiring survey of what he'd been deprived of in not meeting her before then. When his gaze had made its way from the blond satin cap of hair down to the lowest point of the black V of her neckline, Caroline obeyed a provocative instinct that must have been deep in hiding all these years, buried under ladylike decorum. She leaned a little forward as though to accommodate his gaze and give him a more delectable view of the ripe bared curves of her breasts. The movement was a complex blend of surrender and challenge one could expect only from an experienced woman, not a virgin. It said *Take me if you dare.*

Nick's dark eyes when they returned to her face were ignited with a fire that thrilled Caroline with her female power and yet awakened her first uneasiness, which made reality threaten to intrude. To her immense relief, his next words did not call her bluff. If they had been some equivalent of "Your place or mine?" she didn't know how she would have handled the situation.

Instead, he asked with a kind of abstracted intensity, "How long will you be here in Freeport?" and waited for her answer in such a concentrated manner as to suggest that it had immense importance for him in planning his itinerary for the rest of his life. Actually Nick was contending with the dismaying knowledge that he wasn't feeling up to a bedroom scene at the moment. He shouldn't have had the Scotch and soda on top of the earlier gin and tonics. His stomach felt queasy. His head was muddled. His lungs couldn't seem to get enough oxygen from the casino air. God, what a damnable time to get tight, just when he'd met the woman of his fantasies and she seemed ready and willing. If he couldn't through an act of will sober up and get hold of himself, he'd blow everything.

Totally oblivious to Nick's problems, Caroline was reassured that she was dealing here with a man much too sophisticated and knowledgeable in the game of seduction to force the issue of sex before time and place were perfect. He would know exactly what to do and when to do it so that everything would be so natural and inevitable that she need have no qualms about her inexperience. She could continue to experiment with exercising her female wiles without worrying about the consequences because she was in the hands of a master, just where she wanted to be.

"My plans for the whole summer are pretty indefinite." She lifted her shoulders in a graceful little shrug and took a sip from her stemmed glass, which had some magic tendency to remain full, no matter how much she drank from it. "I'm just playing it by ear. What about you? How long will you be here in Freeport?" The delicate archness in her smile and the tone of her voice said that his plans could have some effect upon her own.

"I had planned to be here just a few days." Nick put subtle emphasis upon *had*. "I've never been here before during the off-season. I had no idea what I might be missing."

"Nor did I," Caroline returned softly and leaned toward him again. This time the movement caused her some trouble because her body seemed to want to topple off the stool instead of coming upright again. It came to her in a rush of insight that she'd had too much to drink. Somehow the sips of white wine and Cassis had eased her body's alcohol content up past the level of sobriety. Fortunately Nick hadn't seemed to notice her temporary loss of balance because he'd turned his attention to forestalling the bartender from mixing him another drink and then asked for the check. It was another reassuring evidence to Caroline that he was in control, doing and saying the right thing at the right time.

It had become appallingly obvious to Nick that whatever the consequences, he was going to have to call it a night. Better to try to come up with some excuse and withdraw as gracefully as possible with a proposal for spending the following evening together than to try to continue and end up making a complete ass of himself. He felt as if his very life hinged on getting outside as soon as possible and drawing in a lungful of clean, fresh air. Then he could make it back to his hotel and into bed.

"Awfully sorry to give out so early," he apologized with a grimace, glancing down at his wristwatch and discovering with surprise that it was past midnight. He'd had no notion of the actual time. Normally he'd be in bed by then on a typical Monday evening back in New Orleans. "I just got in today, and I guess the old body's still operating on a different clock."

Even as he spoke the oblique lie, Nick was well aware of the risk he was taking in implying that he was suffering from jet lag, but what other excuse could he offer and still hope to save face? In his befuddled state of mind, he didn't know what his answer would be if she asked him where he'd come from that day. In all probability, she had been all over the globe herself, while this was his first time to travel outside the continental U.S.A. Desperately he tried to remember if it was earlier or later in Europe. He'd look pretty damned stupid if he said he'd flown in from London and was dead tired, if it was only seven or eight in the evening there.

As much as Caroline would have loved to ask him where he'd traveled from that day she didn't dare, because he would name some glamorous spot like Monte Carlo or Zurich and expect her to be familiar with it. She would either have to admit not having been there or try to bluff her way and risk being exposed for a phony. Discussion of travel would be the end of his interest in her. She could just imagine the expression on his face if he discovered she'd never even been outside the United States before this trip to the Bahamas, which was right next door to Florida.

"Isn't jet lag horrible?" she declared feelingly. "I'm glad to know there's someone else who doesn't change time zones easily." She patted her lips in a delicate little fake yawn that might be a result of such a time change she'd experienced that very day herself or might just be provoked by memory. "I think I'll make an early evening of it myself."

Frankly pleased with herself that she'd been so adroit in handling a potentially dangerous subject, Caroline signaled an end to the conversation by getting down from her stool. She was about to congratulate herself for managing that, too, with relative grace, when she discovered the unsteadiness in her legs. It posed a concern. She certainly didn't want to weave and stumble like a drunk leaving the casino. It would be most unsophisticated not to be able to drink and hold one's alcohol.

Nick was quick to slide to his feet beside her. He couldn't quite believe he'd gotten by without being put on the spot. She apparently took it so for granted that the people she met flitted from place to place, country to country, that she wasn't even curious to know where he'd come from that day. It was like a reprieve. The fact that not all was lost was so heartening that he felt better physically as well as mentally relieved.

"At the very least, you'll have to let me see you to your hotel," he declared with a gallant bow, offering her his arm.

Caroline took it gracefully and didn't have a bit of a problem walking out. A number of eyes followed their exit from the casino. They made an exotic couple, he very tall and slender and dark, casually flamboyant in wine-colored silk and gold, she exquisitely blond and chic in a designer gown and the very latest in outsize costume jewelry. It was easy to assume that he had flown in that day from Monte Carlo and she from a shopping spree in Paris. Certainly no one would have suspected that Nick was a certified public accountant appearing in this guise for the first time ever, or Caroline a virgin third-grade teacher who'd splurged on her outfit that very afternoon in one of the fashionable little boutiques in the International Bazaar, right next door to the casino.

Those real identities had threatened to emerge and tarnish the magic of the evening back there at the bar, but as Nick and Caroline walked through the ornate doors of the casino entrance and simultaneously breathed in the tropical night air, they both got a kind of second wind. The constant trade breeze was blowing off the sea, balmy and soft, bringing to their nostrils the scent of lush night blossoms and stirring to life the awareness of being in an exotic place. There, in the bright light of the portico were taxis lined up and a uniformed doorman, on the alert to do Nick's bidding.

Nick gave the man a brief nod that told him to stand by and then bent his head closer to Caroline to ask her where she was staying on the island. He had a resurgence of the sensation that fantasy had turned into reality as he looked

down at her. The scene reminded him of a slick magazine ad
for a luxury automobile, a lovely woman and a handsome
man in evening dress standing on the threshold of a brightly
lighted mansion, in this case the casino, built to resemble a
Moorish palace. The handsome man was actually himself,
Nick Denton. Suddenly he didn't want the fairy tale to end.

"I think this was what I needed, a breath of fresh air."
Nick placed his free hand on her bare arm with casual possession as he smiled down into her face. "Why don't we just
take a little walk to clear away the cobwebs?"

Caroline smiled her ready compliance. With her arm
linked in his, she felt as though walking would be no real
effort. She could just float along beside him, enjoying the
sensual brush of the warm silk of his sleeve against her bare
skin.

"A walk sounds like a wonderful idea," she said.

The doorman was a Bahamian native and had worked at
the job enough years to see tens of thousands of casino pa-
trons of all kinds come and go. After he had bade Nick and
Caroline a respectful good-night, he strolled over to chat
with the little group of taxi drivers, but his eyes followed the
arresting couple with more than usual interest as they
walked away into the night.

Chapter Three

Nick began to feel incredibly better as they strode briskly along the arcaded walkway flanking the casino and the front row of shops in the International Bazaar complex. The fresh air and exercise were exactly what he had needed. His stomach no longer felt queasy, and the fog had cleared away from his head. With the easing of his physical discomforts, he was increasingly aware of Caroline's feminine allure as she walked along beside him and a little confused with the exact nature of his response.

He liked the way she was holding his arm, not just as a token gesture or a provocative contact, but with a light but definite dependency that made him feel male and protective. The element of simple trust that he either perceived or imagined made her seem soft and fragile. Nick thought he must be imagining things, because his perceptions just didn't match up with the confident, sophisticated woman he had met back there in the casino. He replayed in his mind the tantalizing scene at the bar when she'd leaned toward him, issuing a subtle but unmistakable sexual challenge. Memory provided a vivid picture of the low V of her dress framing the delicate rounded curves of her breasts. Nick was aroused all over again and—he had to admit it—a little intimidated again, too. Maybe cowardice as much as the collective effects of alcohol had caused him to try to call it an evening. Well, he was feeling up to the challenge now. As he steered them toward the right in the direction of the Royal International Hotel, where he was staying, Nick discarded his fleeting perception of Caroline as vulnerable. That had surely been some trick of his male imagination. Out of the two of them, *he* was probably the one who was most vulnerable.

Caroline was drifting along contentedly at Nick's side, enjoying the magic of the night and giving no thought to destination. It felt wonderful to be borne along by the steady strength of his arm, so that walking was no effort, and she could just feel the breeze against her bare skin and inhale the faint fragrances of earth and sea that it blended and brought to her nostrils. When she noticed that they seemed to be headed in the direction of the Royal International Hotel, the observation raised only a mild alert, not a sense of panic.

"It seems as though you're seeing me home after all," she commented lightly.

The news that she was staying at the same hotel was unexpected and took Nick a little aback. It was a nice enough hotel, but somehow he'd expected her to be quartered in more exotic luxury, perhaps in some rich friend's private villa or aboard a yacht. What disconcerted him more than the revelation itself was her tone, which seemed to be questioning his intentions.

"My instincts told me you had to be staying at the Royal International, too," he declared with a blasé confidence he didn't feel. "Lady Luck couldn't have arranged it any other way. Tonight is my lucky night all the way around."

Nick didn't think he had been too explicitly presumptuous, not after the come-on she had given him at the casino bar. His words wouldn't have to be construed as a "your room or mine" proposal. But there was no doubt that the slender arm linked with his had tensed and she was silent. Somehow he had blundered.

Between the casino and the hotel was a four-lane thoroughfare divided by a wide grassy median. It had been busy earlier in the day but was quiet now. Nick was thinking so hard of what to say next as he brought them to a halt where the sidewalk intersected with the near two lanes that he almost forgot to look right, not left, for oncoming traffic. It took some getting used to for cars to be approaching from the "wrong" direction, but, of course, that wasn't something he could mention and not appear a rank novice at travel.

Fortunately he did remember at the last moment and inspiration for conversation did come to him as he guided her safely across the highway.

"It's a trade-off, staying here close to the casino, don't you agree? Convenient, but not as nice as being right on the ocean. It's just not the same taking a taxi when the urge hits to go for a skinny-dip in the ocean. Somehow a hotel swimming pool just can't compare, can it? And the managers can be so narrow-minded about such minor things as guests swimming naked in the pool." Never one with a gift for gab, Nick was impressed by his own offhand glibness and encouraged to think that it had repaired the damage wrought by his earlier remarks. The tension in her arm had eased a little, and there was a cautious smile in her murmured agreement.

"You're right. They can be."

"Does a midnight swim sound as good to you right now as it does to me?" In the interest of sophistication, he tried to downplay his genuine enthusiasm. God, a swim sounded great. It would help to sober him up even more and restore his vigor, not to mention that the thought of having her in the pool with him playing sexy water games was highly stimulating.

"I suppose we could even play it dull and safe and wear swimsuits," he added with feigned reluctance, his fingers mentally crossed that should she be in favor of a swim, she'd opt for the swimsuits. Getting arrested for indecent exposure in foreign territory didn't have a great deal of appeal. It was a risk he would take, though, since it was a night for gambles. So far all his bets had paid off unbelievably. He thought the midnight swim idea was paying off, too, judging from the way she had relaxed again.

Caroline's first reaction to Nick's suggestion of a swim had been almost overwhelming relief. Thank God she wouldn't be faced immediately with a bedroom scene. With that threat removed, she was instantly intrigued at the thought of a late-night swim in the hotel pool, which, as Mary the travel agent had promised, was no ordinary rectangle surrounded by lounge chairs. It would be an exotic setting in which Caroline could hope to continue her role of sophisticate, especially since she'd bought the perfect swimsuit for the occasion that very afternoon on her shopping spree, doubtful at the time that she'd ever have the courage to wear it in public.

"I think a swim sounds perfectly marvelous," she declared. "As for whether we wear swimsuits or not, it depends on how curious we are to see the inside of a Bahamian jail. As you probably know, the authorities here tend to discourage public nudity." Caroline's source of knowledge was the packet of information she'd been given with dos and don'ts in the Bahamas, but she managed to sound as though she'd had her share of vacation exploits in various backward locations and could tell amusing horror stories about the insides of jails.

Nick didn't miss the tinge of humorous recollection in her voice, but wariness made him check his natural curiosity. It wouldn't be in his best interest to open up an exchange of anecdotes about close calls with the law. She'd expect him to have some tales to tell himself, and not only was his travel limited, but he was also strictly the law-abiding sort. Back home among friends he wasn't quick to volunteer the fact that he'd never gotten a speeding ticket in his entire life. It seemed more a lack of adventurous spirit than something to be proud of.

"If you don't mind, we can check out the jail conditions here in the Bahamas some other time," he replied carelessly. "Actually I have a real weakness for comfortable beds, and I haven't run across too many of those in jails, not even the most up-to-date ones." Nick's entire knowledge of jail interiors was strictly secondhand. The closest he'd come to seeing one was picking up a less law-abiding friend at a police station.

"Then I guess we wear swimsuits," Caroline conceded with good-natured generosity.

Privately, both were relieved at the decision they'd reached without either of them having to appear conservative or naive. Their silence during the remainder of the short walk to the hotel was absorbed, but not uncomfortable as each of them thought ahead to changing into the swimsuits they would wear for the first time.

Byron had quite insistently made a present to Nick of the new swimsuit that he'd bought for himself when he thought he was making the Freeport trip. Nick had held the skimpy black garment up by its narrow sides and regarded it with such skepticism that Byron had laughed delightedly.

"It stretches enough to cover everything," he'd promised, chuckling.

Nick had gone ahead and packed the swimsuit with no firm intention whatever of wearing it. After all, it didn't take up much room. But now, there wasn't any doubt in his mind that he would wear it tonight, since he'd either have to wear it or one of his own modest pair of swim trunks. Clearly they wouldn't do.

Caroline was glad now that she'd given in to the wild impulse to buy the rose and black one-piece suit that was amazingly similar to the one in her daydream, but more daring. She'd been shocked at her own reflection when she tried it on in the dressing booth. The bottom half, what there was to it, was black. Cut high on the hips, almost up to the waistline, it left a generous amount of buttocks showing in the back. The bodice was a teasing confection made up of two strips of filmy rose fabric that would have been see-through if it hadn't been pleated, and as it was, she has a strong suspicion that the material wouldn't provide much protection when it was wet.

The strips were crisscrossed at the back, then came over the shoulders and straight down over the breasts to the waist. It was clearly not a garment for diving, since there was nothing to keep the strips of cloth in place over the breasts except natural fullness. It was designed solely to drive a man out of his mind.

In the light of the high-ceilinged hotel lobby, Caroline and Nick were impressed with each other all over again and filled with a sense of disbelief that the events of that night were actually happening to *them*. As they walked along a broad L-shaped hallway past the informal piano bar, which was doing a rollicking midnight business, and the entrance to one of the hotel's better restaurants, they both were experiencing a similar need to separate and have a little breather before they met back at the pool, attired in the risque new swimsuits and ready to resume their personalities of the night. Considering the large size of the hotel complex and its layout, it was unlikely that their rooms would be in close proximity.

Despite his gut instinct, Nick, with his ingrained male courtesy, felt he had to offer to see Caroline to her room. "Right or left?" he asked when they'd come out onto an open covered walkway that formed a circle around the hotel grounds, like the inside of a great wheel. It connected to other covered walks that led outward to the detached wings housing guest accommodations. Between the wings were spacious landscaped lawns, giving each wing a feeling of privacy. Either direction they took would bring them eventually to the wing in which Caroline's room or suite was located, but one way might be shorter than the other. On the way, they would be circling the pool area in the center and catching glimpses of it.

Caroline pulled her arm free of Nick's. "Right. But don't come with me. It'll be faster if we meet at the pool." She hoped the breathy sound in her voice wouldn't come across as what it was, nervousness. Before he could answer, she was walking quickly away.

Nick hesitated only a moment, looking after her, and then turned to the left. The location of his room was actually about equidistant in either direction, but he didn't want it to seem as if he was following her, although once she'd started to walk off, he realized in a flash that she could be giving him the brush-off.

Caroline and Nick both got vistas of the pool as they walked along, headed unknowingly toward meeting each other at their common wing. At different times that day they'd both explored the pool area, Caroline at more length than Nick. She had found it utterly delightful, exotic and fanciful and pleasing to the senses.

Separating two large round pool sections was a rugged little man-made mountain with great boulders, palm trees and an artful tangle of tropical vegetation and shrubs. She had recognized hibiscus, croton and copper plants. Waterfalls cascading from the tops of the boulders down into the pool caught the sunlight and sparkled. The rushing and tumbling sound was frolicsome and yet soothing to the ears, providing a kind of intimate cover for private conversations at poolside.

One end of the island had been hollowed into a little cave, cool and gloomy, reminiscent of the many real underwater caves divers came to the Bahamas to explore. There was a little walkway from the tiled edge of the pool into the cave. Caroline had taken it and stood in the cool dimness watching the swimmers as they glided underneath, taking an underwater shortcut from one section of the pool to the other. She'd noticed enviously the way young couples used the cave as a romantic rendezvous point. Their sleek heads would emerge very close to each other and they would tread water, smiling into each other's eyes and kiss.

By night the pool area, along with the rest of the hotel ground, took on a kind of magic because of all the colored spotlights nestled in the foliage. Caroline had noticed the transformation earlier in the evening before she'd walked over to the casino. Now she was even more attuned to the mystery and lushness. Her heart seemed to be tripping in time to the light tap of her high-heeled sandals on the tiled walkway as she walked along quickly, the steady splash of the waterfalls in the pool absorbing the sound of Nick's parallel progress and then his approach until they were close enough to see each other.

Caroline's steps slowed involuntarily and her heartbeat quickened. "Fancy meeting *you*..." she said when they were several yards apart.

"You don't mean to say..." Nick gestured skeptically over to his left where the connecting walkway led to the white rectangular building where his room was located, up on the third floor. In the subdued lighting, he saw the affirmative answer on her face. "Actually I was only joking about Lady Luck and the room assignments." His voice expressed mainly disbelief at the incredible coincidence, which would have been quite understandable to both of them, if they were aware of the actual circumstances. All of the hotel guests on the package trip coming in that day on the chartered flights from New Orleans were assigned rooms in the same area.

As they walked together to their wing, both Nick and Caroline felt awkward and constrained. Nick thought it was pretty obvious that she hadn't been pleased that their rooms were in such close proximity. Considering the encouragement she had given him over in the casino, her attitude roused suspicion that stirred in him pragmatic concern. Was she here in Freeport with a husband or a male companion, but for some reason had gone unaccompanied over to the casino that evening? If so, that would explain why she hadn't wanted Nick to accompany her to her room. Had she left him minutes earlier with no real intention of meeting him at the pool?

Caroline was feeling trapped and panicky. Flirting brazenly with a man like Nick in the safety of the casino was one thing, and being alone with him in the intimacy of her hotel room or his was something else again. What was she going to do if he made a pass at her? Well, she would just hold out strong for the swim in the pool and hope to be able to handle whatever developed out of that.

They entered the wing through double doors at the end and stood near the elevator and the door opening onto the stairs. The light from the plain overhead fixture was unpleasantly bright in contrast to the softer lighting outside. It let them see each other clearly, and they were mutually intimidated. If only there'd been a mirror and they could have seen the apparition of the two of them together, neither of them would have been so struck with a sense of inferiority.

To Caroline, Nick was overpoweringly the urbane male. He seemed even taller and darker and more virile there in the mundane setting than in the casino. The casual splendor of his attire assaulted her senses in the bright light. The deep burgundy color of his silk shirt came alive and gleamed garnet red where the light struck molded planes and curves of shoulders and arms and chest. The gold chain around his neck gleamed against his dark skin, a sumptuous reminder of his decadent life-style. Caroline wondered what on earth had made her think that a schoolteacher from Covington, Louisiana, could contend with such a man. He was totally out of her league.

In the brighter light Nick was able in a quick glance to take in separate details of Caroline's appearance and reaffirm what he already knew: everything about her bespoke the presence of money, and in her case it was money well spent. Her silky blond hair had obviously been styled by an expert in an expensive salon. The black dress was a designer number. The diamond cluster ring that sent out blinding sparkles from the manicured hand holding her black silk purse was no fake and must have cost a small fortune. Even the costume jewelry she wore had an exclusive look about it. Either she had money of her own or else some man was paying the bills, maybe a man somewhere in this very building. The possibility was in the forefront of his mind as he tried to look knowingly quizzical.

"Don't tell me. Let me guess. You're on the third floor."

"No—second floor." Caroline blurted out the answer and then did some quick, desperate thinking, the elevator and the door to the stairs, located side by side, serving as an inspiration. He was obviously on the third floor and the type who would choose an elevator ride over climbing stairs every time. "I never take a room any higher than the second floor. I have this 'thing' about elevators."

For Nick, her admission was a life ring tossed to a man overboard, not necessarily in peril of drowning, but definitely feeling insecure in a great big ocean.

"And I have a 'thing' about stairs," he came back swiftly, trying to approximate her same self-deprecating tone. "It appears we have a dilemma on our hands."

Caroline lifted her shoulders in a little shrug and tried not to look openly relieved. "It's no dilemma. You take the elevator, and I'll take the stairs." She blew him a dainty kiss and moved quickly to open the door to the stairs for herself. "See you at the pool in about five minutes?"

"Sure thing."

Nick was talking to the closing door. He drew in a deep breath as he took the several steps over to the elevator and gave the lighted button a vicious punch. He knew that a good part of what he was feeling was relief and that a man shouldn't be feeling that way when he's been left standing in the hallway of a hotel by a beautiful, desirable woman.

If Byron was there next to him waiting for the elevator, Nick could just imagine the ribbing he would have to take. *Stupid move, pal, letting her take the upper hand like that. Now you don't even know her room number. If she doesn't show at the pool, what are you going to do—go knocking on all the doors on the second floor?*

Hell, man, didn't you notice the funny way she was acting. I was afraid maybe she was married or something. . . .

So wouldn't it have been better to find out than to be left hanging like this? You can't pay attention to every little mood a woman goes through. How many times do I have to tell you a woman wants a man to take over? She wants him to overrule her conscience and common sense and all that kind of good stuff. Take my word for it, pal.

There was no arguing with his friend's ghost just as there was no arguing with him in person. Byron knew women. If he'd been there in Nick's place, he'd not only have taken Caroline to her room, but nine times out of ten he would have managed to get inside it and make love to her before they ever went for any swim in the pool.

But Nick wasn't Byron. Underneath his silk and gold finery, Nick was still Nick, not nearly assertive enough with women. As he rode the elevator alone up to the third floor, Nick was glumly contemptuous of himself for his failings as a man and determined that if Caroline did show up at the pool, he would use Byron for his role model and be the dominant male, let come what may. Then he'd feel respect for himself, whether he got her in bed or not.

In his room he peeled down to the skin and didn't feel much less naked after he had put on Byron's skimpy black swimsuit. To make sure that it did "cover everything," as Byron had promised, he checked his appearance in the mirror and murmured a shocked obscenity at what he saw. The damned chain around his neck covered almost as much as the so-called "swimsuit." He'd feel about as modest in a loin cloth, he thought angrily. At least the thing did fit tight and stay in place. He moved his hips and walked around a bit to make sure.

As he got a towel from the bathroom and wrapped it around his waist, Nick had to admit to himself that the swimsuit felt sexy as hell. Somehow the nerve it took to expose this much of himself gave him a new shot of adrenaline and boosted his male confidence. He thought she would show up at the pool, and when she did, he wouldn't disappoint her or himself this time.

As she fled up the stairs to the second floor, Caroline had very little confidence that the date at the pool would actually happen. She wasn't sure that she'd have the nerve to go herself, and she doubted that he would be interested enough to show up. Not after the skittish way she had behaved. He probably saw right through her disguise and had her tagged as a virgin from Smalltown, U.S.A.

Feeling low in spirits and thoroughly unhappy with herself, she undressed and vacillated as to whether she should just put on her gown and go to bed. Taking the new swimsuit from the drawer where she'd put it, she held it against her naked body and surveyed her reflection gloomily in the mirror.

Even when she impulsively put the swimsuit on, Caroline had no firm conviction that she was getting ready to go out to the pool and meet Nick. But the sight of herself in the daring garment brought the same thrilled admiration and shock she'd felt in the dressing booth that afternoon. It was hard to believe that was really herself, looking that sexy, right down to the come-hither smile on her lips.

Turning this way and that in front of the mirror and striking provocative poses, Caroline visualized Nick's face as he would look when he caught sight of her in the swimsuit. She began to feel incredibly sexy, exactly the way she had felt in her wonderful daydream. His dark eyes would burn with a hot intimate light, and he would undress her with his gaze as he'd done in the casino.

Memory brought to life the make-believe element of her meeting with Nick and made her subsequent fears and insecurities seem ridiculous. It was suddenly unthinkable for Caroline just to don her nightgown and go to bed. She would go out to the pool for a swim, and whether Nick awaited her or not, it would be a bold adventure for her. She'd be proud of herself for conquering her inhibitions, and that was really what this trip to the Bahamas was all about, wasn't it?

On her way to the pool, Caroline breathed in the fragrance of the air, looked appreciatively at the lush, well-tended foliage shown to advantage by the hidden spotlights

and wrapped herself in the delicious awareness of being far
from home on a tropical island. Because of the splash of the
waterfalls, she couldn't hear the sounds Nick made as he
swam laps in the pool. It wasn't until she came close enough
to see him that she realized he was there. Her heart lurched
with the discovery and then beat faster.

As she came up to the edge of the pool, Nick was swimming away from her with long, rhythmic strokes. His head
was dark and sleek, like a seal's. With her eyes on him,
Caroline slowly untied her wrapper and dropped it to one
side. Then she stepped out of her backless, wedge-heeled
sandals and lowered herself gracefully to sit on the edge of
the pool, her bare feet dangling in the water, which felt cool
and silky against her skin.

Anticipation joined with an almost overwhelming pleasure in the scene itself and the awareness that she was really
there, a willing thrall to the night's enchantments. *This is
me, Caroline Ainsley, from Covington, Louisiana,* she had
to tell herself dreamily as she tilted back her head and took
in a deep breath. When she looked again, he was turning
around.

Nick was invigorated by the swim, just as he had
expected. Added to the physical pleasure of strenuous exercise was the sensory awareness of the setting. That
afternoon he'd looked over the pool area and had been impressed with all the expense and trouble that had been taken
to make it something different from the ordinary hotel
swimming pool, but he hadn't known that by night it could
turn into such a dreamy setting for seduction. With the
clever use of lights, the landscaped island in the middle
evoked the magic of a tropical paradise. The waterfalls
created by pumps were brilliant cascades of diamonds.
Overhead was a huge dark sky. In his almost-naked state, he
was a virile pagan awaiting the appearance of the bare-
breasted beauty of the tribe.

When he glanced up ahead and saw Caroline sitting on the edge of the pool, his heart thundered in his breast, sending the blood surging through his long body. As he swam toward her with slow, powerful strokes, he could feel the tightness of the abbreviated swimsuit across his crotch, and the constriction was an added stimulation. Nick had never before in his life felt so totally, aggressively male.

Chapter Four

The pool was shallow where Caroline was sitting. Nick swam up close and then stood in front of her. The water poured down his long body, causing it to glisten in the soft, bewitching illumination of the hidden lights. To Caroline he looked all hard planes and sinewy male muscle, sleek and dark and dangerous. But he didn't frighten her. Out here in this make-believe ambiance, she was the woman in her daydream, sexy and confident. The way he was looking at her more than satisfied her expectations.

"Aren't you supposed to say, 'Come on in. The water's fine'?" she asked when his eyes finished their lingering inspection and came back to her face. Her voice was all soft, husky challenge.

Nick registered the fact that she had not only changed into a swimsuit more sexy than the black dress, but had also reverted back to the seductive woman he'd met in the casino.

"Come on in. The water's fine," he parroted obediently, holding out his hands for hers.

Caroline gave him her hands and let him pull her forward from the edge of the pool into the water. "It's cold!" she protested with a little gasp, but put up no resistance when he drew her toward him until they were standing so close together their bodies were almost touching.

Nick was still holding her hands, with their arms downstretched. Male admiration gleamed in his dark eyes as he deliberately looked her over with a kind of bold possessiveness.

"It's a shame to get your hair wet. It's so beautiful, like spun gold. But—" He smiled as his gaze lowered from her hair to the bodice of her swimsuit. "I'm looking forward to seeing what the water does to that little number you're wearing. Here goes—"

With that warning he backed up, pulling her with him into the deeper water. When Caroline tugged to get her hands free, he released them so that she could swim. They swam over to the island in the center and passed back and forth under the waterfall, gasping and laughing with the impact of the water pouring down on their heads and shoulders.

Caroline was the first one to get out of breath with the exertion and swam a little distance to safety, where she held on to the edge of the pool. Nick wasn't long in following her. He swam up close, the devilish grin on his face serving as a warning even before he grasped her at the waist and lifted her up out of the water. Caroline shrieked and held on to his shoulders.

"Let me down!" she demanded, but there was no conviction in her voice. She glanced down and saw what Nick was enjoying with open male interest. The strips of rose fabric had turned to the consistency of wet tissue paper and were molded to the curves of the breasts that they more or less covered. The one over her left breast had shifted far to the outside so that it just barely covered her nipple, which was stiff and erect. The one over her right breast had bunched up over the inside curve and left the outside of her breast exposed.

Nick's laugh was all male and exultant. "I knew I was going to like this swimsuit wet!"

Still holding her firmly by the waist, he lowered her and brought her closer, taking his time so that Caroline could tell in advance what he intended. He nuzzled aside the limp rose fabric covering the hard peak of her left breast and took the exposed treasure in his mouth and sucked it hard.

Caroline's gasp was a mixture of shock and pleasure. "Nick—" She meant to remind him that despite the illusion of privacy, they were actually subject to public view. Someone could walk up at any moment and see them. Before she could get the warning out, it suddenly seemed too unimportant to mention. Nothing else really mattered except the delicious sensations spreading through her body.

Long before she was ready for him to take his mouth away from her breast, Nick was lowering her down into the water and pulling her with him out into the center of the pool, where she found herself completely and delightfully at his mercy. Not nearly so much at home in the water as he apparently was, she had to move her arms and legs to keep from going under. Nick glided around her like a long-limbed merman, brushing against her, entwining his long legs with hers, exploring her body with bold, caressing hands.

The swimsuit was no protection. If anything, it was provocation, enhancing his enjoyment of touching her feminine curves. He would slip his hands beneath the clinging rose panels and cup her breasts or rub his palms across the stiff, sensitive peaks. He slid the high-cut bottom of the suit even higher until it was free of her buttocks so that he could fondle and squeeze the firm roundness at length.

Caroline was loving every minute of the underwater assault, so much so that it sapped her strength. When treading water to keep herself afloat became too much of an effort, she headed over to the edge of the pool, with Nick gliding effortlessly beside her, still stroking and fondling to his heart's content.

She was out of breath by the time she stood in the shallow water, unself-consciously aware that her swimsuit clung like a filmy skin. It was more provocation than modesty that made her give careful attention to arranging the wet rose strips over her breasts, tugging them this way and that without managing to conceal the rounded fullness that swelled with her deep breaths.

Nick was fully aroused as he rose to his feet by her. He glanced down along with her to note the distended shape of his abbreviated little swimsuit. Amazingly enough, it had managed to stretch enough so that he wasn't exposed, but it wouldn't have mattered to him anyway. Nick had never been more conscious of the power of his manhood, and it was a fantastic feeling, one that he wanted to prolong and revel in as long as possible before nature took over and insisted upon an explosive conclusion.

"You're a beautiful, sexy woman," he told her, stepping up close in front of her and drawing her wet body against his. "I don't have to tell you that you're driving me completely wild." On the last word he slid his hands down to her buttocks, slipped his long fingers up under the clinging material of her swimsuit and lifted her up against his loins. "Do you see what I mean?" he whispered, and held her against him, hard enough for her to share his male excitement but not so hard as to intensify the throbbing ache beyond endurance.

The control he held over his passion made Caroline feel safe enough to practice her feminine powers upon him with even more daring. She slid her arms up around his neck and whispered in a throaty voice, "And you're a very sexy man."

Following an instinct whose sheer brazenness gave her a shocked sense of pleasure, she pressed her chest against his and rubbed her breasts slowly side to side so that he could feel stiff abrasion of her hard nipples. "Do you see what I mean?"

She felt the shiver ripple through him and knew how Delilah must have felt with Samson. What was happening was just like her daydream, only far more exhilarating in reality. There was no anxious thought given to what her success would inevitably lead to. Surely the culmination to all this would be instinctive and wonderful, too.

Nick groaned as he wrapped one leg around the outside of hers, anchoring her against him while he hugged her close in a paroxysm of passion that made him helpless for a moment or two. "God, you're some woman," he told her, and then held her head between his hands while he kissed her, saving the sweet fullness of her mouth and then the rough warmth of her tongue as he took full advantage of her parted lips.

In her years of dating, Caroline had done her full share of kissing and was familiar with a wide range of male techniques. In some instances she had enjoyed kissing and occasionally she had even been mildly aroused, but it had never been anything like this. She'd never felt hungry and eager and hot. The weakness that had overcome her out in the middle of the pool came on again so that she had to hang on to Nick for support.

During the long kiss, Nick's intoxicating sense of male leisure deserted him and was replaced by an urgency the likes of which he hadn't experienced as an adult. He couldn't remember having felt quite the same way, even as a sex-crazed adolescent, because his pleasure in holding Caroline close and kissing her was more than anticipation of sexual conquest. There was a sweetness blended with the boldness of her lips and tongue that made him want to go on and on kissing her until he had solved the puzzle of her woman's essence. How could a woman be experienced and innocent at the same time?

Her uninhibited response had him aroused to a state of exquisite pain, where the primitive need to couple his body with hers threatened to block out all other considerations. But warring with that primal instinct was Nick's reawakened perception of Caroline as soft and vulnerable. Something about the way she had her slim, bare arms wrapped around his neck seemed oddly *trusting*. He'd had that same fleeting sensation about the way she held his arm when they were leaving the casino and walking to the hotel.

Tearing his lips reluctantly free of hers, Nick drew in a deep, audible breath, while he mentally shook his head to clear it of what his intelligence told him was a wrong impression. Caroline was no innocent in need of male protection. He had only to remind himself of the swimsuit she was wearing and the events of the past half hour.

At some time during the kiss, Caroline had stopped being Delilah. She was simply herself, the way she'd never been before, filled with mindless bliss at being in the arms of a man she trusted utterly. She wanted Nick to keep on kissing her, to keep on holding her close, for ever and ever. When he pulled his lips away from her she was patient only long enough to draw in a restorative gulp of air, and then she tried to bring his face to her again. When Nick resisted, she applied gentle force and urged him in a murmur, "Kiss me."

It sounded enough like a willful command to clear the ambivalence from Nick's mind. His faint sense of disappointment came distinctly as a surprise, but it was quickly gone as he kissed her hard and deep and without tenderness, the way a man who is sexually aroused kisses a woman his equal in sexual experience, who is sharing his own sharp urgency. When he broke the kiss off with the same abruptness that he had begun it, he stated in blunt terms the situation that he assumed was as clear to her as it was to him.

"Either we go somewhere pretty soon, or else I'm going to make love to you right here in this pool."

Caroline was reeling with the depth and fire of his kiss, which had verged on brutality. She hadn't meant for him to kiss her that way, and she didn't want him to speak to her in that brusque tone, raw with suppressed passion. Both the kiss and the blunt words threatened to destroy the magic of what she had been feeling in his arms. They set off an alarm she didn't want to heed.

"No," she murmured in protest, and grasped Nick's head again and drew his lips to hers. She took the lead in kissing him, playfully at first and then with tender passion. For her there was none of that knife's edge of pleasure that drew an agonized groan from Nick as he eased her hips a space apart from his. She would have nestled close to him again to share in his arousal, but he slipped one hand down between them and forced a separation by curving his hand to fit the mounded curve between her legs.

Caroline's first instinct was to push against his hand as a protest against the separation, but when he tightened his hand and squeezed, she discovered a new, devastating intimacy that destroyed her complacency. A soft moan came from deep in her throat as he kneaded his fingers against the narrow crotch of her swimsuit. She was so distracted that she forgot all about kissing when she felt him slip his hand beneath the thin, wet material, which had been little protection as it was. Nick's male sound of satisfaction at what he found mingled with Caroline's little gasp of pleasure.

"We're going to be great together, baby," he whispered against her lips.

Caroline could only murmur a little shocked "Oh," as she felt her thighs open for him, quite of their own account. It was the first time they'd ever invited a man's invasion. Always in the past they had clamped instinctively closed.

With the gentle rubbing motion Caroline's pleasure took on an uncomfortable edge. She writhed her hips mindlessly as he caressed her, and felt at a loss when, with a final delicious stroke, he withdrew. For the first time in her life, Caroline had a taste of the same kind of sexual frustration her dates through the years had experienced.

"Please..." she begged softly, with no clear notion of the exact nature of her request.

Nick came within a hair of overriding his inhibitions. For both of them, the moment was perfect to make love. They could go a little deeper into the pool or sink down nearly out of sight in the shallow area where they were. So far no one had joined them in the pool, and if there had been other people besides themselves abroad on the hotel grounds, he hadn't been aware of them. But then it was impossible to hear footsteps with the waterfalls splashing into the pool. Someone might have paused within view of them and looked, without their knowing.

That possibility was his undoing. As impatient as he was of the delay, he knew he would be more comfortable making love with her in the privacy of her room or his. That reluctant decision having been reached, he gave her a quick, final hug and then released her to take her hand.

"Let's go, sweetheart."

Under the spell of his voice and touch, Caroline let him help her out of the pool and stood docile while he took his towel and blotted her dry with the confident solicitude of a lover. Then he carelessly dried himself and tied the towel around his waist. With caressing hands, he helped her into her wrap and then kneeled on the hard tile to place her feet in the wedge-heeled sandals. She felt adored and cosseted as he slipped a protecting arm around her waist and led her away. But the feeling wasn't to last.

If Nick had understood the real situation, he might have done or said whatever he could to reassure Caroline and keep her fears from taking over, but he assumed that she was in as much a hurry as he was to reach the nearer of their two rooms and take up where they'd left off in the pool. He set a steady pace that she would be able to match with her shorter stride and didn't make any effort at conversation, since none was necessary and small talk didn't seem appropriate under the circumstances.

Propelled along at his side with the sound of the waterfalls receding into the background, Caroline could feel the delicious languor of her body easing away and tension replacing it. What had been magical and romantic back there in the pool was fast turning into stark reality. They were making a beeline for their wing, where he would take her to either his room or hers. There he wouldn't waste any time making love to her, expecting her to be an equal sexual partner.

What was he going to say when he discovered she was totally inexperienced, a virgin? What was his reaction going to be? Would he be incredulous, scornful, pitying, bored? Should Caroline let him discover her condition for himself, or should she tell him so that he would be gentle? If she told him, that could well be the end of things. He might just look at her with contempt and walk out.

Dear God, now that she'd gotten herself into this, what should she do?

Caroline's fears intensified into panic when she and Nick walked inside the entrance of their wing, as they had done approximately an hour and a half earlier. Once again they paused under the cruelly bright light. It hit her that she was actually about to go to bed with a total stranger, a man she'd never seen before that night. Her mind was crowded with all the dangers, Why, he might be a pervert, a sadist or some such thing. He might be a carrier of venereal disease. She'd have to be out of her mind to take all these unknown risks, added to the others, not to mention the matter of conscience. When it came right down to it, Caroline knew in her heart she was probably going to feel immoral having sex with a man who wasn't her husband. *Dear God, what would Aunt Sarah say if she were alive and knew what her adored Caroline was about to do?*

The physical and moral dangers of what she was about to do simply outweighed all the reasons in favor of it, now that her passion had cooled, now that fantasy had slipped away and been replaced by reality. The question was how to handle the situation without humiliating herself totally.

Nick couldn't quite believe what he sensed was happening again. There was something about walking through those double doors into the entrance of this wing that transformed them into wary strangers. This time he wasn't giving up so easily. He didn't want to leave himself open to another bout of ridicule from Byron's ghost, and his body was still clamoring for what it had been promised back there in the pool.

Ignoring the fact that Caroline's hold around his waist had gone quite lax, he hugged her tighter and bent his head down intimately close to hers as he spoke.

"Since we're either going to have to take the elevator or the stairs, it looks like one of us is going to have to compromise, hmm? Well, I don't think it'll bother me at all climbing stairs with you."

The lover's warmth in his voice didn't do a thing to thaw the chilly atmosphere. Caroline's body was as responsive to his encircling arm as a department-store mannequin. The smile she mustered felt about as natural on her face as a mannequin's smile looked. It was the perfect accompaniment to the regretful politeness of her reply.

"But I couldn't let you do that tonight." She exerted a slight but steady force to free herself of his arm. "You'd be putting yourself out for nothing, I'm afraid." She patted her lips in a fake yawn. "I've had a perfectly marvelous time. Believe me, I have, but all of a sudden, I'm just feeling dead tired. I don't believe I can manage to stay awake longer than another five minutes."

Nick held fast to her for a moment and then let her slide free while he battled his sheer disbelief. So she'd had a "perfectly marvelous time," had she? Now that she'd done everything but make love to him in the pool, she was "dead tired" and meant to slip up to her room and go to sleep, leaving him to cope with his sexual frustration the best way he could. What the hell would Byron do in a situation like this one? He wouldn't let her walk out on him without putting up a struggle, that was sure. And neither would Nick.

There wasn't time for Nick to decide the exact nature of the "struggle" he intended to put up, because Caroline, with another mannequin's smile and a murmured good-night, was headed for the door to the stairs. With two long strides Nick reached it the same time she did and opened it for her.

"Allow me," he said smoothly, and thought he heard ghostly approving handclaps in the background. He followed after Caroline and took her arm in a gentle but firm grasp when she began a rapid ascent of the stairs. "What's the big hurry? You'll fall in those backless shoes and break your pretty neck. We can't have that, now, can we?" Nick sincerely hoped Byron's ghost was trailing behind within earshot. He didn't think Byron himself could have improved on the indulgently male, chiding tone.

Caroline tried to slow her stampeding heartbeat as well as her steps, but her voice still came out breathless. "I really wish you wouldn't put yourself out like this, especially feeling the way you do about stairs—"

"Walking up a set of stairs with you isn't putting myself out." Nick gave her arm a little squeeze for emphasis. "Tonight I think I could make it all the way to the penthouse level of a New York apartment building and not mind a bit." *Not bad, huh, Byron, old pal? I doubt you could do any better yourself.*

The honeyed persistence in his voice along with the firm touch of his hand on her arm deepened Caroline's panic into a kind of fatalistic terror. What on earth was she going to do? She didn't think he was going to leave her at her door any more than he had let her take her departure down in the entrance, as she'd made it clear she wanted to do. If he insisted on coming inside her room, how could she prevent him? Once he was inside, he would insist upon making love to her, and she would be exposed for what she was: not a sophisticated woman of the world but a virgin third-grade schoolteacher! *What was she going to do to escape him?*

Nick tried not to let her agitated silence unnerve him as they reached the second-level landing, but his jocularity sounded forced to him as he announced, "Here we are, all safe and sound, with no broken ankles." He opened the door with an exaggerated flourish as though he were attired in black-tie formality, not a skimpy wet swimsuit covered by a damp hotel towel.

As he accompanied her down the dimly lit corridor, he couldn't prevent an ebb of confidence in how to handle the situation when they arrived at her door. If only she would *say* something to give him a clue as to her real mental state. A woman like her couldn't be suffering an attack of nervousness over having a man come to her room, could she? And yet he could swear she seemed nervous. Her whole body was tense. The slender arm he held was rigid in his grasp. The warm, sexy enchantress who had seduced him in the pool had pulled a disappearing act. Nick could scarcely believe that if he stopped her and opened up the front of her wraparound robe, he'd find underneath it the rose-and-black swimsuit that had heated his blood to boiling on the first sight of it.

What was responsible for this hot and cold business? Did she have a husband in her room? Was she some kind of mental case, all come-on and tease, turning into ice when it came time to pay off her promises? If he tried to be forceful the way he knew Byron would be, would she turn hysterical and start screaming her head off? God, he could just imagine a scene like that, doors opening and people poking their heads out to see what was the matter. Someone would call the management and report that a woman was being assaulted. Nick might even end up seeing the inside of a jail for the first time.

Normally Nick wasn't so imaginative in conjuring up fears, but the night hadn't been a run-of-the-mill night for him. It had been a night when anything could happen. He was making an effort to dispel his uneasiness and trying to think of what to say when Caroline stopped without any warning in front of one of the numbered doors and fumbled in the pocket of her robe for a key.

"Well, here we are." She got the words out, keeping her jaws clenched tight so that her teeth wouldn't chatter. Suddenly she was freezing cold.

"Here. Let me." Just as Nick held out his hand for the key, he saw a shiver ripple through her body and was instantly concerned. "Did you catch a chill? We'd better get you inside and get you into a hot shower."

Caroline stared at his extended hand and swallowed. "I guess maybe I did." She looked up into his face beseechingly. "I'm just so very tired. . . ."

Nick's immediate instinct was to put his arm around her shoulder and reassure her that everything was going to be all right. Looking down at her from his height, he was conscious of her diminutive size. With her hair wet against her head, she looked small and young and defenseless. He had to remind himself that she wasn't a whole lot younger than he was and definitely not defenseless. This had to be some kind of act she was putting on to get rid of him. Undoubtedly she'd used it in the past on other men and perfected her performance because it was certainly convincing enough.

What would Byron do if he were here in Nick's place? He wouldn't let her get off scot-free, thinking she'd taken him for a sucker, that much was sure. He'd say something light and cynical like, "Hey, sweetheart, you know what we guys call babes like you that lead a man on and then turn into an ice cube?" Then he'd tell her the answer in the kind of crude male language Nick had never used with a woman before. Nor was he going to use it now, he realized as Caroline put her room key in the palm of his hand and stood there looking like the accused waiting for her sentence to be carried out.

The best Nick could manage in the way of keeping his self-respect intact was to inject a little sting of irony in his parting actions and words. He stuck the key into the lock, gave it a twist and pushed open the door for her. Then he backed up, bowed stiffly from the waist, said, "Believe me, it's been a most entertaining evening," and left her standing there as he strolled away down the corridor in the direction of the elevator. He could feel her eyes following him and hoped that his efforts to project nonchalance were successful.

Halfway to the elevator he heard the quiet closing of her door and could stop pretending not to care that she'd made an ass of him. His shoulders took on a discouraged slump as he stood waiting for the elevator, and his thoughts were largely self-condemnation. Ginger had been right about him. He was "too nice," all right. Translated, that meant he was one of those men women could always manipulate to their hearts' content. He was the perfect candidate for all those weak male stereotypes that were favorite material for cartoonists and comedians: the hen-pecked husband, the cuckold, the recipient of the famed "Dear John" letter.

Nick wouldn't have been so hard on himself if he'd known how convincingly, from Caroline's point of view, he'd carried off his parting scene. Her initial relief at being left alone at her open door was quickly gone, swallowed up in disappointment as she watched him walk away from her down the corridor, the man of her daydreams, so tall and dark, so carelessly masculine and yet so intense. He had made her feel like such a woman, awakening in her emotions and sensations so pleasurable that she was frightened by their power. She'd been a match for him only in her daydreams, not in reality. His walking away from her seemed tragically conclusive. It was a door of opportunity shut in her face, probably forever. Through that door she'd glimpsed forbidden, unimaginable delights, but simply hadn't had enough courage to walk through it.

As she walked through her hotel door, alone and disconsolate, Caroline reminded herself of all the legitimate reasons for her behavior and told herself she'd done the wise, safe thing not going to bed with a strange man. She'd be relieved the next morning when she awoke and looked back upon the evening. Tonight, though, she just felt empty, terribly empty, and unfulfilled.

Mightn't it have been worth all the risks to be initiated into womanhood by a man like Nick, the first man who had ever transported her beyond an awareness of the here and now with his touch and his kisses? Sinking down on the edge of the nearest of the two full-size beds, Caroline closed her eyes and quite easily recaptured the sights, sounds and feelings of being in Nick's arms in the pool. He had been so warm and strong and passionate. There was nothing ugly or frightening in the memory of the delicious sensations he had aroused with his caresses and kisses.

What was frightening was the thought that it might be too late for her ever to yield herself to a man, no matter how persuasive he might be. Perhaps the years of saying no had made her into a spinster, like Aunt Sarah and her friends who'd either not married at all or else settled into widow-hood without any regrets for the loss of the marriage bed. That night might be the closest Caroline would ever come to making love with a man. She couldn't imagine that a woman could be any more aroused by a man than she had been aroused by Nick, and yet she had panicked, followed the pattern of years and said no with her actions.

Would she have another chance with him after tonight? She strongly doubted that she would, but if she did, the outcome would be different. She promised herself that. Perhaps it was the lateness of the night and her agitated state of mind, but to go back home to Covington still a virgin seemed to Caroline like accepting a life's sentence of spin-sterhood.

Chapter Five

The next morning it all seemed like a dream to Caroline, an exotic dream with more pleasant than unpleasant associations. In recollection, her feelings of tragic loss at the end of the evening seemed blown out of proportion. Thinking back over exactly what had been done and said between the time she and Nick had left the pool and parted at her bedroom door, she had no reason to think he had been all that terribly upset. Sure, he had been annoyed that she hadn't invited him into her room, but he was a worldly man and in control of his passions and emotions. All was not lost. She didn't think that upon encountering her again, he would hold a grudge.

In view of the civilized manner in which he had handled her abrupt change in behavior, her fears about him seemed particularly ludicrous and outlandish. She'd just gotten cold feet when faced with the imminent prospect of going to bed with a man. That was all.

As she mentally outlined her plans for the day, Caroline
had no expectation of running into Nick. In her mind he was
a night person. She didn't have any inkling of how he would
pass away the daylight hours, but she simply couldn't imagine him in ordinary clothing doing what ordinary vaca-
tioners like herself did during the day. The assumption that
she wouldn't encounter him gave her a pleasant sense of
purposeful leisure, the end of each activity not merely enjoyment but preparation for the evening when she would
undoubtedly see Nick again, in the casino.

After a midmorning breakfast, she took advantage of the
hotel transportation provided and went to the beach to get
a couple of hours' sun, wearing not the rose-and-black one-
piece swimsuit she'd ventured out to the pool in last night,
but a bikini that wouldn't have been considered scandalous
by most of the citizens back home in Covington, Louisiana.

Then she returned to the hotel, showered and dressed in
a casual skirt and blouse outfit to venture over to the casino
for her next step in preparing herself for the evening ahead.
The previous night she had been too befuddled by the wine
she'd drunk at dinner and too overwhelmed by the feeling
of being in a totally alien habitat to try her hand at gambling, as nearly every tourist coming to Freeport does, just
for the fun of it and for the telling upon returning home.
Caroline had a reason other than either of those two. She
wanted to familiarize herself with Nick's habitat so that she
could give the appearance of being at home in it herself.

At the casino she cashed in the twenty-dollar voucher
she'd been given as part of the Royal International Casino
package trip, conservatively opting for quarters, not dollar
coins, since the former should last longer and she didn't
want to dip into her own spending money until it was necessary. Before she chose a slot machine she wandered along
the rows of gleaming metal and bright-colored lights and

studied the various kinds, stopping at a discreet distance and watching when she would approach someone playing a particular machine. Occasionally there would be the jangling of coins and excited whoops when a player would hit a jackpot.

Much to Caroline's surprise, the undercurrent of hopeful suspense that permeated the casino, even in the daytime when the stains in the carpet were faintly visible, was infectious. By the time she stopped in front of a slot machine that for unknown reasons was *the* machine, she could feel the tingle of excitement in her fingertips as she dug into the paper cup and took out a quarter.

At first she put one coin at a time into the machine, but after she'd won several small jackpots, she became more reckless, feeding two or even three quarters into the coin slot on a single pull. Every time she'd get down to just a few quarters left in the cup, she'd win enough to replenish her betting store. When twinges in her legs made her wonder how long she'd been standing there, she glanced down at her watch and noted with astonishment that she had been playing the slot machine for over an hour! The time had melted away.

With the idea that she'd go ahead and feed the greedy machine the several dollars worth of quarters she had remaining, she started putting in four quarters at a time, the maximum. On the second pull of the lever, the jackpot light started flashing. When Caroline read the amount she had won on the credit meter, she felt a resurgence of the excitement that had started to ebb. Pushing the payoff button, she stood there and grinned while the quarters poured into the metal coin tray. Players in her vicinity cast congratulatory and envious looks in her direction before they turned their attention back to their own machines with renewed concentration.

As she scooped up the quarters that wouldn't all fit into her little paper cup, Caroline reflected with amazement about how quickly she had lost the feeling of strangeness and begun to feel quite at home here in the area where the slot machines were located. It was time now, she felt, to broaden her gambling education while the gaming tables weren't busy and the few dealers looked idle and bored.

When she left the casino two hours later, Caroline was thoroughly pleased with her afternoon's activities. She still had her original twenty dollars from the voucher and another twenty besides. It wasn't big winnings by anyone's standards, but she was familiar now with blackjack and roulette. The dealers had been most helpful, especially the blackjack dealer, a pleasant young man who'd spotted Caroline as a novice at once. He had routinely mentioned the sum of the two cards she'd already been dealt when it was time for her either to request another card or stand with those she had. Caroline could tell by the tone of his voice what the odds would dictate that she should do.

Once she felt relaxed playing blackjack, she'd moved over to a roulette table where it was obvious at a glance that the few players gathered around it were in her same category: tourists enjoying their first time at gambling in a casino. The dealer was patient at answering questions and permitted a more leisurely pace of placing bets than he would allow later in the evening when there were serious gamblers present. Caroline guessed shrewdly that the tables were probably open during the afternoon mostly as a kind of initiation opportunity for the novices who might be discouraged from stepping into the betting action during the evenings when the casino was crowded and the pace much faster.

Before she returned to the hotel, she walked through the International Bazaar, puzzling over the question of whether she could get by with wearing the black dress again tonight. Nothing else that she had brought along could even compare to it in style or sophistication, and she couldn't justify spending the money for another dress that she was unlikely to wear when she returned home. Deciding that perhaps a change of jewelry would do the trick, she remembered a display in one of the small shops she'd browsed in the previous afternoon and searched the shop out. The crystal and jet earrings that dangled almost down to her shoulders weren't cheap for costume jewelry, but they would be a perfect accept for the ultrasophisticated dress. So would the matching bracelet.

As she paid for her purchases with a charge card, Caroline attracted the attention of other shoppers. Her exposure to the sun at the beach had given her a light golden tan that looked great with her blond hair and blue eyes, but it was her animation that made her so much prettier than usual. The sparkle in her eyes and the smile on her lips were those of a young woman with a marvelous secret. When she noticed the attention she was getting, not just there in the shop but on her walk back to the hotel, it only added to her general good feeling about herself and her optimism as she thought ahead to the evening. Tonight was going to be even more wonderful than last night, she thought happily. She was prepared tonight and determined not to cheat herself because of loss of nerve.

If Caroline hadn't detoured through the International Bazaar before returning to the hotel, she would have stood a very good chance of running into Nick, dressed as himself in khaki walking shorts and a navy knit shirt. He'd just turned in his rented moped at the little thatched-roof hut adjacent to a native straw market on the hotel grounds and was returning to his room, windblown and looking forward to a shower and watching the early evening news. His afternoon riding around the populated Freeport-Lucaya section of the island on the moped had darkened his skin several shades.

It had been restlessness and the need to pass away the time until evening that had prompted him to rent the moped. He simply wasn't the type to sit around a pool all day or lie on the beach, especially not by himself, and after what had happened the night before, he wasn't exactly geared to walk out of his room and start picking up strange women. The more he thought about the previous night, the less he could believe that any of it had happened. It all seemed like a dream. Caroline seemed like a glamorous mirage.

The first half of the day he'd kept an eye out for her everywhere he went, at breakfast, at the pool when he strolled all around it before walking over to the International Bazaar to browse with the idea of buying some souvenirs. The fact that she wasn't anywhere to be seen brought more relief than disappointment. In his daytime guise Nick wasn't up to a face-to-face encounter. He didn't think for a minute she'd be interested in him for the person he really was. Hell, she might walk right past him and never recognize him, for that matter.

If Nick had seen Caroline enter their wing with a bouncy step some fifteen minutes after he had taken the elevator up to the third floor, he might have needed a second look to recognize her. Dressed in a soft shade of blue and carrying her parcel, she looked more like a pretty, wholesome sorority girl looking forward to a big date that night than the sophisticated, sexy woman whose picture he carried in his mind.

To his amazement, Nick discovered he was looking forward to dressing for the evening and assuming his night personality. Gone was his former repugnance at the idea of donning the slick garb Byron had coerced him into bringing along. In its place was a faint anxiety. Nick hoped the Cinderella trick was going to work again!

It was no accident that he caught sight of himself in the mirror that evening. After he had gotten dressed he checked

out his appearance and whistled at what he saw. He was
wearing the same dark fitted trousers, burgundy silk shirt
and Byron's gaudy rope chain, but he also put on the cream
silk jacket he'd left hanging in the closet the previous night
for fear of being too flashy. He'd been right. The combination was flashy, more so this night than it would have
been the night before, with his skin darkened by the
afternoon's exposure to the sun. Nick couldn't decide
whether he looked like an indulged younger son of a Mafia
don or an actor auditioning for the role of a modern Italian
prince. What pleased him was that he definitely didn't look
anything like Nick Denton of Denton and Sinclair, Certified Public Accountants. He'd wear the jacket.

"Man, you're some dude," he told his reflection, shaking his head and grinning. "I just wish the folks back in New
Orleans could see you in this getup. They wouldn't believe
their eyes."

When it was time for Nick to leave his room, he turned
out all the lights except for one, just as he had done the prior
evening. Whatever he looked like on the outside, he still
couldn't see being needlessly wasteful.

Nick felt great as he took the elevator down and went to
dinner at the Rib Room, located there in the hotel. He and
Caroline had walked past its entrance the previous night on
their way to the pool. Along the way and inside the En-
glish-pub-style restaurant, he attracted notice from both
men and women. From more than one of the latter, there
were appraising glances with secret, flattering messages.
Nick had had women he was escorting look at other men
that way. He'd always pretended not to notice, just as these
women's male companions were doing.

The general feminine attention made him all the more
watchful for the one special woman he hoped to encounter
during the evening. She was still somewhere in Freeport, he
just knew it in his bones. They had to come together again.

Fate had to give him another chance with her or else he'd leave Freeport with an intolerable sense of anticlimax, even if he broke the house bank over at the casino, and he intended to give that a good try tonight.

In this optimistic frame of mind, Nick enjoyed his prime-rib dinner thoroughly, despite the fact that he was eating it alone. Afterward he walked over to the casino, a route that was considerably more familiar than it had been the previous evening. Ahead he could see the entrance of the casino, its Moorish dome and fanciful cupolas ablaze with light, the whole facade looking like a movie set of a fairy-tale palace, all the more charming for Nick because it was so outlandishly fake.

He fully realized that he was fake, too, going to a masquerade of sorts, wearing the disguise of a rakish prince of the night, but the make-believe element made it all the more fun. It was great to shake his real identity and be somebody more daring, more exciting than his dull self. He had never felt so reckless and carefree in his entire life, and there was no harm in it, none except possibly to his bank account if he got carried away gambling.

Nick looked for Caroline when he first arrived at the casino, and when he didn't see her anywhere, he turned his full attention to wooing another lady, Lady Luck. Feeling comfortably flush with his winnings from the night before, he took a place at one of the blackjack tables with a twenty-dollar minimum. An hour later, when the balance of wins and losses had left him with about a hundred dollars less than he had started out with, he decided to try his luck at a roulette table.

He'd lost another hundred by the time Caroline entered the casino and spotted him. The sight of him set off little sensory shock waves. He was taller, darker of complexion and more rakishly handsome than she remembered. Before she could lose her nerve, she sucked in a deep breath and walked right over to the table and eased herself into the space at his side. He was leaning forward placing his bet and didn't see her until he straightened. She met his glance with a smile of greeting and watched the light of recognition flare up in his dark eyes. That first look laid to rest any fears about whether she was welcome.

"Having any luck tonight?"

"Not much. Not until about five seconds ago."

Caroline's lips parted in unconscious provocation as he lifted one elegant, long-fingered hand and toyed with her crystal-and-jet earring. Then he touched her bare shoulder with his fingertips and drew them down her arm in a feather stroke that heightened the intimacy of his tone as he murmured, "Welcome. I've been looking for you all day."

She had to suppress a shiver of pleasure at his touch and the warmth in his eyes. Being so close to him, even in so public a place, triggered the same physical weakness she'd experienced in the pool last night when he had aroused her with his kisses and caresses. Exclamations from the other players at the table and the little fringe of watchers gave her the perfect excuse for diverting the attention away from her for a few moments while she grasped the table edge for support.

"Look! You're a winner! Perhaps I have brought you good luck tonight."

Nick turned back to the table to see that, sure enough, the croupier was shoving over in front of him several stacks of the red and white chips he was playing with. His exultation was genuine, even though he was taking advantage of the circumstances as he slipped an arm around her shoulders and squeezed her close against him. She felt soft and feminine and luscious.

"No doubt about it, honey. You're definitely lucky for me."

"Good." Caroline pursed her lips fetchingly and made a little smacking kiss sound. For a delicious, suspenseful moment afterward, she didn't know whether he was going to follow up on the urge to kiss her that she could read in his face. "It's time to place your bets," she murmured, hazily aware of the croupier's voice somewhere far in the background. Her voice was as much temptation as reminder of the present.

"Why don't you bet for me?" The offer was merely a vehicle for all the intimate messages he wanted to convey.

"I'd rather watch you bet, if it's all the same to you. I'll just stand here close and concentrate."

In the interest of impressing her with his daring, Nick abandoned the cautious strategy that had served him well the night before and placed a straight-up bet, putting a whole stack of chips on number twelve. When he lost, he just smiled and with a careless shrug, put out another stack on twelve. Actually he didn't really give a damn about losing. That was what was surprising.

"I was closer that time," he said cheerfully when the white ball landed on nine. He was about to pick up another stack of chips when Caroline stopped him by laying her hand over his.

"Don't. At this rate you're going to lose all your chips, and I'll feel terrible."

Nick raised his eyebrows and grinned. "How terrible?"

With a smile of mock reproof, Caroline drew back her hand. "I get it now. You want me to feel guilty so I'll have to make it up to you somehow. What a villain you are!"

"Ladies and gentlemen, last call to place your bets," the croupier advised in a bored tone.

"Not a villain, just a gambler. One last try, and then we'll have a drink at the bar. Come on, now, lovely lady. Think lucky for me." Nick looked every inch the role he was playing with gusto as he picked up a third stack of chips, placed it on the number twelve, hesitated and then, as though listening to an inner voice, shoved the stack over to the line between eleven and twelve so that he was betting a "split," with seventeen to one odds rather than the thirty-five to one chance he would be taking again with just the number twelve.

"This time you did it!" he exclaimed when the little white ball came to rest on eleven. While the croupier pushed his winnings over to him, Nick took his own prize. Right there in front of everybody, he kissed Caroline, taking her by surprise and tasting again the intoxicating sweetness of her lips. It was the kind of bold impulse he would have been unlikely to follow under ordinary circumstances when he was dressed and acting as himself. Once he got started kissing her, it was hard as hell to stop. He didn't really care about the situation being so public. He didn't really care about anything except having her in his arms.

When their lips finally did come apart and they looked into each other's eyes, Caroline and Nick both were a little dazed and skeptical at what had happened. Neither of them was the kind to kiss a stranger in a crowded gambling casino and have the world just fall away under their feet so that they might have been alone, holding on to each other.

"I guess we'd better have that drink." Nick's voice was unsteady.

Caroline swallowed and cleared her throat. "Yes, I guess we'd better."

By the time Nick had cashed in his chips, stuffed the bills carelessly into his wallet and led Caroline over to the bar at one side of the large room, they had stepped back into role and were on guard, though not in any strained, unpleasant sense. Both were more confident than they had been the previous evening and less apprehensive about handling the revealing turns the conversation might take.

Caroline was feeling secure enough to order a frozen daiquiri, the alcoholic beverage she came closest to actually liking. When she told Nick her preference, he didn't raise an eyebrow or indicate by any subtle expression that he thought the choice unsophisticated.

"A frozen daiquiri for my lovely companion here," he told the bartender, and then tapped long fingers nervously on the polished surface of the bar while he hesitated, as though trying to make up his own mind. Actually he was asking himself if he would do inestimable injury to her opinion of him if he ordered a lowly gin and tonic. He decided to take the risk. The thought of force-feeding himself with Scotch again tonight made him want to gag. "And give me a gin and tonic. Make that Beefeater's." Caroline was sitting on one of the comfortable high stools with upholstered arms and backs. Nick chose to stand close to her even though it was a kind of delicious torture. His physical awareness of her was even more intense than it had been the night before, and subtly different. It had taken on possessive overtones, as though by touching her so intimately in the pool and arousing pleasure in her body, he had staked some sort of claim.

Now as his eyes strayed down to the bold V of her dress, the visual enticement was augmented by sensual memory. He had cupped her bare breasts in his hands, squeezed the delectable fullness, felt the rasp of her hardened peaks against his palms. He had caressed all the delightfully feminine curves of her small, shapely figure and found them perfectly to his liking. His approval was in his eyes and in his voice as he toasted Caroline with his drink.

"Here's to incredible luck two nights in a row."

Caroline smiled a gracious acceptance of his male admiration and paid some compliments of her own with her eyes and her tone as she gracefully touched the fragile bowl of her daiquiri glass to his tall gin and tonic.

"I'll drink to that." She sipped her daiquiri and found it tart and yet sweet, with no strong alcohol taste. "Perfect," she murmured, a queenly connoisseur of daiquiris blended throughout the world.

"I'm glad it's to your liking." Nick managed to imply that it had been a major concern to him that the drink should measure up to her complete approval. Now they could move on to other matters. He gave her another admiring once-over and touched his fingertips to her lightly tanned cheek. "Wherever you were hiding from me today, it must have been in the sun. You look marvelous. I'm surprised you tan with that peaches-and-cream complexion."

Caroline had no trouble translating for herself the unspoken part of the compliment: he'd like to see the rest of her tan that was covered by her dress. As though to accommodate him as best as she could, she slid her bottom a little forward on the stool and sat with her shoulders well back so that her breasts strained against the low-cut bodice of her dress. She felt wonderfully provocative.

"I have to be careful. If I'm not, I can burn to a crisp." The rueful admission was accompanied by an admiring survey of his sun-darkened skin, offset by the gold chain around his neck. "I'll bet you never have that problem. You look like the kind with a year-round tan."

Nick shrugged a careless agreement and did some quick thinking about the conservative story his tan lines could tell. When it came time to take his clothes off tonight, he thought, he'd have to make sure the light was dim.

"Actually I'm more of a night person," he declared. "The sun just seems to have a way of tracking me down."

His words fit in perfectly with Caroline's conception of him from the very first. He was the dark lover of her daydreams who had stepped out of the shadows. He was sophisticated, worldly, experienced and yet, miracle of miracles, he didn't frighten and intimidate her. His admiration warmed her like a silky cocoon. His belief in the glamorous self she wished to project gave the role such credence that she half believed in it herself.

This was a night of magic, just as she'd wanted it to be. This was a night when she would make her too-long-delayed passage into womanhood, and there was no sense of anxiety because she had only to let matters take their natural course. Nick was in control. He would take care of her.

Secure in this intuitive optimism, Caroline let herself go as she had never done with a man before. The glances she freely exchanged with Nick, her smiles, her conversation were filled with sexual promises that made Nick's blood hum. All it would have taken was the merest hint that she wanted to go somewhere and make love and he would have suggested that they leave the casino, but she seemed to want to stay and gamble, and he would have done anything in his power to please her.

They both played blackjack, sitting side by side at a table with a twenty-dollar minimum, with chips Nick bought for them with his dwindling winnings. Despite the fact that they paid more attention to each other than to the cards dealt them, they managed to win enough to keep playing for an hour or so. When all the chips were gone, they laughed and moved on to a roulette table. Neither, it turned out, had any interest in craps. Actually, neither had gotten around to figuring out the intricacies of betting at the craps table.

Two hours and many turns of the wheel later, Nick's winnings were gone and he was out of pocket for another couple of hundred bucks. But he really didn't care about losing his money. It had been sheer exhilaration, betting with her, exulting over the wins, groaning over the losses, watching the piles of chips grow and diminish with the caprices of luck. Still, enough was enough. He wasn't inclined to dig deeper into his pocket, when other pleasures beckoned.

"I've had about enough of this," he told Caroline, drawing her back from the roulette table with his arm around her shoulder. "What about you?"

Caroline's heart gave a little lurch. "I have, too. I just feel bad about losing all your money."

Nick's answer, accompanied by a careless shrug, would have brought incredulous expressions to the faces of all his friends and business acquaintances back in New Orleans.

"Don't feel bad. It's only money."

Caroline reached up and gave his cheek a caressing pat, mainly because she wanted to touch him. "Maybe we'll be lucky and win it all back tomorrow night."

Nick caught her hand and brought it to his lips. After he had kissed it, he held it tighter.

"I feel like I'm a big winner tonight," he said softly. "Shall we go?"

Caroline felt her heart pick up the tempo of its beat as she held Nick's gaze and read his meaning.

"Yes," she said, nodding. "Why don't we go? I'm ready."

Her words, with their clear implication, were what Nick had wanted and been given good reason to expect to hear. His gladness at hearing them was almost excessive. He felt as if he'd just conquered the world as he walked out of the casino with Caroline on his arm. It was an effort to moderate the length of his stride for her benefit, not because he was in a hurry, but because he felt so damned good.

If he'd had any premonition of the revelations awaiting him before the evening was over, his long legs might have slowed his progress. But there was no premonition, not even any anxiety about performing to the peak of his male powers for her enjoyment and his own. This time, he hadn't consumed too much alcohol. This time everything was going to be perfect, just as it had been up to this point.

Borne along on the tide of Nick's controlled energy, Caroline felt only the mildest form of apprehension about what lay ahead and wasn't concerned at the presence of those subdued fears. It was natural that she would be a little nervous, but she was confident that Nick would be fully in charge and would take care of everything. In his arms she would be the kind of woman he wanted, the kind of woman she longed to be, if only for this one night.

The same doorman from the night before was on duty outside. He started to raise his fingertips to his gold-braided hat and parted his lips to ask Nick if he wanted a taxi, but seeing the situation for what it was, he lowered his hand and shrugged. His head nodded knowingly as he watched the absorbed couple walk off, oblivious to his very presence. He recognized them from last night and didn't need a script to know how they had progressed in their relationship.

Chapter Six

Aren't the fountains beautiful?'' Caroline's voice was dreamy. "This place looks like something out of *Tales of the Arabian Nights* the way it's all lit up at night, doesn't it?''

Nick laid his hand over hers that clasped his arm. "I was thinking something of the same thing tonight on my way over to the casino.''

After that satisfying little exchange, they were silent for a while as they walked along, both full of thoughts and feelings about each other and themselves that they couldn't share without revealing too much. Nick's perception of Caroline as soft and fragile was back again, stronger than ever, awakening his protective instincts that could, he well knew, be too easily activated where women were concerned. He guessed Byron was right. It all came out of his background, which was upper-crust old South. Born and reared in Natchez, Mississippi, renowned for its antebellum mansions and steeped in Southern tradition, he had been taught courtly manners and respectful attitudes that weren't easily shaken. In any social gathering he automatically came to his feet when a female, especially one his elder, entered the room. It was also second nature to him to screen obscenities from his language when he was in feminine company, despite the fact that so many liberated young women cursed fluently.

But not Caroline. He hadn't heard her speak the first mild obscenity, not even a *hell* or a *damn*. If it weren't for opening up the subject of backgrounds, he'd like to ask her where she was from. Now that he thought about it, he wondered if she weren't from the South or hadn't at least spent some time there. While she didn't have a pronounced Southern drawl, her speech sounded so completely familiar that it hadn't drawn itself to his attention. And her manner was ladylike, despite her sophisticated style of dress.

Caroline was walking along beside Nick marveling that she could feel so close to a man who not only was a stranger but wasn't the companionable type. A tropical night could obviously do strange things to a woman's judgment because Caroline felt as though she could just keep on walking wherever he led as long as she could lean on the strength of his arm the way she was doing now.

"This is quite different by night than by day, isn't it?" she mused when he brought them to a halt to check for traffic before crossing the near two lanes of the highway.

"Yes, it is." Nick stopped himself before he added unthinkingly, "You should try it on a moped during the height of traffic." He didn't want to mingle the happenings of day and night. That had been his day self riding around on the rented moped, mulling over what had happened last night. Now he was his night self, assured and in control.

"This whole island is different by night, haven't you noticed?" Nick caressed her hand on his arm to reinforce the husky intimacy of his tone. "For example, I walked by the pool today, and it wasn't the same place I remembered at all. What about you? Did you go out to the pool today and find it changed?''

He meant to evoke sensual memories that would serve the purposes of seduction, not disrupt the magic of the evening with recriminations and demands for explanation of past behavior. But a serious undertone had crept into his voice, posing a question he hadn't consciously intended to ask at all: *why did you change your mind last night?* Feeling Caroline's hand tighten on his arm, Nick mentally cursed himself for being a fool and spoiling things, but yet he couldn't bring himself to break the silence that hung between them like a huge question mark.

Caroline was taken completely off guard and didn't know what to say. She answered the stated question first. "Yes, I did walk by the pool today, and you're right—it wasn't the same place by day.'' She met his glance uncertainly in the semidarkness and was forced by his silence to keep talking. "A lot of things seem different in the daytime, don't they? When I got up this morning and remembered last night, it was hard to believe that it all happened. I didn't know if you'd even speak to me the next time we met. Not after the way I'd acted.''

The shamed reluctance in her tone was an effective plea to Nick to step in and close the subject, which she found painfully embarrassing and didn't want to continue. He wanted to say something light to ease over the awkward moment for her, and the urge wasn't altogether an unselfish one. His male common sense told him it was better to discuss what had gone wrong the night before *after* he'd taken her to bed. Yet no soothing blandishment came to mind. Despite all the sound reasons for doing so, Nick found that he just couldn't let the matter drop. He had to have some answers, now, before they went any further. He did what he could to soften the inquiry with his apologetic tone and phrasing.

"What did go wrong last night? Was it something I did or said?"

"No, it wasn't your fault at all." Caroline's denial was quick and sincere, but then it left her faced with the first, difficult question to answer. She was struck with a powerful urge to blurt out the truth, but the embarrassing words wouldn't come and a quick glance over at Nick did nothing to shore up her courage. How could you tell a man like that he'd been taken in and was escorting a twenty-eight-year-old virgin to his hotel, not a sophisticated, experienced woman? Caroline winced at the thought of the expressions that would cross his urbane countenance. She could hear the chiding skepticism in his voice. "A *virgin*. Come now. You're kidding me."

So what besides the truth could she offer as a convincing excuse? After a quick, fruitless search of her mind, Caroline had to fall back upon the same weak lies she had used the night before.

"Really, Nick, I was just bone tired last night, but I'm all rested up now. I feel wonderful tonight." She took in a deep audible breath and exhaled just as noisily as though offering some kind of proof of her rested state and exalted spirits. Then she rushed on, taking reckless courage in hand.

"You know what I'd like to do? I'd like to pretend last night didn't happen, or at least the part after we left the pool. Why don't we do it all over again and this time have it perfect from beginning to end?" Caroline's heart was beating so hard at her own incredible temerity that the last words scraped past her throat but, amazingly, came out sounding sexy, not frightened. Her quick smiling glance up into his face told her she'd gotten a positive reaction to her proposal. His dark eyes, black in the night, seemed to burn her countenance.

Nick wasn't at all satisfied with her vague explanation of what had made her change her mind about going to bed with him the previous evening, but that didn't keep his heartbeat from picking up its tempo at what she promised with her voice and her smile, or his body from making a strong male response.

"You mean meet in the pool again as we did last night?"

"Yes, that's what I mean."

Her quick reply spoken almost in a whisper raised goose bumps on Nick's skin underneath his silk shirt, but some stubborn, nagging reservation remained. He wanted more explicit assurance that there wouldn't be a repeat of last night's hot and cold treatment.

"And you're sure a swim won't tire you out too much tonight?" He put subtle emphasis on *sure*.

"I'm sure."

Her answer came breathless again and too fast. Nick still wasn't satisfied, but the entrance of the hotel was just ahead and the demands of his body overpowered those of his mind. A replay of the last night's rendezvous in the hotel pool had enormous appeal. He couldn't wait to see her again in that bathing suit, especially after it got wet and was plastered to her small curvaceous body. He couldn't wait to caress her and kiss her in that make-believe setting.

"You'll wear the same swimsuit?" His voice told her the provocative nature of his thoughts.

"Yes, I promise I will."

Caroline's soft reply came readily and contained little sexual nuance. To Nick's ears it sounded oddly serious, as though she were making a pact with him. For Caroline, the certainty in her own voice removed the last shadow of doubt from her mind about what she intended to do tonight.

She was going to shed the innocence that she had come almost to hate. This night she was finally going to make love with a man, and not just an ordinary man, either, but one who was a master in making love to women. Though her fears and insecurities hadn't magically dissolved in the presence of her certainty, the burden of decision had been lifted. Walking along beside Nick, she felt as giddy and nervously expectant as a bride leaving the church on the arm of her groom.

If she had truly been a bride entering the hotel foyer with her brand-new husband, Caroline probably would have chattered confidingly. Was he struck as she was by the vastness of the lobby, which seemed to dwarf all the furniture and the people in it? Had he ever seen an Oriental rug as large as the big round one in the center? Didn't this place have a real "thing" about roundness, anyway? But she kept all these inconsequential but vivid impressions to herself because they weren't the thoughts of a well-traveled woman, but the thoughts of the person she really was, and that person wouldn't interest a man like Nick.

On the way past the discreet entryway of the Rib Room, with its printed menu posted behind glass, Nick thought about mentioning the fact that he'd had dinner there tonight, but then he quickly suppressed the impulse because he couldn't possibly share with her his real pleasure in his dining experience, all the flattering attention he'd drawn with his exotic night appearance and the sense of embarking on another evening adventure that had given a new dimension to taste. He'd be limited to comments about the food and service and such. She'd be bored with such talk, bored with him. It was better to say nothing than to reveal himself with talk of the mundane.

"Which way?" he asked when they walked through the glass doors leading out onto the tiled, covered walkway that circled around the central pool area, connecting the various wings. The inquiry was a conscious, amused parody of his words the evening before, inviting her to smile with him over the way they'd parted and encountered each other again so unexpectedly. Caroline laughed softly and pulled her arm free of Nick's, the way she had done the previous night.

"This way," she said, and walked quickly away to the right as she'd done the night before, but tonight there was laughter in her voice.

Nick grinned, looking after her a moment before he strode away to the left, a spring in his step. He felt incredibly good at the expectation of meeting her up ahead again.

Tonight he must have walked a little faster because he got to the walkway leading outward to their wing before she was in sight and had to stop and wait. His pulse quickened when he could make her out in the dim, magical light, a glamorous vision of womanhood coming to him, a smile of mystery and promise on her face.

"Fancy meeting you here," he called out softly.

When Caroline came up close he reached for her and took her into his arms. She came into them so willingly that the sheer wonder of what was happening as well as his physical reaction to her closeness set off a rippling sensation along his spine, a kind of hot chill of pleasure.

"You're not supposed to do this yet," Caroline whispered, and then promptly undermined the protest by surrendering her lips to his. She was conscious of a delicious familiarity about the intimacy of his embrace and yet a newness that arose from the barrier of his rich clothing. Indulging herself in sheer tactile pleasure, she lifted her hands to his chest and ran her palms over the smooth, warm silk of his shirt, touched the heavy gold chain around his neck and then moved upward to his shoulders, where the incredible softness of the material of his jacket was enhanced by the solid warmth of his man's body underneath the luxurious layers of cloth.

"You're different from any man I've ever known before," she whispered breathlessly when his lips had ravaged hers thoroughly and moved across her cheek to her earlobe and then down to the curve of her neck.

The kiss, combined with the sensory reaction to her hands and her warm response, had Nick so quickly and thoroughly aroused that he couldn't see any reason to stick by their original game plan. Gone were all his value reservations about the sincerity of her intentions.

"I've never wanted any woman the way I want you," he murmured between taking tastes of the perfumed satin of her skin. He felt as drugged as he sounded. "Let's go to my room and make love, sweetheart. Then we can go swimming afterward."

He didn't have to wait for words to know her answer, which in his state of blind confidence jolted him with disbelief. He could feel in the involuntary reactions of her body her instant rejection of his impassioned suggestion. The hands caressing his neck and shoulders went still. Beneath his lips he could feel the cords of tension tighten in her neck. Her body stiffened in his arms. With all these negative signs to assure him of her refusal, her verbal compliance came as still another shock.

"Okay." A pause. "Or perhaps we should go to my room."

Nick lifted his head slowly and levered his upper body back from her as he straightened. He held her loosely by the waist as he took in a deep breath and expelled it while he studied her face closely in the dim light, searching for some clue as to what the hell was going on in her head. He'd be damned if she didn't look *scared*.

"Caroline, are you sure there isn't something you should tell me before we take this any further?"

The wariness in his voice made Caroline's heart sink. She thought, he must *know*. When she froze up like that, before she could stop herself, he must have put two and two together and concluded that she was a phony, a virgin masquerading as a woman. As soon as she confirmed his suspicion, that would undoubtedly be the end of it. He'd probably just shrug, say something with a quiet bite to it and walk off. She didn't want that to happen. She didn't want this to be the end.

The strength of Caroline's feelings made her tighten her arms around Nick's neck and press closer. The unmistakable evidence that he still wanted her came as a reassurance of sorts.

"I don't want to tell you anything, Nick. I don't want to talk at all. I just want you to make love to me."

There was far too much fervor in her voice, but she was speaking the words Nick badly wanted to hear.

"That's what I want, too, sweetheart, more than anything in the world right now." He kissed her and was swamped again with a yearning hunger that he knew she shared. A woman couldn't fake that kind of response. The confidence that he could rush matters if he chose permitted his male generosity to come to the fore. "But I also want everything to be perfect, for both of us. If you'd rather meet in the pool first, the way we said earlier, that's what we'll do."

"Are you sure you don't mind?"

Even before she answered, Nick had felt the instant relaxation of her body against him and knew that for some reason she was still bent upon a repeat of last night. The soft blend of relief and gratitude he heard in her voice revived the little nagging suspicion that something was wrong, but he undermined it with the resolve not to make the same mistake he had made the previous night. He would overcome his inhibitions and make love to her in the pool when the two of them were hot and ready, as they had been last night. Let the world look on with envy, Nick didn't care.

"Of course, I mind," he told Caroline, releasing her with a reluctance that was like a caress. "But the thought of seeing you again in that sexy bathing suit is some consolation. Run along and change, now. Don't be too long."

"Aren't you coming?"

His smile was provocative and teasing. "In a minute. I don't trust myself to go in with you. I might give in to savage male hunger and pull you into the first empty room."

Nick didn't want to risk the hazard of the brightly lit entrance to their wing. Besides, he could use a minute or two to recover his equilibrium. He watched her walk with quick, light grace away from him, waited until her figure was illuminated in the shaft of bright light from the entry door and had disappeared inside. Then he took a deep steadying breath, blew it out and followed behind her.

Caroline didn't dawdle in undressing and donning the same outfit she'd worn out to the pool the previous evening. She didn't give herself more than a quick appraising glance in the mirror, and then she concentrated her attention upon tidying her room. She'd decided that when they left the pool tonight, she'd feel more comfortable coming to her room, not Nick's. Then he would be the one to have to leave eventually, when their lovemaking was over.

Her sense of propriety was offended by the idea of bringing a man into her room with stockings and underwear draped over a chair and personal toilet articles littered over the counter in the bathroom. It didn't take her long to establish perfect order, and when she was finished, she took the next step in setting the scene by turning out all the lights except for the lamp on the dresser, which she left on low. At the door she stopped and looked back to take in the atmospheric effect.

Her heart beat so fast at the thought of herself and Nick in the room making passionate love that she pressed her right hand over her chest and sucked in a calming breath. Then she went on out to the pool, looking forward to what she was considering a sensual interlude before the advent of the real thing.

Nick was already in the pool when she got there, but he wasn't swimming laps tonight. He was floating on his back near the side she approached and came right over to the edge as soon as he saw her. Caroline took a second, closer look at his face and then understood the annoyance in its expression when movement at the other side of the pool drew her attention and made her realize that they didn't have the pool to themselves. Another couple was over in the shadows near the waterfall, with only their sleek wet heads and her arms, wrapped around his neck, showing. They were kissing and carrying on a lover's exchange of words and laughter that was just a murmur beneath the sound of the waterfall.

With a glance over in Caroline and Nick's direction, where Caroline, in disregard of their prior claim, was taking off her short wraparound cover and stepping out of her sandals, they apparently decided to seek privacy elsewhere. After swimming to the far side, they climbed out and disappeared, arms wrapped around each other's waist and dripping wet. It seemed to Caroline that they had left behind them an atmosphere of easy, relaxed intimacy, and for that, she was grateful to them.

She laughed softly as she sat down on the edge of the pool. "I wish you could have seen your face. You looked positively outraged, as though they were intruders in your private territory."

Nick's answering grin was boyish. "That's exactly the way I felt, too." He held out his hands. "Come on in with me. I can't wait to get that swimsuit wet again. I want to see it plastered against you."

While he talked in a voice full of sexual innuendo, he came closer, his dark eyes holding her gaze. Caroline gave him her hands, her lips parted with the anticipation of the shock of sudden immersion.

"I know it's going to be *cold*!" She shrieked as he gave a jerk and pulled her off the edge into the water.

"Don't worry, sweetheart, I'll get you warm again," Nick promised, pulling her into deeper water.

Caroline came with him unresistingly, expecting him to draw her underneath the waterfall as he had done the previous night, but she braced herself for its impact for nothing, because tonight he took her straight over to the inner edge of the pool that rimmed the central island.

"Aren't you rushing things a little?" she gasped in laughing protest as he grasped her by the waist and lifted her up clear of the water.

Nick's laugh was exultant. "What do you mean, rushing things? I've been waiting for you out here for centuries tonight. Believe me, sweetheart, it was worth it." His eyes examined the effects of water upon the bodice of her swimsuit with male satisfaction. The rose strips had turned to tissue thinness and molded the firm curves of her breasts. Twin hardened peaks stood out in irresistible invitation.

Nick made a hungry growling sound as he brought her chest to his face and nipped at each hard point in turn. Her soft whimpering responses brought a little grimace of pain to his features, and he groaned as he lowered her into the water and hugged her close against him, grasping her buttocks and grinding her hips hard against his.

"You are driving me crazy, sweetheart, you do know that?" There was real pain in his voice that came from the sharp urgency of his need and the necessity to restrain it awhile longer.

"Kiss me," Caroline demanded softly, wrapping her arms around his neck. She was most pleasantly stimulated, but not as aroused as Nick was.

"Okay, sweetheart, I'll kiss you. I'd like to kiss you lots of places, but for right now this will have to do." Nick kissed her on the mouth, deep and hard, plunging his tongue inside to couple roughly with hers. Breathing hard, he murmured to her the other alternatives for kissing while he touched the parts of her anatomy under discussion. "I'd like to kiss you here." His hands cupped her breasts, and he took a hard nipple between each thumb and forefinger and rubbed them briskly. Her moan against his lips brought an answering sound of primitive male pleasure from his throat. His hands then slid down her waist and hips and one of them sandwiched between her thighs and curved itself intimately to the mounded shape. "I'd kiss you here."

Caroline murmured his name in a shocked tone as he slipped his fingers beneath the crotch of her swimsuit, but her thighs opened for him as they had done the previous night.

The extended foreplay was sheer torture for Nick because he was so fully ready to make love to her. But she reacted to his stroking and caressing with such quivering pleasure that he didn't want to hurry her. He wanted her to be wild with need when he entered her, ready for a reasonably quick climax.

Caroline suffered the onslaught of physical weakness that she had come to associate with her sexual response to Nick's lovemaking. She felt pleasantly dissolved with sharp pleasure points at strategic areas of her body. Since she and Nick were standing in the shadows at the central edge of the pool and in water up to their shoulders, she put up only the weakest resistance when he started taking her swimsuit off, pulling the clinging rose strips off her shoulders and free of her arms. She thought at first that he only wanted to have her breasts uncovered entirely and open prey for his hands.

But after he had caressed them at length and ducked his head down below the level of the water to suckle the nipples, he applied himself to tugging the swimsuit lower.

"Nick!" she murmured in protest, too late. He had the swimsuit down past her hips. She clamped her legs together to stop it at her knees, but when she took her arms from around his neck to reach her hands down and retrieve it, he took her hands in his.

"Here. You can help me," he urged and carried her hands down to where his swimsuit rode low on his hips. "I can't hold off much longer. I need you."

While Caroline hadn't ever had intercourse with a man before, she wasn't ignorant of the commonly known biological facts about the sexual nature of men—and women, too, for that matter. She thought that Nick had reached the point where he wouldn't be able to wait for lovemaking and that he was asking her for help in getting his release.

In compliance with his wishes, she slipped her fingers beneath the thin tight fabric of his abbreviated swimsuit and eased it down his hips, taking care to maneuver the swimsuit delicately free of his manhood. When she had the swimsuit down around his thighs, she left it there and hesitated before moving on to the next step, hoping for some guidance from Nick.

"Please. Don't be shy." Nick took both her hands and brought them to his groin. Later he would remember the way she had touched him and know that her tentativeness had been a dead giveaway, but now, in his urgency he assumed that hers was a knowledgeable and selfish gentleness. He thought that consideration of her own pleasure made her want to avoid pushing him over the limit of his control.

"Are you ready for me, sweetheart? As you can feel for yourself, I'm ready for you." Nick's question was nine-tenths passionate rhetoric. He was confident that she was ready. When he slipped his hand between her thighs, caressing them apart, and thrust several fingers up inside her, deeper than he'd gone before, it wasn't to assure himself of her readiness, but to heighten her need for him. The obstruction that he encountered was so unexpected that he disregarded it and pushed harder. It took her little whimper of pain to make his discovery dawn clear for what it was and the truth hit him like a truckload of bricks. The shocked expletive that he muttered was a violation of the Biblical commandment that forbade taking the name of the Lord in vain.

"You're a *virgin*!"

He stared at her unbelievingly, as though expecting her to deny his accusation.

Caroline shrank back against the side of the pool and felt the cold tile press against her bare back. She folded her arms protectively across her chest and tried without any success to muster a mantle of dignity.

"I'm sorry. I guess I should have told you."

Nick couldn't stop staring.

"You're a *virgin*," he said again. "Of all the goddamned—unbelievable—" Words failing him totally, he broke off and shook his head before he made another attempt at verbalizing his utter incredulity. "So that's why—last night—but why the hell didn't you *tell* me? A man has a right—he needs to know something like this, for chrissakes." Even in his upset state, Nick had to remind himself that his language was crude for a woman's ears, especially a woman who'd never even been to bed with a man.

"I'm sorry," Caroline said again, completely miserable. "I thought about telling you, but I was afraid that if you knew, you wouldn't be interested in, well, you know what I mean."

"You're dam—darned right I wouldn't have been interested," Nick informed her angrily, and then resented the fact that he had blurted out a truth that made him seem oldfashioned.

He reached down into the water and jerked his swimsuit up. When he ran into his own personal bodily obstruction, it seemed an affront, proof of what a gullible fool he'd been.

He had to clamp his mouth closed and grit his teeth to keep from uttering another obscenity not fit for a woman's ears.

With fumbling fingers Caroline followed his suit. She had never been more humiliated and embarrassed in her entire life, but, surprisingly, her strongest impulse, now that she'd been exposed, wasn't to escape his anger and contempt, which she thought he had the right to feel and express. She didn't want to grab her things and flee to her room, where she could be alone with her shame. Along with having the truth come out into the open came a certain relief. She supposed a criminal felt the same way confessing a crime. Like a criminal having once said, "I did it," she wanted to tell all and felt a certain urgency about the matter, since from Nick's manner, he might be the one to rush off abruptly. He seemed far more upset than she was.

"I'm not at all who you think I am," she told Nick as she struggled to pull the wet strips of tissuelike rose cloth up over her arms and onto her shoulders. "Gosh, this thing is hard to put on when it's wet!"

"It's not so easy to get off, either," Nick muttered unsympathetically, suppressing his instinctive impulse to help her, along with the cutting comment that came to mind, *Believe me, it wasn't worth the trouble.* His initial shock had subsided enough that his inbred courtesy toward members of the opposite sex had reasserted itself. As much as it galled him, he just couldn't help being a gentleman. "Who are you, anyway?"

"I really am Caroline Ainsley. I'm an elementary schoolteacher. I teach third grade." Caroline's reply was faintly distracted because having managed to get the swimsuit back on, she was concerned about arranging the rose panels decently in place across her breasts.

Nick shook his head slowly from side to side as he watched her peering downward toward her chest, while she fussed with the swimsuit, unable to judge the success of her efforts since the water level was up around her shoulders. Her sudden modesty reinforced her matter-of-fact revelation.

"A third-grade schoolteacher. I guess you're here on one of those cheap package trips." The quiet bitterness of his voice matched his thoughts. *No wonder she had been impressed with him. She'd have been impressed with any phony she ran across. And he'd thought she was a wealthy jet-setter.*

Having done what she could to attain maximum coverage, Caroline ceased her tugging and pulling on the swimsuit and turned her full attention to Nick.

"That's right. I am. It was only two hundred dollars, airfare and hotel included. There was even a voucher for money to use for betting in the casino."

Her apologetic tone awoke Nick's first feeling of guilt, but something, he guessed it was pride, kept him from speaking up and telling her that she didn't have to describe her package trip to him. He was fully aware of all the details since he'd come to Freeport on the same deal himself.

Caroline didn't read anything but restraint into his silence. There wasn't any hope in her heart that he would have any interest in her when she was finished with her full confession, but she was still bent upon telling him everything. The words poured out of her as though she'd been administered a truth serum.

"This is actually my first time ever to travel outside the United States. My Aunt Sarah, who was my guardian and like a mother, since she raised me from just a little baby, died in December. I've gotten used to the fact that she's gone, but the house is so big and empty with just me living in it. Once school was out, I had all summer ahead of me.

"Of course, I have lots of friends in Covington—that's a little town in south Louisiana, where I've lived my whole life, except for the four years when I went to a women's college in Mississippi. There's the youth group at church that I co-sponsor and the Art Association and Friends of the Library." She paused and sighed apologetically. "Gosh, I can just imagine how dull all this sounds to you, but maybe you can understand how exciting it was to someone like me to come here to Freeport and meet a man like you. You won't believe this." Her voice grew sheepish. "Once I decided to come to Freeport, I had this wonderful daydream about myself and, of course, a man, and the man looked just like you. He was tall and dark and very sophisticated." Nick made a movement that Caroline interpreted as restlessness with probably a touch of embarrassment on her behalf. Sensing that her time was limited, she talked all the faster.

"I know I should have told you the truth about myself, but it was so much fun to pretend I was someone else, someone glamorous and well traveled and, you know, *experienced* with men. It was only a matter of time before you would find me out, but it was fun while it lasted. I'm not really sorry."

Nick was in a state of shock. She was not just any third-grade schoolteacher, but one from Covington, Louisiana, located on the north shore of Lake Pontchartrain, a mere thirty- or forty-minute drive from New Orleans via the causeway. Nick was acquainted with any number of people who lived over in that area and commuted to New Orleans on a daily basis. Hell, he had clients from over there. If she was like the majority of people who lived on the north shore, she probably came into the city or at least its outlying suburbs and shopped and went to restaurants and movies and, since she was a schoolteacher, cultural performances. Nick could have run into her a hundred times. Maybe he *had*, and they hadn't noticed each other, ordinary people that they both were.

But the coincidences grew even more incredible. She didn't have to tell him the name and location of the women's college in Mississippi that she'd attended. It was his mother's alma mater! She'd managed to talk two of his three sisters into going there. It would be the thrill of his mother's life if he ever married a girl who'd graduated from her own school. And to think how close he had just come to deflowering one of her younger alumni in a swimming pool in a resort hotel on a tropical island! It was all too much. He was speaking the truth when he commented with an irony Caroline wasn't well-informed enough to comprehend, "I really don't know what to say."

"I guess there isn't much else to say," Caroline suggested sadly.

It was Nick's perfect opening to make some honest revelations about himself, but he let the moment pass. He just couldn't make himself speak the bitterly ironic words that came to mind: *You couldn't be more wrong. There's quite a lot to say.* He wasn't really sure what was behind his silence. Perhaps he lacked the courage to match her honesty and come in for his own share of outrage and contempt. Maybe he just didn't see any point in carrying things any further. They were a couple of dull phonies who'd been taken in by each other, and that was the end of it. Nick was disappointed and totally dispirited.

"I don't know about you, but I've had about enough of standing here in this water," he remarked in a stiff, polite voice. He didn't have to reach down and touch himself to know that it was safe for him to make his exit from the pool. Truth had totally extinguished his passion.

"I know what you mean. I'm beginning to feel shriveled."

Nick had to harden his heart against the chord of sympathy she aroused with her pathetic little effort at cheer. He couldn't speak consoling words of forgiveness to her without feeling like even more of a hypocrite than he already felt, and pride kept his own secret locked inside him.

Sharply aware of the ironic humor in the situation and of himself as a kind of ridiculous Don Quixote type, he took Caroline's arm politely and escorted her out of the pool. With the same detached courtesy he stood there and waited while she slipped into her short wraparound robe and stepped into her backless sandals.

"There's one thing I am rather curious about," he remarked with pointed delicacy as they were leaving the pool area.

Caroline felt her face grow hot with embarrassment. She was glad for the semidarkness.

"I think I know what it is. And the answer is yes. I did give some thought to taking precautions."

"It's the kind of practical matter a man often forgets to think about in these liberated days."

Sensitive to her embarrassment, Nick tried to suppress what was more than just idle curiosity, considering how close he'd come to having intercourse with her. The need to know how close he'd also come to possibly being a father won out in the end. What did an elementary schoolteacher, whose age he guessed to be between the mid-twenties and thirty, who'd never been to bed with a man and didn't bother to inform her about-to-be lover of that fact, choose as a method of birth control?

"If you don't mind my asking—"

Caroline knew her reaction was outdated, but she was still mortified. As a single woman living in a straitlaced small town, it wasn't the kind of subject she had call to discuss with anyone and certainly not with a man.

"The trip came up suddenly—there wasn't time, you see, to schedule an appointment with a doctor over in New Orleans. I'd have been too embarrassed to go to my doctor in

Covington. So I just went to a drugstore and bought some things. Over in the city on a shopping trip," she added.

"Oh, my God," Nick muttered in real horror. She had bought some patent products out on the market.

"You have to understand that I didn't really think anything would happen!" Caroline protested. "It was all just a pipe dream, coming here to Freeport and having a fling with an exciting, sophisticated man. I didn't really think I'd meet you, in the first place, and certainly I didn't think there was a prayer that you'd actually be interested in me. Please don't think that if I'd gotten myself into trouble that I'd have held you responsible."

"Well, fortunately, nothing did happen. But I would advise you to be more careful in the future. And next time, be sure to tell the guy what's what."

Nick would have used the same tone with a younger sister. He delivered his stern little lecture as he was opening the door into the brightly lit wing entrance. He could see the crestfallen expression on her face as she replied sadly, "I don't know if there'll ever be any 'next time.' I think maybe I just waited too long. I'll probably just stay a virgin forever."

The light was cruel as it had been on the other occasions, forcing upon them the brutal realities of life that neither of them could prevent or change. Nick was particularly mindful of the facts, since he was in possession of both sides of the story. Caroline was a wet little blond schoolteacher who'd reached out for romance and had it slip from her grasp. Nick was a tall, skinny accountant wearing his partner's gold chain and skimpy swimsuit. They were ordinary, dull people longing to escape the limitations of being themselves. For a few wonderful hours they had succeeded. They had helped each other enjoy the illusion of being glamorous and exciting, but fantasy couldn't hold up under that bright corridor light. If only it had been a chandelier, as it probably would have been if they were the real thing and staying in more expensive lodgings.

The farewell remarks they exchanged were stiff and polite, typical of well-bred Southerners who don't forget their manners, no matter what.

"I'm sorry if I hurt your feelings out there in the pool," Nick told her with sincere apology. "And please don't feel bad on my account. After all, it's not the end of the world."

Caroline mustered a grateful little smile for his kindness. "You're being awfully nice about this."

After that, there was just the matter of executing the actual parting, which they both looked forward to now that it was imminent and would end the horrible awkwardness. Caroline assumed the lead and relieved him of his male responsibility to see her to her room.

"Well, good night. I guess I'll take the stairs."

Nick inclined his head in a courtly gesture that came natural, no matter what he was wearing.

"And I guess I'll take the elevator."

He held the door to the stairs open for her, and watched her slip through it, a small, vulnerable figure. Then he stood there, a bitterly disappointed man, while the heavy door slowly closed itself.

Chapter Seven

The chaste order of her room, softly illuminated by the one lamp turned to its lowest beam, mocked Caroline. She had left the room with such breathless anticipation only a short time earlier, confident that it would be the setting for her first time to make love with a man when she returned there with Nick.

How depressing it was to come back alone, feeling so utterly undesirable. What had happened in the pool was more than just the ultimate in embarrassment. It seemed a kind of prison sentence to Caroline, locking her forever into her state of virginity. All those years she'd hoarded her sexual innocence, like a treasure, and when she finally got around to offering it to a man, it was rejected.

She couldn't help feeling bitter about the situation, and yet who was she to blame? Aunt Sarah? Her Sunday-school teachers? Society? Her own need for approval or her ease in conforming?

Sighing, she went into the bathroom to peel off the wet swimsuit. Holding it up gingerly between thumb and forefinger, as though it were an object of repugnance, she made a distasteful face and threw the sodden garment into the tub. In her present state of mind, she couldn't imagine ever wearing it again.

Methodically Caroline got herself ready for bed, following her usual routine of cleaning her face and brushing her teeth. Nick had been right, she thought, when he had said that what had happened tonight wasn't the end of the world. Life would go on. She guessed she should take more consolation in that thought, but it didn't lift the heavy weight of her depression as she got into bed and propped herself up with a magazine she knew she wouldn't be able to read with any concentration.

Just as she'd expected, she found herself going over and over the happenings of the night. She recalled wistfully the exhilaration, the sense of perilous adventure, the delightful physical stimulation her body had known and then cringed to remember her later acute embarrassment and shame. Her final thought, each time she came to the end of the mental replay, was that she had been fortunate indeed in her accidental choice of a man. Nick, for all his initial shock and indignation, had been kind. There was so much that he could have said and hadn't. A man who was less a gentleman could have left her feeling far worse about herself than she did.

Nick's opinion of his character was considerably less favorable as he took the elevator up to the third floor and let himself into his room. The evening hadn't done wonders for the self-image he'd come to Freeport hoping to bolster. He didn't think he'd ever want to get mixed up with another woman again in his entire life. He'd go back to New Orleans and concentrate on business. With the time and money he'd save by giving up on a personal life, he could probably make a fortune in investments, he thought wryly. Surely that would be some consolation, to be rich.

No sooner had the door closed behind him than he was peeling off Byron's swimsuit and unfastening the gold chain. It was childish and irrational of him to place any blame on his well-intentioned partner for what had happened, but Nick still resented Byron for pushing him into the trip and encouraging him to make a fool of himself. From now on, he vowed, Nick would tell Byron where to get off.

After he had showered and gotten into bed, knowing that he'd lie there sleepless, thinking, Nick found himself feeling worse by the minute about the way he'd acted with Caroline—all pompous and righteous, when he was as much an impostor as she was. The truth about himself would certainly have spared her feelings somewhat, but he had been too caught up in the injury to his own precious ego to give consideration to her.

By the time he finally dropped off to sleep, Nick wasn't feeling like much of a man, but he was honest enough with himself to admit that he didn't have any intention of seeking Caroline out and telling her the truth about himself. As far as he was concerned, the whole episode was something he wanted to forget. If he encountered her accidentally during the next two days, he would speak and go his way.

Nick's sleep might have been even more fitful than it was if he'd known how soon the accidental encounter he foresaw as a possibility would occur: the very next morning at breakfast. A person of habit, he awoke early, at his usual hour. Remembering the previous night's happenings, he discounted any thought of trying to go back to sleep. He'd get dressed and have breakfast and make it his business not to be around the hotel all day so that he wouldn't be likely to run into Caroline.

By the time he had shaved and dressed, Nick was looking forward to the day with moderate anticipation. Along with the disappointment of having banished his more exotic alter ego came a certain comfortable relief in just being himself, Nick Denton. Wearing Bermuda shorts, a short-sleeved shirt and sandals, he set out for breakfast, a current professional magazine tucked under his arm. It had come in the mail the day before he left for Freeport, and he hadn't gotten around to reading it yet.

At that early hour the Garden Café, where breakfast was served, wasn't crowded. The hostess guided Nick over to a table next to the outer glass wall so that if he cared to enjoy the view, he could look out at a portion of shady brick courtyard and also have seen anyone passing alongside the restaurant on the covered tiled walkway.

But this morning Nick wasn't interested in people watching or gazing out at the courtyard, where greedy little birds, filled with memories of yesterday's tidbits, were scouring the swept bricks in vain. He gave the breakfast menu a cursory glance, ordered, and then opened up his magazine. When his waitress bustled up with a pot of coffee, he looked up long enough to thank her politely when she filled his coffee cup and then he went back to reading his article, oblivious to the fact that Caroline was passing along outside and entering the restaurant.

Like Nick, Caroline was accustomed to rising early every morning at precisely the same time, and the habit was hard to break at the beginning of the summer. She'd actually been up as long as he had, but it took her a little longer to get dressed than it took him. Otherwise, they probably would have arrived at the Garden Café together.

She didn't see Nick as she passed within a couple of feet of him because her smiling attention was drawn to the flock of chattering birds in the courtyard. The day before she had observed their boldness in begging food from hotel guests lunching and snacking at the patio tables. The early morning energy of the birds and the clean fragrance of the air she was drawing into her lungs reinforced Caroline's generally optimistic outlook upon the day. No matter what had happened the previous night, there was something to be said for being in such a lovely place for a few more days. She would get as much enjoyment out of her remaining time in Freeport as she could manage, she thought happily.

There was probably no matchmaking involved in the hostess's decision to seat Caroline next to Nick. Guests could be depended upon to prefer sitting at a table near the windows, if one was available, and it was standard procedure to any experienced hostess to take full advantage of seating capability. The only small table available at the window was the one next to the tall dark-haired man reading his magazine with frowning absorption while he sipped his coffee and waited for his breakfast to be served.

Caroline spotted Nick as soon as the hostess headed off in his direction. Making a rapid adjustment to the fact that he was up and about at such an early hour, she got a smile in readiness for the moment when he would look up and see her. But he seemed entirely oblivious to the proximity of other human beings as the hostess seated Caroline facing him and left her with a menu and the promise that her waitress would be there shortly.

The suspense of knowing that Nick had to look up at any time and see her made Caroline ill at ease. She wished, once she was already sitting, that she had done what would have been the natural thing for vacation acquaintances and greeted him upon her arrival. But she realized, that might have caused some awkwardness, too, if the hostess concluded wrongly that the two of them might enjoy sitting at the same table.

Caroline studied her menu and took surreptitious glances over at Nick. He looked so different in the daytime in plain-tailored casual clothes that it was difficult for her to believe this was the same man in the wine silk shirt and ornate gold chain, the same man in the tiny little black bikini that left almost nothing to the imagination. He looked like a clean-cut young professional man with an intellectual bent, a lawyer, perhaps, or a junior executive type.

Nick didn't look up until his waitress brought his food, and then he still gave no sign that he was aware of Caroline's presence. He glanced up at the waitress with an absently polite expression and moved his magazine over to one side so that she could place his plate of scrambled eggs and bacon in front of him. Caroline decided for her own piece of mind that she would have to force his notice of her, or else she'd never be able to eat her own breakfast with any enjoyment.

"Good morning," she called over to him cheerfully.

Nick's head snapped up and he gazed at her, first with open astonishment and then with a reserve that didn't leave much doubt in Caroline's mind that the sight of her hadn't brightened his day.

"Good morning," he replied with stiff courtesy. "I'm afraid I didn't see you."

"So I noticed. I would have spoken sooner, but I didn't want to disturb your reading. You seemed to be so interested in your magazine. But, please, don't let me interrupt. Go ahead with your breakfast and your reading." Caroline dismissed him with a smile as cheerful and forced as her tone and turned her attention to her breakfast menu, as though she hadn't already decided what she would order. She just wanted to reassure him that she had no intention of intruding any further upon his privacy.

Nick was relieved and did as he was bade, but his enjoyment of both his food and his magazine was ruined. He didn't like the fact that she had been sitting over there watching him when he was totally unaware and unguarded. It made him feel awkward to know that he couldn't look up without chancing that he would meet her glance. Nothing was more uncomfortable than having to try not to look at someone and yet not appear to be under that constraint.

Caroline sneaked looks at Nick while she sipped her hot tea and waited for her breakfast of hot croissants and melon to be served. More used to his appearance, she nevertheless was still struck with the marked change. Of course, she wouldn't have expected to meet him abroad during the day in his rich nighttime attire, but the colors he was wearing this morning were such quiet, muted colors, and his throat was bare of any jewelry. Usually a man who wore a chain would wear one all the time.

He was clean-cut and attractive in a quiet, wholesome way, but definitely not strikingly handsome as he had been at night. It was hard for her to believe that this wasn't the conservative twin of the rakish gambler she'd seen with her own eyes as he stood at a roulette table over in the casino and bet hundreds of dollars on a single turn of the wheel. Caroline's puzzlement grew in direct proportion to her curiosity, but she was resigned to the good possibility that she wouldn't be getting any answers from or about Nick.

She had brought along some brochures about various sightseeing tours and day trips and pulled those out to peruse them while she ate. Meanwhile Nick had finished eating and was about to refuse another cup of coffee from his waitress when he noticed that Caroline was paying no attention whatsoever to him and decided to have another cup after all. He was really in no hurry, having formulated no definite plans for the day. It was his turn to sneak glances over at her and note the changes in her day appearance, which were in keeping with what he'd learned of her identity the night before. She looked like a pretty young elementary schoolteacher from a Southern town in Louisiana.

Her blond hair didn't show up so well during the day as it did at night under artificial lights, but it looked clean and soft with a healthy sheen. The color was either natural or else it had been done by an expert. He was inclined to believe the former since she had the complexion of a true blonde, delicate and fine. She was wearing very light make-up and pale pink lipstick that went well with the pastel colors in her blouse. Her jewelry was so dainty that it wasn't evident on first sight how much of it she was wearing: little dangling pearls in her ears, a gold filament chain and pearl pendant around her neck, a feminine gold watch on one arm and a chain bracelet on the other, several rings on her hands, but none of them the large diamond cluster. The overall effect was soft and feminine.

The word *ladylike* came to Nick's mind as he surreptitiously looked her over and watched her eat with impeccable table manners that reminded him of meals at his mother's table back home in Natchez, Mississippi. There wasn't a doubt in his mind that Caroline could walk into his mother's house and be perfectly at home. His mother would approve of Caroline, as she looked right now, wholeheartedly, especially when she learned the name of Caroline's college alma mater.

For the type of small-town Southern girl that she was, Nick had to admit that he himself found her pleasingly attractive. Considering her attributes—her blond prettiness, her nicely proportioned figure and her evident good breeding—he couldn't understand how she'd managed to remain unmarried when she was certain to have had her share of offers. Even more incredible was the fact that she'd stayed a virgin. It would be different if she was the frigid type, but he knew from firsthand experience that she could be passionate and hotly aroused.

In view of the speculative nature of his thoughts, Nick was embarrassed when Caroline lifted her gaze unexpectedly from the brochure she was reading and caught him looking at her. To his relief, she didn't look affronted at the fact that he had been staring at her. The wistful expression on her face arrested his attention, but didn't prepare him for her question.

"Have you ever been diving?"

"Diving? You mean with scuba equipment and all that?" Caroline nodded. "Why, yes, I have been diving a time or two."

Caroline's sigh was envious. "I wish I had the nerve to try it, but I don't. I'm not even a good swimmer. It would be such a thrill, I think, to go right down into the world of beautiful fish and strange underwater plants. Look at this." She turned the brochure around so that he could see the underwater camera shot of a diving scene that took up the whole page.

She sighed again, this time with a tinge of self-consciousness. "Maybe I'll go back home to Covington and take some of those diving lessons in a swimming pool and give diving a try at some later date. For now, I guess I'll stick to a safer excursion, along with all the senior citizens, and go out in the glass-bottomed boat." She folded up the brochure with the scuba diving scene, dropped it and picked up another brochure, which she pretended to be studying with interest. Her comments had been totally spontaneous, arising out of the adventurous side of her spirit, which she assumed every person had. She hadn't meant to sound self-pitying.

Nick waited for her to look up and give him a natural opening, and when she didn't, he cleared his throat and spoke to her anyway. "You know, there's a very safe alternative to scuba diving that's more adventurous than a glass-bottomed boat: snorkeling." Caroline's expression was politely doubtful. "You don't have to be a strong swimmer, either, not in saltwater. It makes you naturally buoyant. You get to see the same thing you see when you dive down. The water's crystal clear." *Not cloudy like Lake Pontchartrain or muddy like the coffee-colored bayous and rivers in south*

Louisiana, Nick could well have added, but didn't. At least he felt truthful talking about diving and snorkeling even though his experience had been limited to exploring the reefs off the eastern coast of southern Florida. He'd gone on a couple of diving and snorkeling trips down to Key West.

The discreet doubt on Caroline's face was joined by her earlier wistfulness, but Nick was a Southerner himself and knew her reply was pure politeness.

"I have a couple of brochures here on snorkeling excursions. Perhaps I'll give it a try. Thank you for suggesting it." She took a final sip of her hot tea and began to gather up her brochures in a tidy stack in preparation of leaving.

"Could I take a look at those snorkeling brochures?" Nick asked, surprising himself as much as her.

"Why, certainly you may."

While Caroline shuffled delicately through her stack of brochures with her long-nailed, perfectly manicured hands, Nick came over to her table and sat opposite her. The fact that there wasn't a hint in her face or her eyes, the latter a really lovely color of blue-gray in the daylight, that she was aware of the impulse that had hit him somehow made it take hold all the more strongly. Why not take her on a snorkeling excursion today? he asked himself. She wouldn't go by herself, and he'd enjoy being out on the water himself. The notion rather appealed to him to make it possible for her to fulfill her longing for a taste of adventure.

"This one looks good, the one offered by the Underwater Explorers Society. See the picture of the boat here." He leaned closer and held the brochure where she could see. "The big platform across the stern makes it easy to get down in the water with your flippers on. They tend to make climbing down a swimming ladder a little difficult. That's my main reservation about this other trip on the trimaran, even though it sounds like more fun sailing out to the reef."

Caroline nodded to assure him that his judgment sounded good to her and tried not to look doubtful as to how it applied to her. She didn't dare let herself hope that an invitation was being implied, but there was still a pang of disappointment when he handed the brochures over to her and shoved his chair back in preparation for getting up.

"Well, how about it? Want to give snorkeling a try?" Any reservations Nick was still feeling when he issued his offhand invitation were swept away by the animation that lighted Caroline's features. She looked like a little girl on Christmas morning.

"I'd love to!" was her immediate spontaneous response, but then it was followed up by the reluctant reminder, "I was serious when I said I'm not a very good swimmer."

"And I was serious when I said you don't have to be a good swimmer," Nick reassured her gently. "Don't worry. I won't let anything happen to you. I promise."

As soon as he'd spoken, Nick was self-consciously aware that his words might be taken by many women as a brand of male chauvinism, but Caroline apparently wasn't in the least offended.

"Then my answer is yes," she declared happily.

"Good."

They smiled at each other like any ordinary young man and woman finalizing plans for an outing that promised to be fun. Then they briefly settled the mundane details, with Nick taking the lead. He would make the reservation for a midmorning trip. They would meet in the side lobby at the excursion desk and take a taxi over to the marina from which the boat departed. He recommended that she be sure to wear or at least bring along a T-shirt, which she might even want to wear in the water to prevent severe sunburn on her back.

"I've seen people on snorkeling trips get some pretty serious sunburns, and you look like you might have delicate skin."

"I do," Caroline admitted unhesitatingly, taking the remark as subtly complimentary, the way it was intended. "I tan if I take it easy and get out in the sun a little while each day, but I can burn to a crisp if I'm not careful. I brought along some good sunscreen."

When they parted outside the restaurant, Nick promised to let her know if he encountered any problems in making the reservation.

"With any luck, they'll still have room for a couple more people. If not, we should be able to figure out something else to do."

The casual assumption that they would spend the day together made Caroline's step springy as she returned to her room. She hoped the snorkeling trip materialized, but the possibility that it might not didn't dampen her high spirits. Her sense of anticipation at the prospect of Nick's company for the day was different from the keen excitement she'd felt upon venturing over to the casino the previous night. The dangerous element was gone now that her identity was out in the open, but in its place was a warm, pleasurable glow that was really very nice.

Nick felt good about the day ahead, too, until he thought about the questions that would naturally come up about his background. He wished that he'd been forthcoming the night before and told her the truth about himself. The fact that he hadn't spoken out made a belated revelation damnably awkward.

There were some pragmatic considerations, too. He and Caroline were virtually neighbors, living on opposite sides of Lake Pontchartrain, and the proximity caused him some concern. It wouldn't surprise him in the least if they even had acquaintances in common. If news of his masquerade got back to New Orleans, he preferred to relay it himself in a manner that wouldn't cause him embarrassment. Without any undue conceit on his part, there was also the possibility that Caroline might try to pursue a relationship upon their return home, and her virginal state would prevent his wanting to get involved with her since it was commonly known that a woman is susceptible to becoming emotionally attached to her first lover.

The more Nick thought the matter over, the clearer the answer seemed to be. He would do well to quell his conscience and keep his identity secret for a few days, thereby avoiding all manner of later complications. As a point of honor, upon his return to New Orleans he'd never mention Caroline's name or even relate the details of their meeting in any way that she could find objectionable if she knew. Meanwhile he'd go all out to see that she had a good time for the rest of her vacation, and when the two of them left, she'd have pleasant memories and stories to tell to her friends back home. He would have his privacy, and, indeed, some good memories of his own. That would be the end of it.

Once Nick had worked it all out in his mind that to remain a man of mystery would be beneficial to him and not harmful to Caroline, he looked forward to the day even more than he had before, and he wasn't disappointed in the way it turned out. He enjoyed himself thoroughly and was glad a dozen times over that he'd given into his impulse and invited Caroline to go snorkeling.

Her enthusiasm was lovely to see. She couldn't seem to stop smiling on the taxi ride to the marina as she looked eagerly out the window. "This is so exciting!" she murmured after they'd signed in at the Underwater Explorers headquarters and were collecting their snorkeling gear out back. On the ride out to the reef she kept drawing in deep breaths of the fresh sea air and took an obvious delight in the scenery, her eyes moving from the receding shoreline to the open sea and then upward to the cloudless blue sky. "It's such a beautiful day, isn't it?" she demanded of Nick several times, and he could only agree.

Early on, the possibility had occurred to him that she might be one of those wimpy females, like a few he'd seen on other snorkeling excursions, requiring a lot of persuasion and reassurance before they would ever get down into the water, but that turned out not to be the case at all. Having listened with rapt attention to the instructions given by a bronzed young Adonis, who made Nick feel like a tangle of bony arms and legs, she was quick to put on her gear once the boat was anchored over the reef.

"I'm scared," she confided to Nick, but her blue-gray eyes were asparkle with excitement, and she let him and the young god help her off the platform and into the water.

Nick stayed close to her to make sure that she was going to be all right and give some calm reminders of the instructor's advice. After some initial problems with adjusting her mask and getting the hang of breathing through the mouthpiece of her snorkeling tube, she relaxed somewhat, reassured that just as Nick and the instructor had promised, she was quite buoyant and would stay afloat with no effort whatever. Noticing that she lifted her head up often and looked around for the boat, Nick sensed that she must still be a little nervous about her limited swimming ability.

"Don't worry," he told her. "I'll stay with you and make sure we don't get too far from the boat."

It must have been the reassurance she needed because after that she devoted her attention utterly to the underwater world beneath them. True to his word, Nick stayed close by her and from time to time had to steer her in a circle and back in the direction of the boat. For him, it was companionable gliding along over the surface of the water, side by side, each of them pointing when they caught sight of a fish

or a coral formation that they wanted to make sure the other
one saw. He thought that he could feel her wonder like a
tangible force, and it brought back for him the thrill of his
own first snorkeling trip.

For Caroline it was the most transcendent experience of
her life. She was enthralled by the exquisite colors; purples,
blues, reds and yellows, some delicate and some brilliant and
luminous like millions of incandescent little pinpoints of
color pigment. She was enchanted by the endless variety of
form and shape, ranging from the most graceful to the gro-
tesque. Movement had never brought her such pleasure, and
there was constant movement, darting and swift, ponder-
ous, so slow as hardly to be discerned by the eye. The scene
beneath her was everchanging. Great swarms of tiny fish
would glide into sight so that there seemed to be millions of
them and then just as quickly they would be gone. Solitary
shy individuals would ease into sight out of the labyrinth of
coral caves and then slip into the shadows again. Down on
the floor of the sea were the sinister sea urchins, black and
spiny, and occasional strange crawling creatures. It was a
world of fascination and total quiet.

Caroline was so immersed in it that she wanted to float
forever there on top of the sea and gaze down at the sound-
less symphony of color, shape and movement. With Nick
beside her, she felt safe to enjoy it. When she would point
at some especially spectacular sight and he would reach his
hand down and clasp hers to signal his appreciation, her
satisfaction went so deep that it brought an ache of happiness.

She was the last person to climb aboard the boat again.
When the call came for everyone to get out of the water, she
heard it and heard the good-natured shouts of those who
complained that they hadn't seen enough. Caroline just
feasted her eyes on the underwater drama below her with a
kind of farewell intensity. Her face had a dazed, other-

worldly look as she finally climbed aboard, gratefully accepting Nick's help.

He helped her remove her flippers and mask with the attached snorkeling tube and then led her forward to a bench under the canopy that provided protection for the steering station. Caroline sank down gladly and smiled happily at Nick as he sat next to her. He was indulgently prepared for an exuberant outpouring like those he was hearing from the benches in the stern. The first-time snorkelers in particular wanted to describe the strange wonders they'd seen. Caroline's fervent expression of gratitude was unexpected and sweet.

"I can never thank you enough for bringing me on this trip," she told him softly. "It is truly the most wonderful thing I've ever done in my life. I'm sure that I shall never forget it."

Under different circumstances, Caroline would have been embarrassed by her appearance. The cotton T-shirt she'd worn in the water over her bikini was sodden and shapeless. Her blond hair hung in wet hanks. Her light makeup had washed off in the sea, leaving her face fresh and shiny. Her lips were the delicate pink that nature had made them. And yet Nick had never felt any stronger urge to kiss a woman. Since it was one of those crowded, intimate situations, he didn't fight it.

"I'm glad." He smiled into her eyes and leaned over to kiss her tenderly on the lips. "I enjoyed it myself."

The exchange was warm and simple and left them both feeling good. As they leaned their backs against the hard fiberglass bulwark, their shoulders touching companionably, neither was marking the moment as any important milestone in their relationship, but they felt easier in each other's company. Their conversation was pleasantly relaxed on the short ride to the picnic site on a sandy beach, where they would be served lunch.

It was there, after everyone had waded ashore from the shallow anchorage, helping to carry the lunch supplies, that Nick had to field his first questions from Caroline about his identity. He'd thought they would have come much sooner, but up until now she had been too involved in the excitement to give way to her inevitable curiosity.

While the boat crew was grilling the hot dogs and hamburgers for lunch, Caroline and Nick were among those who went for a leisurely stroll along the beach. "Don't go off too far," the bronzed Adonis shouted out good-naturedly from his squatting stance on the sand by the portable grills. "Another five minutes and we'll be eating." The hungry replies all claimed imminent starvation.

Five or ten seconds later Nick's stomach growled loudly and then, as though on cue, Caroline's made an answering sound. The two of them burst into spontaneous laughter.

"I sure hope they brought enough food," Nick declared with a sincere fervor, rubbing his flat belly. "My breakfast has been long gone."

"Mine, too."

The casual mention of breakfast brought back to each of them the awkward meeting that now seemed a long time ago. Aware of its comic elements upon retrospect, Caroline slid a sideways glance at Nick to get a hint of his thoughts and connected with his own glancing gaze. She felt confident enough at this point to grin impishly and tease him.

"You should have seen your face when you looked up and saw me sitting across from you this morning." She giggled at the recollection. "You'd have thought I intended to snatch your breakfast away from you. Or maybe your magazine. What were you reading with such interest, anyway?"

"I'm not much of an early morning conversationalist," Nick retorted, ignoring her question.

Caroline would have let the question about the magazine drop if a picture hadn't flashed into her mind from the scene at breakfast. When they were ready to leave the restaurant, Nick had picked up his magazine from the table, folded it so that the cover was hidden and held it down against his leg. At the time she'd been too excited about the snorkeling trip to take much notice, but now her curiosity was aroused, and she wondered if he hadn't deliberately concealed the magazine from her.

"Come on. Tell me. What were you reading?"

"Oh, just a financial magazine." It was truth of a kind. Any trade magazine subscribed to by an accountant dealt after a fashion with money.

"What was the title of it?" Caroline persisted, amused that he was being evasive about something so unimportant.

"Why this strong interest in my reading material, anyway?" Nick countered.

"It would be nice to know *something* about you," she came back at him gaily. "Do you realize that you're a total mystery to me? You know virtually my whole life history, and I don't know the first fact about you—where you live when you aren't on vacation at some glamorous place, what you do for a living or even if you *do* do something to earn a living. For all I know, you could be a professional gambler."

There it was, the moment Nick had known would come. For just a split second he wavered and considered telling her the truth. Unwittingly Caroline herself quelled the impulse. His brief hesitation made her realize that he actually might be deliberately concealing from her the facts of his identity. The thought was naturally intriguing, especially when the picture of him the way he looked at night in the casino flashed into her mind. He might be someone with a behind-the-scenes notoriety.

"I think maybe you're afraid I'll find out who you are and come out with an exposé in one of those gossipy newspapers in the supermarkets," she accused him, only half-teasingly.

Her eagerness to be fascinated and even shocked by his identity filled Nick with a deep sense of irony at how disappointed she would be if he told her the dull truth.

"Take my word for it, those gossip rags couldn't be less interested in yours truly. My story is just too dull to tell. We'd both fall asleep before it was half over." He injected a lighter, carelessly joking tone into his voice. "Do me a favor and imagine that I'm an exciting fellow, maybe one with a checkered career. I'll forget everything you've told me about yourself and pretend that you're a foreign princess in disguise. We'll have a wonderful, glamorous time and then go our ways and live happily ever after. How about it?" He rubbed his stomach to circle the conversation back to its beginning. "I wonder if those hot dogs and hamburgers aren't done yet."

As he caught her by the shoulder and turned her around to head them back toward the picnic site, Nick had to admire the way he'd made skillful use of the truth in his deception, and yet he felt lousy, a feeling he attributed to guilt. It was another product of his upbringing that lying just didn't come easy to him, even when it didn't hurt anybody involved. He was almost irked at the ease with which he'd deflected Caroline's curiosity.

"You'd better watch your every word," she warned him gaily. "I'm going to be looking for clues as to who you are." But he could tell that she liked the game of pretence he'd suggested, and in some totally irrational way, he was hurt that she didn't persist in learning his true identity.

What Nick didn't know was that Caroline was counting her blessings. Here she was in paradise with a man she was liking more all the time, having new experiences and living out the promises of the brochures she'd gotten from the travel agency back home in Covington. Now he'd just as much as told her they'd be spending the rest of her precious few days in Freeport together. The sun was warm on her face, the sand silky underfoot and the mouth-watering aroma of food pervasive in the air. The only thing that could have improved upon the moment was the knowledge that she could trap it somehow in a container and keep it forever.

Chapter Eight

The atmosphere was convivial at the picnic site, with a lot of laughing and joking while the food was being served. After she had her paper plate loaded with a hot dog and potato salad in one hand and a paper cup of fruit punch in the other, Caroline looked around for a place to sit while Nick finished serving himself. Most of those who'd been ahead of her in the food line were just sitting down on the sand in the bright sunlight. She assumed that she and Nick would do the same.

"Why don't we go over and sit under one of those trees in the shade," he suggested when he came to stand by her side. "Even with that sunscreen you're wearing, I'm a little worried about what this tropical sun can do to your skin. You wouldn't want to get sunburned and have the rest of your vacation spoiled."

"No, I wouldn't want to do that," Caroline agreed at once and followed his lead.

It occurred to Nick as they were settling down under one of the twisted, stunted trees with broad flat leaves, that it was damned comfortable to be with a woman who didn't constantly have to take issue with a man's every act and word just to assert her female independence. Yet she wasn't a clinging-vine type, either. As evidenced by her behavior on the snorkeling trip, when given the opportunity, she welcomed a new experience and plunged into it wholeheartedly, even if with some reasonable trepidation.

They both ate hungrily and conversation for several minutes consisted mainly of comments about their state of hunger and the good taste of the food. The situation was a far cry from breakfast.

Nick sat back with a satisfied sigh when he'd finished his plateful of food. "I think I might live now." He drained the fruit punch in his paper cup. "Care to try some of that Bahama Mama concoction now?" They'd both chosen the nonalcoholic punch to drink with their lunch instead of the one laced with rum.

"Sure," Caroline agreed promptly and lounged back comfortably while he went to dispose of their paper plates in the plastic garbage bag provided and refill their paper cups with rum punch.

She choked on the first swallow. "That's strong stuff! I'm not much of a drinker, I'm afraid."

"I'm not, either." The words were out before he could stop to think, and they drew an incredulous look from Caroline.

"Anybody who drinks Scotch is a drinker in my book!" She made a face and shivered her distaste. "I hate Scotch. It's so nasty I don't see how anybody can enjoy the taste of it."

Nick was in such complete agreement with her that he had to take care to keep his own repugnance for Scotch from his voice as he remarked, "I guess it's an acquired taste. Actually I like gin equally as well," he added a bit too emphatically, paving the way for the evening, when he had no intention of force-feeding himself with Scotch.

"That's right. You did drink gin and tonic last night." Caroline's voice was dreamily relaxed. She set her cup down in the sand and leaned back on her hands with her head tilted back. "Even on a full stomach, this Bahama Mama stuff is making me light-headed. I feel so good, like I could just float back to town. What about you?" She turned her head sideways and smiled at him, with no conscious provocative intentions whatever.

Perhaps the fact that he had been aroused to the point of lovemaking two nights in a row and not satisfied was responsible, but Nick was finding her posture and her voice sexy. He was keenly aware of the grains of sand on her bare thighs. The way her breasts were rounded against her T-shirt made him want to slip his hands up under it and reacquaint them with the soft fullness. The curve of her throat was a tender invitation. He was telling himself that he'd have to wait until they were back at the hotel when he remembered her innocence and knew he'd have to wait a lot longer than that. The realization didn't make him happy. Why had he gotten himself mixed up with a virgin schoolteacher, for heaven's sake?

"This stuff *is* potent," he said abruptly and sat up erect, directing his eyes firmly out at sea and away from Caroline, who followed his gaze, blissfully unaware that anything might be amiss. The combined effects of excitement, sun and rum really had made her quite light-headed and deliciously languid.

She drew in a breath of air and exhaled it, taking conscious pleasure in the normally involuntary act of breathing. "Look at the boat out there," she told Nick in the same dreamy voice that was like the rub of soft fur against his kin. "It's just bobbing away, tied down to that anchor. That's the way I've been my whole life, tied down to an anchor.

Not that I'm blaming anyone but myself, because it was a lot my own fault. This was my first little trip out to sea, you might say, and believe me, it won't be my last. I feel like the whole world is out there, just waiting for me to come and explore it."

She sighed again. "This trip to the Bahamas is just the beginning. I have lots of school holidays and vacation time. From now on, I intend to go places and do things. I intend to meet wonderful, exciting men—like you."

She turned her head slowly to smile at Nick, expecting to find any one of several varieties of indulgence on his face. The sharp disapproval she saw there instead took her aback, and she eyed him with surprise.

"Just keep in mind that you're going to find more than pretty fish out there in the sea," he told her shortly. "There are also some big, dangerous sharks with teeth as sharp as a razors and an appetite for pretty little schoolteachers from Covington, Louisiana."

Caroline blinked and with another deep breath sat up and stretched luxuriously, not at all displeased with Nick's curt warning.

By the time they arrived back at the marina, Nick had conquered his fleeting ill humor over his fated bad luck with women. He was looking forward to the evening with Caroline, even though it would have a platonic end. Her enthusiasm was genuine and endearing, a pleasant contrast to the bored attitude that became a matter of chic with young women her age.

During the taxi ride to the hotel, Nick finalized plans for the evening, even to deciding upon the restaurant where they would have dinner: Ruby Swiss. They'd both heard it mentioned enthusiastically and seen its ads claiming an outstanding menu with both Continental and native specialties. After dinner they would take in the casino show.

"I'm really looking forward to the show," Caroline commented enthusiastically. "Don't forget I have a free pass that came with my trip." Nick had one just like it, but naturally couldn't make mention of the fact.

For all his realistic acceptance of what would happen when they arrived at the hotel, Nick wouldn't have been a normal man if he hadn't given at least fleeting thought to how nice it would be for the two of them to go up to either his room or hers—it wouldn't matter which—take a short shower together and make love. Afterward they could have a nap and then wake up refreshed to get dressed to go out for the evening. There was only one circumstance preventing that most appealing chain of events: the fact that Caroline was a virgin. What made matters more difficult for him was that the obstacle raised itself only in *his* mind, not in hers, giving him the full burden of restraint. Given her present adventurous outlook upon tasting life's pleasures, he didn't think he'd have to do much more than suggest that they continue the day together, on a more intimate basis, and she'd be game to give lovemaking a try.

Her very innocence made it all the more impossible for Nick to give in to his male lust. He didn't know what was behind the abstracted expression on her face or her evident haste as they walked together to their hotel wing, but there wasn't a hint of self-consciousness in her manner, as he knew there would have been if she'd been keyed into his thoughts.

"Where's the fire?" he chided her teasingly. Normally he had to moderate his long stride for the benefit of her shorter legs.

"I want to change clothes and do some shopping." Her impish look up into his face was younger than her actual years, at variance with the light self-disparagement of her voice. "A princess in disguise wouldn't want to wear a schoolteacher's clothes, and yet I don't think she'd wear the same dress three nights in a row either, do you?''

Mention of the black dress didn't help Nick much in holding on to his honorable intentions. His glance down at the front of Caroline's T-shirt, dried by the sun now, was pure male reflex.

"I certainly don't object, not if we've both got the same dress in mind."

Carline's blush was more one of pleasure than embarrassment. "That's good to know, just in case I don't have any luck."

Nick himself would have been sharing Caroline's concern about wearing the same clothes three nights in a row if he hadn't taken the opportunity that morning to buy himself another shirt to wear with the dark trousers and white jacket. This one was dark green. He'd found it in the same men's shop there in the hotel where he'd bought the swimsuit he was wearing, a plain red nylon tank suit, not as racy as Byron's bikini and not as stodgy as Nick's own swimming trunks.

Memory of his covert shopping trip helped him to put matters firmly in perspective and conquer any remaining temptation. He was reminded of that promise to himself not to take advantage of Caroline in any way with his secrecy about his identity. To take her maidenhead without telling her who and what he was seemed a violation of that promise. Looking ahead to the evening, Nick tried to shore up the moral strength he thought he was going to need by giving himself an ultimatum: *keep in mind, pal, that if you make love to her, you've to tell her who you are.*

It occurred to Nick that he might find it easier to hold on to his restraint if Caroline didn't wear the black dress that evening or some new outfit equally as daring. She would be cute as a button, but not nearly so provocative in one of the dresses she'd brought from home, and there was really no call for her to spend her money needlessly.

"You don't need to go shopping," he told her. "Wear something you already have and save your money."

"Maybe that was a financial magazine you were reading at breakfast today," Caroline mused teasingly. "You sound like old Mr. Clarence Boudreaux, Aunt Sarah's tax accountant. He always acted like Aunt Sarah was spending his money, not hers, when she'd call on him for advice."

Nick's momentary flash of disbelief went unnoticed, he was sure. There was no way he could confirm, without asking her, whether her aunt's conservative old tax man wasn't a male relative of the Clarence Boudreaux who was a contemporary of Nick's and had been in his and Byron's class at Tulane. Nick had run into Clarence recently and found him as obnoxiously boastful as ever. The chance that Caroline might have some connection with him made Nick deeply thankful for his discretion. If there was anyone Nick would prefer *not* to have any information on him that could make him look ridiculous, it was Clarence Boudreaux.

"Who am I to give advice to a princess in disguise?" he said lightly, throwing up his hands. "Go ahead and spend your millions." Grinning, he reached out a finger and tapped her gently on a sun-reddened nose. "I just don't think I'd recommend a red dress."

As it turned out, Caroline took Nick's advice and didn't do shopping that afternoon. By the time she got to her room and took a shower, pleasant exhaustion settled in and she took a nap instead, rationalizing that it would be better to stay alert that night, no matter what she was wearing, than to yawn all evening or fall asleep over her dinner.

Getting dressed for dinner turned into a major decision-making process. She tried on every dressy outfit she'd brought, including a couple of her best silk dresses that were in the same price category as the black dress. What distinguished the black dress from the others was its simple, bold style and the fact that she couldn't possibly wear it to church. Remembering the expression in Nick's eyes when he'd given his ready permission for her to wear it again, Caroline decided to take him at his word.

Next there was a matter of jewelry. Since she was wearing the same dress, she thought, she could at least try for a different look. It was too bad that she didn't have some really fabulous diamonds like a real undercover princess should have, but her diamond studs were nice and made quite a show when worn with the diamond "jackets" Aunt Sarah had given her for her birthday two years ago. With diamonds in her ears and the big diamond cluster on her finger, she would go for a simple, classy look, with no other jewelry besides her tiny gold evening watch.

Nick came by her room for her at the time they'd prearranged. When Caroline opened the door, she just stood there for a long moment adjusting to the transformation he had made back into his exotic night personality. He was the same man who'd been with her most of the day and yet he was an intimidating stranger, so tall that he loomed above her, so deeply tanned by the day's outing in the sun that the gold chain around his neck gleamed with a more wicked luster and the soft white of his jacket was luminous in the dim hallway.

Caroline had to swallow before she could speak. "You look very handsome."

Her wide-eyed awe brought a smile to Nick's face. "And you look very beautiful, Princess Caroline." He inclined his head with mock formality.

Caroline relaxed immediately at the teasing note beneath the gravity of his voice. The glamorous stranger was Nick.

"You know, I just can't get over the difference in the way you look during the day and the way you look at night," she marveled. "It's a regular Jekyll and Hyde kind of transformation. Not that either one of you is a monster," she added laughingly when Nick's eyebrows shot up with humorous questioning.

"You seem to go through something of a Cinderella act at night yourself," Nick remarked, and let his eyes run admiringly over Caroline's appearance, giving due notice to the revealing neckline of her dress and making her glad of her decision to wear it.

On the way to the restaurant, she light-heartedly pursued the truly intriguing subject of his two contrasting faces. "Which one of you is the real Nick Denton?" she demanded. "Is it the one who wears silk and gold and gambles away thousands of dollars at the casino or is it the fellow who wears khaki shorts and sandals and eats hot dogs and potato salad on a picnic?"

Nick shrugged and made a carelessly grandiose gesture with his hands that belonged totally to his nighttime personality. "Maybe both. Maybe neither. Which one do you prefer?"

Caroline gave the question some smiling thought before she gave what was intended to be a diplomatic, but truthful answer.

"Today you were perfect the way you were, but tonight you're the answer to a woman's dream of the perfect escort. You're the mystery man out of my daydream, dark and handsome and worldly, a man who has been places and done all sorts of things, *wicked* things." Her laugh was a lightly self-conscious acknowledgment of her enjoyment of the game of pretense he had initiated earlier in the day. "Tonight you're just the kind of man a princess in the disguise of a schoolteacher comes to a tropical paradise hoping to find."

From his point of view, Nick couldn't have asked for a warmer, lovelier, more delightful companion for the evening. He couldn't even bring himself to wish that she was less physically appealing. It was a temptation he couldn't resist to play to the hilt the role that she wanted him to play—that of a handsome and irresistible stranger. He said romantic, flowery things that would have stuck in the throat of down-to-earth, conservative Nick Denton. Caroline answered in kind. The script for their make-believe drama was enjoyably mixed with the real. From time to time they laughed at themselves, were even confident enough to poke light fun at each other.

Nick had never had a better time with a woman in his life or desired one more than he desired her, as the evening progressed. Once or twice he mentally prodded himself with the facts, but reality couldn't bring him down to earth. Caroline, on her part, knew she was falling madly and foolishly in love and couldn't seem to care. For her it was a night of enchantment with no worries about repercussions. It was the kind of night every woman wants to experience at least once in her life, and Nick was the kind of excitingly handsome, attentive escort a woman is likely to know only in her romantic fantasies.

Ruby Swiss turned out to be a perfect choice of restaurant. The atmosphere was exclusive, the service unobtrusive, and the food delicious. They made different selections and shared them.

"I want to try the conch," Caroline remarked when they were studying the extensive menu. "But what if I don't like it? I don't know about you, but I'm starving again."

"If you don't like it, we'll simply snap our royal fingers and have them take it away and bring something more to your liking," Nick replied pompously, and then grinned in response to her appreciative giggle.

"Seriously."

"Oh. Seriously. Why don't we order a safe alternative for each course. That way we'll get to sample strange culinary delights and be assured of not starving to death, too. For a

soup course, we can get the conch chowder and—'' He
looked at her under raised eyebrows.

"French onion soup."

"Excellent choice. Now, let's see. How about the Cracked
Conch—that has a barbarian sound about it, wouldn't you
say?—for an entrée and, for our safe alternative . . .''

"Steak and baked potato."

The test choices turned out to be their favorites. The
conch chowder was spicy with chewy chunks of the shell-
fish that was a Bahamian food staple.

"Hmm, that's good,'' Caroline said at once when she had
taken a tentative taste.

"Delicious."

They alternated taking several more spoonfuls before she
asked, "How shall we do this anyway?'' She'd never shared
a bowl of soup before.

Nick understood at once that she was dealing with a
problem of table etiquette and managed to smother his grin
while he dipped into the bowl and then ate another spoon-
ful. "I don't know . . .'' he began gravely and waited for her
spoon to clear before he dipped his again "I guess—'' A
pause while he ate. "We had better think of something—''
Another pause for the next bite. "Before it's all gone.'' As
it almost was by that time.

Caroline realized then that he was having fun at her expense, but the fact didn't bother her in the least. "Being a
princess and all, I'm just not used to eating out of the same
bowl with my subjects,'' she declared loftily. "Pass the
French onion soup over, and let's see what that tastes like.''

Nick hastened to do her bidding. "Do all princesses have
an appetite like yours?'' he wondered aloud.

The cracked conch turned out to be outstanding, too.
Their Bahamian waiter explained that the filets had been
pounded to tenderness, breaded and browned to the golden
color in melted butter. The flavor was delicate and the con-

sistency succulent. Caroline and Nick each devoured their portion of that entrée before they paid any attention to the steak, which turned out to be quite palatable, too, but ordinary fare by comparison.

Caroline sighed contentedly over her after-dinner coffee. "I hate to think what I would have missed if I'd just have had the steak and baked potato, and that's probably what I would have ordered, or something else equally as safe, if I'd been on my own." Her smile and the expression on her face completed the message that was more, much more, than just gratitude for a good dining experience.

"I'm glad you weren't on your own," Nick told her softly. He picked up her hand and carried it to his lips and kissed it, not because the act was in character with his role but because deep inside he wanted to and his dashing role gave him the freedom.

There were no bad moments for Nick during dinner that would give him cause to feel uncomfortable about his secrecy. Fortunately Caroline hadn't even brought up the subject of the distinctive New Orleans cuisine with which both of them were familiar, so that Nick wasn't faced with whether or not to claim having visited New Orleans during his assumed travels. She seemed blissfully content to be caught up in the here and now and not at all concerned with probing Nick for mundane facts about his background.

At the casino he did have a bad moment when it came time for him to get their tickets to the show. He couldn't let Caroline accompany him to the window, or she'd know that he was using a free show admission, just like hers.

"Why don't you sit at the bar and have a drink while I get the tickets," he suggested when they arrived at the casino.

Caroline glanced at her watch.

"It's only thirty minutes before the show, and we're served two drinks during it for the price of admission." Nick quickly resigned himself to spending the extra twenty or thirty bucks, whatever it was, for a ticket, but then Caroline saved him the expense when she looked over at the line forming outside the casino theater and suggested that she might get in line and wait for him there.

"We want to be sure and get good seats."

Nick felt hypocritical walking off and leaving her there, but by the time he returned, the length of the line had grown, proving her suggestion to have been an excellent one. They were able to get choice seats in the first tier of the small semicircular theater. Caroline ordered a daiquiri and Nick ordered a gin and tonic, and they sat sipping their drinks while they waited for the show to begin.

"The travel agent who sold me this package trip raved about the show," Caroline remarked. "She said the costumes are fabulous."

Nick had overheard some enthusiastic remarks about the show himself that morning in the men's shop. They had been about what the female dancers's costumes didn't cover.

"You do realize that this is a Las Vegas type of revue?" Nick's eyes dropped to the front of Caroline's dress. "In some of the numbers there are topless dancers." And not much to the bottoms of the costumes, either, he silently added, according to the lusty male comments he'd heard.

"No, I didn't know."

Nick couldn't tell if she was faintly shocked at the news or just interested. He had a hard time once the show began keeping his eyes on the stage as much as possible. Caroline's reactions were so much more interesting to him than the dance numbers, even though he had the normal male's appreciation of a lavish display of shapely female bodies.

As Caroline's travel agent had promised, the costumes were brilliant, with a lot of sparkle and color and a profusion of feathers, but with the exception of the capes, they didn't leave a great deal to the imagination. It was during the third number, one that featured a great deal of running on and off the stage, that the dancers returned minus the tiny spangles that had been covering their breasts.

A reflex glance over at Caroline told Nick that she was embarrassed. She was sitting very straight and still with her eyes firmly fixed on the stage. As he turned his own eyes back to the dancers, Nick was undeniably stimulated by the sight of bouncing breasts and flashing thighs and gyrating buttocks, all in time to loud rousing music. But the specific object of his desire wasn't one of the smiling girls flaunting her body up on stage, but Caroline herself. He was subjected to tormenting visions of undressing her very slowly and gently and seeing her shyly naked before his eyes.

Caroline had felt Nick's eyes on her and sensed that he was aware of her embarrassment. During the brief intermission midway through the show, she decided that she'd probably feel much less awkward if she openly admitted her reaction and held it up to ridicule.

"I know this is going to sound like an elementary schoolteacher, but I really can't imagine getting up in front of a whole room full of people with no more clothes on than that!" she said, meeting his eyes squarely and expecting a teasing light in them. What she found instead was a warm intimacy that brought the whole discussion of nudity down to the two of them.

"You don't look like any elementary schoolteacher I've ever known, not in that sexy dress," Nick told her, smiling.

Caroline looked down with him at the daring bodice of her dress and then raised her eyes slowly, bracing herself for another intimate connection with his gaze.

"You can't imagine how 'exposed' I felt the first time I wore this dress." Her voice made fun of her modesty. "Every time a man looked at me, I wanted to cover myself with my hands."

"Now that you've worn it several times, you no longer feel that way?"

Caroline looked straight into his eyes.

"Tonight I haven't noticed any other man but you, and I like having you look at me. Do you know what I was thinking during the show? That I'd like to be naked for you."

"Caroline—"

It was just as well that the curtains on the stage opened and music filled the small theater again as the show was resumed. Nick knew he would have gotten bogged down once he was past speaking her name with that impassioned mixture of protest and longing. He fixed his eyes on the stage and took quiet deep breaths to slow down his runaway pulse, while he made desperate reminders to himself of all those reasons he should be strong and conquer his carnal nature. It didn't help him to know that he didn't have just himself to fight, but Caroline's sweet womanly submission, too. Perhaps the honorable man in him might come out the winner if he could just keep reminding himself that she wasn't really offering herself to *him*, but to some exciting man she'd been able to fabricate with her romantic imagination, thanks to Nick's silence about himself.

When the show ended at midnight, Nick was armed with several suggestions of what they could do next, none of them the option that the man in him would have preferred.

"The night's still young. Would you like to do a little gambling? The casino doesn't close for another three hours. Or we could go somewhere and dance. There's a lively disco place in the Royal Tower next door. If you feel like something a little more laid back, there's the piano bar over at our hotel. We could have a drink and sing along."

Caroline hesitated out of politeness. None of the choices appealed to her, but she would make herself amenable to whatever he was in a mood to do. Her guess was that his first offer would be his choice.

"Why don't you gamble and just let me watch? Every time I've bet for you, you've ended up losing all your chips.

Either I'm unlucky or else I just don't know any betting strategy.''

Nick couldn't have agreed with her more. The accountant in him was deeply relieved at her lack of enthusiasm for what could have been the most costly entertainment alternative.

"I'm not much in the mood for gambling tonight. I'd rather do whatever you would enjoy doing."

"I'd just like to go for a walk. The show was fun, but it was noisy. It would be nice just to get a breath of fresh air and enjoy the peace and quiet. How's that for an exciting suggestion?" Her smile was self-disparaging, but the message in her blue eyes endearingly honest. She wanted to get away from all the people and be alone with him.

Going for a walk had a strong and similar allure for Nick, but for both their sakes, he tried to sound as though he was merely indulging her as he agreed.

"A walk, it is."

As they walked outside into the black velvet of the tropical night, he couldn't have been more aware of the dangers than if he'd just agreed to take her on a midnight skydiving jaunt.

Chapter Nine

Caroline held his arm in that feminine, trusting manner that had given Nick an instinctive male pleasure right from the first. She seemed to float alongside of him with effortless grace. Lulled into a sense of manly confidence that he could handle whatever arose, he relaxed and took in a deep breath.

"The air's nice, isn't it, with the scent of the ocean and the flowers?"

The use of understatement was intentional, meant to be a kind of antidote for the potent charms of the night, but it quite obviously had no effect on Caroline, who was a most willing slave.

"Isn't this wonderful?" she declared in that dreamy, unconsciously sexy voice that had given Nick some problems earlier in the day on the snorkeling trip. "The only thing that could be better would be walking barefoot on the sand along the edge of the ocean instead of on concrete. I remember what you said the night we met, that you usually like to stay on the ocean. The next time that's what I intend to do, too." Her gurgle of soft laughter was like a feather brushed over Nick's nerve ends. "Maybe I'll even go skinny-dipping in the ocean at night." She looked up at him with an archly reminiscent smile.

"Remember you suggested we go swimming nude in the hotel pool," she continued, "and I was too inhibited. Well, maybe—"

"I remember that we discussed the very real possibility of being hauled off to a foreign jail," Nick cut in briskly, fearful of letting her finish her conjecture. His repressive tone had no noticeable effect upon Caroline, who just giggled.

"Were you really taken in by me?" she demanded skeptically, and then didn't pause for an answer. "I can't believe that you were. You must have known the business about jail was a big bluff on my part. I've never seen the inside of a jail in my life except in news pictures or on the TV or movie screen." She sighed wistfully. "It was all such great fun pretending to be someone terribly sophisticated, terribly experienced."

Her quick look upward combined with the way her voice altered told Nick that she'd made a leap forward in memory to the scene at the pool, when he'd discovered her virginity. He was feeling sharply uncomfortable with the turn the conversation had taken.

"No harm was done," he put in quickly.

"You're just being nice." The soft gratitude in her voice made Nick want to squirm, but there was worse to come. "I don't know who you are, Nick Denton, but it doesn't really matter to me where you're from or what you do. As far as I'm concerned, you're the nicest man I've ever met, along with being the most handsome and the most fun. I'll never forget you as long as I live."

"Caroline, please—"

Caroline attributed the desperate entreaty in Nick's voice to embarrassment and made a swift apology that only made him feel more like the world's greatest hypocrite.

"I'm sorry! I know a man like you is embarrassed to death by this kind of naive feminine emotion. It's just that I feel so great about everything that's happened, it's hard not to say what I feel."

Nick envied her the freedom of her candor. The burden of his imposture weighed upon him like a ton of lead that he saw no opportunity of shrugging aside. With every spontaneous word, she was making it more impossible for him to be honest with her. How could he admit that he had been totally taken in by her in the beginning because he was no more a world-traveled sophisticate than she was? How could he reveal at this point that his primary disappointment in discovering her true identity had been a matter of ego: he had been crushed to learn that the gorgeous, sexy blonde who found him so fascinating was an innocent school-teacher?

It had been the combination of shock and male pride that had kept Nick from speaking out in the pool the previous night, when the moment had actually been right for making his own confession. Then that morning he had had a second chance at honesty and opted for what he had chosen to think of as discretion. He hadn't foreseen the human complications. He hadn't expected to find her so warm and companionable and refreshingly feminine. He hadn't known she would look at him in such a way as to make him want to go out and slay dragons in her path. His innate honesty made him want to blurt out the truth to her, and yet his courage failed him on two counts. Not only did he cringe at the thought of her contempt, now that he had come to value her undeserved admiration, but he hated to be the source of her disillusionment. The truth about him would spoil her wonderful tropical vacation.

As he looked ahead and saw the familiar lighted entrance of their hotel, Nick felt like a man who'd dug himself a safe trench to hide in, only to find that it had turned into a deep black pit.

"Well, look where we are. It's as though we're both a couple of homing pigeons," he observed with a false heartiness. "Now that we're here, we may as well have a drink in the piano bar." He didn't feel like having a drink or sitting in the midst of a noisy crowd, but anything would be better then continuing this conversation or following along the dangerous path it was leading them.

The wistful quality of Caroline's little silence didn't bode well for Nick's escape plan.

"I thought you might be about to suggest another midnight swim in the pool."

"We've both had about enough time in the water for one day, don't you think?"

Her silence this time was secretive. Nick braced himself for her next words, knowing that she would be unveiling a counter plan.

"You're right. We probably have. In that case, I think I'll just call it a night. It's been a long, wonderful day and I'm a little tired."

She told him all he needed to know with her soft, languid tone. The transparency of her simple ploy was oddly touching. She would agree to let him accompany her to her door, kiss him good-night and trust that nature and romance would take over from there. His wisest course, he surmised, was not to argue with her, but to play right along and get her safely deposited in her room.

"Are you sure you wouldn't like a nightcap?" The inquiry was polite, with no real persuasive content.

"I'm sure, but thank you, anyway," Caroline answered politely.

"Then I'll walk with you to your room."

"You really don't have to, you know."

"I know I don't have to. I want to."

Nick could feel her satisfaction and knew the courteous exchange had gone quite according to plan. She made no further efforts to dissuade him. Her next words were on an entirely different subject.

"Have you ever seen such a huge round Oriental rug before in your life?" she demanded of him as they entered the main hotel lobby. The secretive, happy undertone in her voice made Nick's heart drag on the polished tile floor at the disappointment he was conscience bound to cause her.

"No, I don't think I have."

In the full light of the hotel lobby and then the broad L-shaped corridor that took them out into the semidarkness again, Caroline sneaked looks at Nick that deepened her sense of wonder and yet her certainty about what she meant to happen when they got to her room. Tonight she would make love with that tall, dark, strikingly handsome man walking beside her, a virtual stranger, about whom she knew nothing. The realization thrilled her to her fingertips and toes, and yet there was more than reckless abandon involved in her decision to give herself to him. There was a solid sense of the rightness of it that defied everything she'd been taught by church and society.

Not that she was fooling herself into any illusion that something permanent would ever come of what happened between them tonight. She knew nothing would, but she also knew deep in her heart that making love with Nick would be meaningful and beautiful. She felt like the most fortunate of women to have met him at exactly the right time.

Nick's reticence didn't cause her any great concern, since she believed that his constraint was related to the fact that she hadn't been to bed with a man before. If anything, she admired him for not wanting to take advantage of her. Being a virgin didn't keep her from having all the normal female perceptions, and she was sure that Nick desired her, even knowing who and what she was. During the day she had felt the physical attraction flare up between them, and then during the casino show it had been electrifying. Now she would simply have to take the initiative and convince him that she knew full well what she was doing.

If Nick had been hoping that the overhead light just inside the entrance to their hotel wing would do its trick and turn Caroline into ice, as it had done before, he was disappointed. She smiled up at him and wrinkled her nose in a cute gamin expression.

"Shall we take the elevator? It's faster."

Nick's heart beat faster in response to the shy insinuation in her voice and eyes, but he just raised his eyebrows with mild enquiry and tried to keep his reply gallant and clear of any answering innuendo.

"There's no big hurry, is there? I wouldn't want to rush an evening like this one to a close."

Caroline held his gaze long enough for Nick to see her gathering up her courage, and then she glanced away as she made her follow-up attempt in a quick, breathless voice. "My hurry is not to bring it to a close." As soon as she'd gotten the words out, she looked back up at him with startled questioning, to see his reaction.

Nick wanted more than anything in the world to take her into his arms right there and kiss away every trace of feminine uncertainty, but he knew he couldn't afford to indulge the tender impulse because it was too dangerous. She might look like a sweet child-woman in her sexy black dress, but once he felt her in his arms it would be the woman that he would respond to, and then there would be hell to pay in turning down her invitation to spend the night with her.

Caroline forgot to breathe as she watched the fire flame up in Nick's eyes, but then, disappointingly, he lowered his gaze and gave her hand clasping his arm a friendly pat as he urged her over in the direction of the elevator. She was glad that he at least didn't make small talk. The silence between them could allow her mentally to take a preparatory breath and get ready for the moment when they would arrive at her door. It was clear to her now that shy hints wouldn't do. She was going to have to be bold, probably even spell it out with words. He wanted her—of that she was certain—but he wouldn't take her unless she somehow overcame his reservations.

Nick was prepared for another tentative overture at her door and preferred to forestall even that, to be on the safe side.

"Good night and sweet dreams," he said lightly, taking her by the shoulders and bending to kiss her on the forehead. "No more thank-yous are necessary. Anything I've done to give you enjoyment today or tonight was pure selfishness on my part. I've had a great time. Now get yourself a good night's sleep so that you can be bubbly and pretty at breakfast again in the morning." He took his hands away from her shoulders slowly, as though he'd just stood a prized piece of sculpture on the shelf and wanted to make sure it would stay there, safe. At the same time he was retreating a half step backward to wait while she got her key out of her little evening bag.

Caroline gave every appearance of being cooperative, taking out the key and handing it to him so that he could unlock her door. But when he had pushed the door open, she made the overture Nick thought he had bypassed, and there was nothing tentative about it.

"Don't I even get a 'real' good-night kiss?" she demanded in a sultry tone that by itself spelled trouble. Before Nick knew what was happening she had her arms around his neck and her body pressed close up against his.

"Caroline, you don't know what you're doing." Even as he voiced the desperate warning, Nick was giving in to the temptation he'd warded off downstairs and was putting his arms around her. He shut his eyes against all the consequences and for a long, delicious moment, hugged her hard against him, savoring the forbidden pleasure of the feel of her soft womanly curves. He'd just hold her like this and then let her go, he convinced himself. No harm would be done.

"Kiss me, Nick." Caroline's soft plea brought his eyes reluctantly open, and he gazed down into her face, seeing her sweet urgency and her lips parted in an invitation more eloquent than any words.

Nick didn't figure that a kiss would do a whole lot more damage in giving his body false hopes than holding her close had already done, and the truth of it was that he just wasn't strong enough not to kiss her. He'd wanted to kiss her too many times during the day, an urge that had grown steadily more powerful during the evening. Even as he bent his head and covered her lips with his, he knew the weakness of his rationale: one kiss wasn't going to satisfy his urge, not even two kisses or three. His hunger was a man's hunger that went too deep for satisfaction from kisses.

As far as Caroline was concerned, the moment Nick's arms closed around her in the hard, convulsive bear hug her case was won. She melted against him and gave herself over to his care, free to immerse herself in the pleasure of his touch and his kisses with no worries about what would come next. She would be content to stand there in the hall kissing, leaning her body into his and hanging on around his neck, until he took them into the next stage, which she assumed would be in her room.

When Nick groaned and pushed her face into his shoulder, she made no struggle but stood there quiescent, feeling the thud of his heartbeat. When he took her by the shoulders some seconds later and put her back from him, every pulsing nerve and cell in her body screamed a protest to the separation, but her still-functioning brain assured her it was temporary. Her smile was dazed, but confident, as she voiced what she assumed was in his mind.

"We'd better go inside my room, where we can have a little more privacy."

When Nick started shaking his head slowly from side to side, Caroline stared at him blankly until he said, "No," once and then again, with more violent emphasis. *"No."* He held her tight by the shoulders, as though to make sure that she didn't buckle, and then dropped his hands away with an experimental slowness. "You don't know what you're doing."

Caroline gave her head a little shake to clear away the haze of confusion. "But I do know what I'm doing. I'm twenty-eight years old, Nick, not sixteen. What's wrong? I don't understand. You do want to make love to me, don't you?" She looked into his eyes searchingly.

"What I want has nothing to do with it."

"Yes, it does." Her quick denial matched the feeling in his voice. Still holding his gaze, she reached down for his hands and brought them up to her breasts and held them there. Her voice was hardly louder than a whisper. "Tonight I could tell that every time you looked at the front of my dress, you wanted to touch me here. And I wanted you to." Nick looked with her down at his hands spread across her breasts, and no power on earth could have kept him from moving his fingertips, even though stroking the satiny curve of her bared cleavage was death to his good intentions.

"Caroline—" He jerked his hands away from her chest and held them in fists down by his side. "Honest to God, Caroline, I wish you'd listen to me, for your own sake. You've never been to bed with a man before, and now you're willing to make love with a man you don't even know. You don't know anything about me. You don't even know if Nick Denton is my real name."

"I don't care, Nick!" Tears were coming to Caroline's eyes. Her confidence was fast ebbing with the sense of everything having gone horribly wrong. "Is the fact that I'm a virgin really such a big deal to you? Well, it isn't to me, except as an embarrassment and a hindrance. If it weren't for that, we wouldn't be standing here like this, having this discussion, would we?"

The reluctant truth was written on Nick's face for her to read. Disappointment and mortification made the tears well up in Caroline's eyes and spill over down her cheeks. Her only defense was anger.

"I'd just like for you to tell me what I'm supposed to do to get over this undesirable state of being a virgin if no man is going to touch me as long as I am one! That's the very reason I didn't tell you in the first place. I was afraid you wouldn't be interested, as you very obviously aren't." She drew in a long unsteady breath and held her shoulders very straight. "We might as well not waste any more time standing here." It was a pathetic bluff since she didn't make a move to leave.

Nick clenched his fists tighter. No matter how much he wished he could take her into his arms and hold her tenderly to ease her hurt, he knew he didn't dare. As rotten as he felt at that moment, he knew he was doing the right thing by her. His mixture of frustration, apology and anger at the situation was reflected in his voice and did nothing for his cause.

"Caroline, please believe me, this isn't easy for me, either," he began, and paused when he could see that his words weren't helping.

"I'm sure it isn't," Caroline came back at him proudly, drawing herself up to her full height, unimpressive as it was. "I can only assure you that it won't happen again. If I have to stay a virgin my whole life, I'll never throw myself at you again, Nick Denton. And don't go feeling sorry for me, either!" she blazed, seeing the stricken look on his face. "I came here to Freeport to find a lover, and I'm still going to find one!" It took some courage for her to stand her ground when Nick took a half step toward her.

"You know you don't mean that, Caroline."

His terse disapproval might have given her more satisfaction if it hadn't been mixed with his deep concern. How could a woman hope to work up a case of angry indignation against a man with such decent instincts? There was little conviction in Caroline's parting words, with their imminent threat of tears.

"Whether I mean it or not is no business of yours. Just go away and leave me alone. I don't ever want to see you again."

With head held high, she turned her back on him and marched through the opened door, remembering at the last minute to stop and snatch the key out of the lock. It seemed the final evidence of a totally cruel universe when the key stuck and she had to jerk on it, losing her last shred of dignity. Nick heard her muffled sob as she finally succeeded in pulling it free and closed the door behind her with a bang.

He stood there five or ten seconds, staring sickly at the door, adjusting to the fact that of all the times he had bungled with a woman, this had to be the worst and the most painful. How could a man make such a mess of things with the best of intentions?

Not sure of how he was ever going to straighten out the tangled web of his relationship with Caroline, but positive that she was in no mood to listen to explanations that night, he finally stirred himself to movement and walked disconsolately down the hall to the elevator, took it up to the third floor and went to his room. As guilty as he felt for having caused Caroline such unhappiness and as anxious as he was over the possibility of not being able to set things right, he was still frustrated as hell physically and irritated that she hadn't been able to appreciate how damnably hard it had been for him not to take her up on what she'd offered him. If she knocked on his door right now, his honor and her well-being would both be in trouble. A man could turn on and turn off again, with no satisfaction, just so many times before he reached his explosion point, and Nick was about there.

He felt better mentally, if not physically, as he decided that he'd make a clean breast of it with Caroline the next morning at breakfast. He'd tell her everything. If she went back home and took out a full-page ad in the Sunday edition of the New Orleans *Times Picayune* exposing Nick to everyone north and south of Lake Pontchartrain, he would only be getting what he deserved. But he didn't think she was at all the vindictive type. Now that he knew her better, he realized that there hadn't been any call for his discretion on the grounds that she might cause him embarrassment or prove to be a nuisance on their return home, but that was hindsight. He'd just have to do what he could to set things right.

The next morning Nick awoke early, according to habit, and comprehended almost at once what was behind the feeling that something important was going to happen. He

was surprisingly nervous as he dressed and went to breakfast and attributed his jitters to normal cowardice and
uneasiness over Caroline's state of mind, both before and
after he'd told her. She'd probably be hurt and proud and
unfriendly at first, and afterward, well, he just couldn't
predict how she'd be. Maybe they could laugh over the
whole thing and then enjoy themselves. That was what Nick
was hoping.

He deliberately took along the same trade magazine, in-
tending to use it as a prop. "You were curious about what I
was reading at breakfast yesterday morning," he would say
and show her the cover. "Here. Take a look for yourself. It's
the key to the Nick Denton Mystery."

His plan was to be light and self-deprecating, to try to
make a joke of the whole story, from beginning to end: the
circumstances that had led to his taking his partner's trip, his
daydreams about winning a fortune in the casino and meeting a beautiful blonde, his masquerade in flashy gold and
silk, his encounter with Caroline. Actually, if the telling of
his story went well at the beginning—and that depended
greatly upon Caroline's reception of it—Nick thought he
might enjoy sharing it with her. Everything after Discovery
in the Pool—he intended to label key happenings—he would
gloss over lightly. As to why he hadn't confessed his identity at that time, he'd just be candid and tell her the reasons.

"I'm hoping to be joined by a young lady," Nick told the
hostess when she led him over to the same table he'd had the
morning before. He told the waitress the same thing and said
he'd like coffee while he waited. When thirty minutes had
passed and Caroline still hadn't appeared, he decided to order his breakfast. Expecting her to show up any minute, he
ate it with little enjoyment, had a final cup of coffee and
then left the restaurant, thoroughly disappointed and annoyed and yet concerned. His common sense told him that

Caroline was probably just avoiding him, but there was the nagging, alarming possibility that something might be tragically wrong.

He went straight to Caroline's room and knocked on the door. When there was no answer, he knocked louder and called out her name. Faced with the decision of what to do next, he decided against the high odds of making an utter fool of himself by trying to knock down the door or summoning the management. She was probably up early, just as she had been yesterday, and had gone somewhere besides the Garden Café for breakfast. Or she might be in there ignoring him, too hurt and angry or embarrassed over last night to want to face him and speak to him.

With this latter possibility in mind, Nick went up to his room and had the hotel operator ring Caroline's room, only to get no answer. After that he tried again every fifteen minutes for an hour and began to get seriously worried. Where was she? he wondered. She had had time enough to eat breakfast and return. It was too early for the shops to open. Nick paced the floor, wondering what to do, and then when he asked the operator to ring her room for what would be the final time before he resorted to drastic action, he was told that the lady in room 212 had asked not to have any local calls put through to her room. She didn't want to be disturbed.

The message was a slap in the face to Nick and made him furious at the thought of how he had wasted all his concern. While he was going out of his mind, she'd either been there in the room the whole time or else had returned and just hadn't bothered to answer the phone, figuring it had to be Nick. He was inclined to believe the latter, and the fact that she was going about her business made him all the angrier. If she was feeling like a woman scorned, it was her own fault for not giving him the chance to explain.

Caroline had awakened feeling all of what Nick had
thought she might be feeling that morning and more: hurt
pride, anger, embarrassment and a deep, aching disappointment she was hard put to explain to herself. It was the
latter that made a coward of her. Without it she might have
armed herself with the mix of other emotions and marched
over to breakfast, welcoming an encounter that would allow her to demonstrate supreme indifference. Instead she
yielded to the instinct to avoid Nick and made her actions
acceptable to herself through the exercise of rationaliza-
tion.

Instead of breakfasting once again in the Garden Café,
she would venture over to the Royal Tower and sample its
early morning fare because the walk would be pleasant and
she wanted to do and see as much as possible during her
short trip. It would be a balm to her hurt pride if she could
succeed in enjoying herself, despite what had happened the
night before. In a way, she would be showing Nick Denton
that he wasn't important, whether he even knew or not.

At that early hour most hotel guests were still asleep.
Caroline was aware of the quiet as she left her room and
thought of how she had taken a kind of pleasure in her early
morning aloneness the previous morning. But not so today,
not with the distinct possibility that Nick was up and
abroad, too, and she might at any second encounter him. It
annoyed her to feel like a fugitive. Outside on the covered
walkway, she forced herself not to hurry, but it was a relief
to reach the glass doors opening into the corridor that would
take her to the front of the hotel.

With the front entrance doors closing behind her, Caroline took in a deep breath and looked around her with a kind
of determined appreciation of her surroundings, but she
hadn't gone more than a few steps when it dawned upon her
for the first time that there was only one sensible route over
to the Royal Tower. It meant she had to cover the same ter-

ritory that had been a charmed path for her the three previous nights when she'd floated over it holding on to Nick's arm. She had to take the paved sidewalk that intersected with the four-lane highway in front of the hotel and then the arcaded walkway along the front of the International Bazaar and the Royal International Casino. The walkway would lead her past the big fancy doors of the casino and on to the entrance of the adjoining Royal Tower Hotel.

As she trudged along, Caroline tried halfheartedly to banish from her mind the vision of a glamorous couple, walking and talking and laughing softly in velvety night darkness. She could hear the echoes of their voices, and the sound made her want to cry with despair. His tone was low and masculine, consummately sure. Hers was silvery and excited, musical notes climbing a scale of romantic hope. This morning, with her heart feeling like a big lump in her chest and her feet falling heavy on the pavement, it was hard for Caroline to believe that eager young woman had been herself. Her heart ached with an oddly commiserative sympathy for the enormous disappointment that lay in waiting for her.

"Bastard!" Caroline murmured aloud, and at once felt a little foolish but somehow better for having denounced the man as a villain.

After that she could let the ghostly couple glide past her on their way to the hotel and to their unhappy parting, which was past history to her. As she walked on to the Royal Tower, Caroline thought about the day ahead of her and felt increasingly more cheerful as she made her plans.

She enjoyed her breakfast far more than Nick had enjoyed his and took a grim pleasure in not answering the phone when it rang after she had returned to her room to change into her swimsuit. To make sure that it was the "bastard" who was calling, she checked with the operator immediately afterward to learn that a gentleman in the hotel had been calling her, and then she left the nasty little message that she didn't want to be disturbed by that same "gentleman" again.

It was right after she'd hung up the phone with a little satisfying bang Caroline decided to wear her new one-piece swimsuit out to the pool that morning. Let Nick Denton come looking for her, and he'd find her getting her full share of male attention and not caring that none of it was his.

Chapter Ten

Caroline's nerve might have failed her when she arrived at the pool if it hadn't been so early so that she was one of the first arrivals. She selected a lounge chair with a perfect exposure to the sun and sat down on the edge of it before she eased off her cover-up and stretched out with her eyes closed. In a short time she felt as relaxed as she was pretending to be.

Between the screen of her lashes, she watched other arrivals and both saw and felt the close glances in her direction. She was amused but definitely flattered when a group of college boys trooped by her, stopped for a murmured conference and then circled back to take lounge chairs close to her own.

"I can't wait to see her when she gets that pink-and-black number wet."

"Me either, man."

The lusty whispered exchange came to Caroline's ears, bringing raw memories of a similar sentiment voiced by a more mature male. At that moment she seriously doubted that their curiosity would be satisfied since she didn't have any intention of going into the pool. She already knew that the thin material of the swimsuit turned into a filmy skin when it got wet, and in the bright light of day, it was surely semitransparent, as well.

Three-quarters hour later, Caroline was wishing that she'd worn a swimsuit more suitable for swimming and could take a cooling dip in the pool. So far Nick hadn't appeared and already the tropical sun was hot on her skin. She felt self-conscious even sitting up and applying sunscreen lotion, aware that she was attracting a great deal of male attention, guarded in the case of those who had female companions next to them, but blatantly open on the part of the college students lounging next to her. They were following the movements of her hands over her sun-warmed bare flesh with undisguised lust and were eagerly awaiting a stray glance over in their direction that would give them an opening for a friendly overture.

Caroline had made brisk short work of spreading the sunscreen lotion liberally over her blonde's sensitive skin and was ready to screw on the bottle cap when she caught sight of Nick, passing at the very outskirts of the pool area. Quickly she averted her gaze before he saw her and squeezed another pool of lotion into her palm.

"Where are you fellas from?" she inquired of the college boys with a friendly smile over in their direction as she gave her right thigh a second, more deliberate coat of sunscreen lotion.

The answers came back eagerly, almost in unison.

"We're from Texas."

"Except for Jimbo here. He's one of them Cajuns from down in the bayou country in Louisiana."

The four of them were students at the same university in Texas and were fraternity brothers. Caroline didn't have to ask them what their student classification was to know that they were either freshmen or sophomores. She barely listened to their answers, aware that Nick was threading his way through the lounge chairs in her direction.

"What a coincidence," she told the youth labeled Jimbo by his buddies. His wiry build and dark hair and eyes bespoke his French Acadian ancestry. "I'm from southern Louisiana, too. Where exactly are you from?" She gave Jimbo the full benefit of her smiling interest and ignored Nick's arrival at the foot of her lounge chair. "New Iberia? I've been through there several times. That's big sugar-cane country, isn't it? What made you decide to go all the way to Texas to go to college when you have a state university right there in Lafayette?"

While Jimbo was explaining that he wanted to be a veterinarian and couldn't earn that degree at USL in Lafayette, Caroline appeared fascinated with the information—but she was actually listening to the exchange on the other side of her. Nick was asking the fiftyish woman reading the thickest paperback Caroline had ever seen if she would mind terribly moving over to the unoccupied lounge chair next to her so that he could sit next to his girlfriend. The woman said she wouldn't mind at all, and the sounds that came to Caroline's ears told her the transfer was being made and Nick was settling his long length next to her.

"Well, I'm sure you're all having a good time here in Freeport," she told the college youths in a sugary tone, and settled back again in her lounge chair with her eyes closed, and her face turned slightly in their direction. It took all her will power to pretend that she didn't even know Nick was there. Indignation churned inside her at the very notion that he would muscle his way next to her by telling that woman that she was his girlfriend. The college boys' conversation among themselves was quite obviously intended for Caroline's ears as they discussed their hangovers after a night of competing with each other to see who could drink the most Bahama Mamas. After about five minutes they agreed that it was time to take a dip in the pool. If it hadn't been for the terse presence on her other side, Caroline wouldn't have responded to the hopeful looks in her direction. She opened her eyes lazily and smiled.

"Ready for a swim?" the leader of the pack named Brian was quick to inquire.

"Not yet. I think I'll get some sun on my back first."

Still pointedly ignoring Nick, she sat up on the edge of her chair away from him, took her time about arranging her towel over the plastic webbing and stretched out on her stomach, giving the college boys and anyone else watching a view of bare rounded buttocks whose tender white color made it obvious they hadn't been exposed to the sun before. Not for the world would Caroline have succumbed to her basic modesty and reached back to tug at the thin stretchy black fabric and try to cover more of herself. Instead she wiggled her hips in little sideways movements as through settling herself more comfortably.

Nick watched the whole production along with the college boys, understanding completely their openly lustful interest and yet resenting it. He felt like telling them to run along and find themselves some girls their own age, who he knew would be likely to have a lot more sexual experience than Caroline.

The waves of disapproval Caroline felt coursing at her from Nick's direction gave her immense satisfaction. Lying with her face turned away from him she gave her hips another tiny wiggle, just for good measure and heaved a sigh to attest to her utter relaxation. It was only a pose because she had never felt less relaxed in her life, especially when the college boys had trooped off and Nick's chair scraped on the tile as he jerked it closer to hers. When his voice came from almost over her shoulder, she tensed with the knowledge of his nearness.

Having a distaste for public scenes, Nick had sat up on the edge of his lounge chair and hitched it as close as he could to Caroline's. "Don't you think you're being a little immature?" he inquired coolly and watched her stiffen. His male appreciation of the reflex tightening of her buttock muscles was totally involuntary, as was the sensual memory of caressing her shapely bottom in the pool. Nick didn't choose to be physically attracted to Caroline at a time when he was deeply annoyed with her.

Caroline took her time about raising up on her elbows and turned her head slowly to meet Nick's gaze. Despite the telltale closeness of his voice, his nearness still went through her like an electric shock. He was sitting bent forward, with his arms resting on his knees, his face a mere eighteen inches away from hers so that she got the full brunt of the disapproval in his dark eyes and the reluctant male appreciation, as well.

"You don't take a hint very easily, do you?" she countered, keeping her voice as low as his. With a calculated deliberation intended to irritate, she picked up her oversize sunglasses and propped them on her nose. "After last night, I don't think we have anything to say to each other."

"Maybe you don't have anything to say to me, but I have a lot to say to you," Nick replied grimly. "After I've said it, then I'll leave you alone to carry on with your college pals, although you're wasting your time and theirs. You'd be better off finding yourself a man, not a kid who's all sex drive and no control."

Caroline's gasp was audible. "Of all the nerve! What I do is none of your business! I thought I made that clear last night!" The effort required in keeping her voice low only served to heighten her vehemence.

Grimacing apologetically, Nick said, "You're right. I had no right to say that. It's just that—" He shrugged, finding himself at a loss to explain his motivation.

Caroline pressed her unexpected advantage with a cool aggressiveness that secretly shocked her. She couldn't believe the words or the voice were actually coming from her mouth as she told Nick in a contemptuous undertone, "I thought I had found a *man* who would be the perfect first lover for me, but he turned out not to be interested in making love to a virgin."

Nick's initial surprise at the bluntness and viciousness of her attack flickered over his face, but was quickly blotted out by anger that blazed hot in his dark eyes and tightened his features. Caroline drew in her breath and managed not to give an inch of territory as he leaned his face into hers and made his retaliation between clenched teeth.

"That's how much you know about it, you little idiot. If you had any experience with men, you'd know that I had one hell of a time going to sleep last night because I was so damned horny. That was only the third night in a row I got turned on for nothing. Can't you feel it when a man wants you? That's not something he can fake, you know, or something he can even control. And when he doesn't get any satisfaction, he hurts. But you don't know anything about that, do you?"

The silence was tense with emotion as they stared at each other, their faces so close that every slight reflex movement was magnified. When Caroline wet her bottom lip nervously and swallowed, Nick realized she wasn't being intentionally provocative and yet he was stirred with the urge to kiss her, and it wasn't a tender impulse. He wanted to convey all of his complex anger and his suppressed desire. Abruptly he pulled away from her and sat more upright with his hands braced on his knees.

For the first time Caroline noticed the swimsuit he was wearing, not the sexy black bikini or the red nylon racing suit, but plain, modest trunks made of a dark cotton plaid. They were utterly typical of the kind of swimsuit the average American male wore, in keeping with the tailored shorts and shirt Nick had been wearing at breakfast the morning before, but not at all in keeping with his nighttime appearance. And, as on the previous day, he wasn't wearing the gaudy gold chain around his neck. She had the same thought now that she'd had after first noticing his appearance at breakfast. He was a clean-cut, conservative daytime version of his exotic nighttime self. Which one was the real Nick Denton?

Nick's spurt of defensive anger ebbed under her curious inspection. He had worn the bathing suit deliberately, for the same reason he'd taken the trade journal with him to breakfast: to raise the questions he could sense forming in her mind. Now he just wanted to get this business of confessing over with as quickly as possible.

"This is the real me," he said, lifting his hands from his knees long enough to gesture toward his body. "The other fellow in the fancy clothes is a fake. The chain belongs to my business partner, who was the one who was supposed to come on this trip. He got tied up at the last minute and talked me into taking it instead. He also talked me into buying the slick clothes." Nick paused to give her an opportunity to absorb the news of his deception and react. So far she looked as much interested as surprised, but he wasn't letting down his guard. There was sure to be unpleasantness to come.

"Is your name really Nick Denton or is that your partner's name?" Caroline forgot to be either self-conscious or cautious as she rolled over on her side to face Nick. His gaze, dropping quickly to her chest and pausing there before it skimmed lower, served as an instant reminder that she was wearing the revealing new swimsuit. She gave a hasty glance downward to make sure that what there was of it was in place and then looked up to find Nick watching her with a mirthless smile on his lips.

"Oh, I'm Nick Denton, all right. If you'd met my partner instead of me, you'd have a different story to tell when you got back home to Covington, Louisiana, I can assure you. He's quite a womanizer."

The dry inflection in Nick's tone brought a flush to Caroline's cheeks and put her on the defensive.

"You mean your partner doesn't object to virgins?" she inquired tauntingly, drawing back her shoulder with a provocative little movement that thrust her breasts forward.

Nick's eyes were drawn downward again. He wondered if she had the least idea of the way the design of that swimsuit affected a man. Sight of the tender curves of her breasts peeking out on either side of the pleated rose strips made him want to slip his hand underneath it and make a concealed capture of the lushness he'd already felt for himself. But that wouldn't satisfy for long. Next he'd have to ease the rose strip up over her cocked shoulder and down her arm, unveiling to his gaze the round pink-tipped breast underneath so that sight would add to the sensual pleasure of touch.

Brought back to reality by a familiar ache in his groin, Nick looked abruptly away from the tempting view of Caroline's chest and glanced around the extensive pool area with disbelief. Most of the lounge chairs were taken now, with beach towels and paperbacks and other poolside paraphernalia staking claim for those who were in the pool. It amazed Nick to realize he'd been aroused by his own erotic fantasies in the midst of such a crowd and right in the middle of the confession he'd so dreaded making.

So far that confession wasn't going at all according to his expectation. He had anticipated being bombarded with questions, not seduced. It seemed to him that Caroline was showing a surprising lack of interest in the details of his life that he'd concealed so carefully up until now. Her indifference irritated him. It seemed a matter of pride to resist her physical appeal.

To aid him in that effort, Nick proceeded to put a little more distance between them. "My partner's actually a very nice guy. I'm sure you'd like him," he stated with firm matter-of-factness as he pushed his chair back several inches, ostensibly to give himself room to cross his legs. And then before he could stop himself, he was undermining his new straightforward beginning by adding grudgingly, "All women do."

"Then I guess I'd have to like him," Caroline said peevishly, disgusted with herself that, after all the insult he'd dealt her, she would still turn to mush under his gaze and then be disappointed when he withdrew his attention. "What kind of partner is he, anyway?" she asked irritably, wondering what it took to convince an idiot like herself that a man was bent upon keeping his distance.

Nick had been expecting the question, but her manner of posing it awoke fresh annoyance. She didn't have to make it so plain that the discussion of who and what he was *bored* her.

"Byron and I are partners in our own accounting firm," he informed her curtly. "We're both CPA's. Certified public accountants," he added arrogantly as though elaboration were necessary.

Caroline was finally reacting according to his expectation, he noted with a kind of dread relief. Very slowly she took her sunglasses off and surveyed him with wide-eyed, slack-jawed disbelief.

"A *CPA*? You've got to be kidding me. You're an *accountant*? You fill out people's income tax forms and things like that?"

"Byron and I have some large corporations as clients as well as private individuals," Nick told her with stiff-necked pride. "Our work is far more complicated than filling out income tax returns, though certainly that is a part of our job, too. Actually we feed information into a computer, and it fills out the forms."

Feeling uncomfortably like the stuff-shirted individual she was making him out to be, he waited for the pertinent questions that would follow, allowing him to fill in the rest of the dull details about himself, but, amazingly, they weren't immediately forthcoming. She was apparently so bemused by the knowledge of what he did for a living that she didn't care to know the rest. Rather than sit there squirming under her wondering gaze, Nick decided to go ahead and give her the other relevant facts he felt obligated to divulge. His summary was terse.

"I have a bachelor's and master's degree from Tulane University in New Orleans. I live and work in New Orleans, although I am originally from Natchez, Mississippi, where my parents still live. I'm here in Freeport on the same package deal as yours."

Here Nick was prepared for a much stronger reaction than the one he got. Caroline raised her eyebrows in surprise and nodded slowly while she briefly mulled over the information he'd given her. When she spoke, her voice was reflective with a faint undertone that seemed oddly like sadness to Nick. He found it utterly incongruous with her opening words.

"So that explains our being in the same hotel and our rooms being in the same wing. I wonder if we were on the same airplane from New Orleans. My flight was at ten o'clock."

Nick thought he saw the direction of her thoughts now. His slight shrug was apologetic, but his answer unfalteringly honest. "So was mine. I guess it probably was the same plane."

"And we didn't even notice each other. Not as our actual ordinary selves."

"I got stuck in the back, just a row in front of the smoking section."

"And I was in the second row up front."

Nick watched her guardedly as she sat up and adjusted her lounge chair and then stretched out again, this time at a reclining angle rather than flat on her back. There was no provocative intent in her movements. He wondered as he looked at her closed eyes and composed features what she was thinking. Her relatively calm acceptance of his news should have come as a relief to him, yet he didn't feel relieved. In a way, he felt let down, perhaps because he had been braced for stronger emotions. What bothered him was the thought that *she* was feeling let down, too. To probe her state of mind would be hazardous for his ego, but he either had to take the risk or walk off, and the latter didn't even seem a possibility.

"I guess it's pretty disappointing," he ventured hesitantly. "Finding out who I am, I mean. Maybe you would have rather I hadn't told you."

Caroline moved the shoulder nearest him. "In a way, I guess I would rather that."

The dispirited admission gave Nick a deep wrench that he had been such a source of disappointment to her, and yet it called up his pride, too. He thought she might have given some thought to *his* feelings as well as her own.

"I'm sorry about this whole mess-up," he told her tersely. "At least you can understand now why, when I found out about you, I couldn't—well, you know what I mean."

The silence stretched out until he thought he couldn't stand it another second if she didn't say something. Finally she rolled her head slowly sideways toward him and looked at him through the parted screen of her eyelashes. Her voice was proud and shamed at the same time.

"No, I can't really say I do understand why. But—as you pointed out earlier—I don't know much about men."

Nick glanced around as though frustrated by the awareness of other people all around them, but deep down he knew he was biding for time and inspiration as to how to answer her. No one was paying them any particular attention, but he hitched his chair closer to hers again in a gesture of confidentiality and bent forward over his knees.

"Don't you see, Caroline, that it would have been wrong of me to take advantage of you when you thought I was someone I wasn't?" His low, urgent tone pleaded with her to be reasonable and accept what he believed to be an honest explanation.

Caroline repeated the little isolated movement of her shoulder. "How could you have been taking advantage of me when I'm an adult and it was what I wanted?"

Nick sat up in frustration, gave the pool terrain another irritable survey and then hunkered over again, with his elbows resting on his knees, resigned to having to probe deeper below the surface of his motives.

"All I can tell you is that it felt wrong. Maybe it's male pride not to want to make love to a woman who thinks you're something you're not—"

"But what if I'd been the woman you thought I was at first and not a schoolteacher from a little Southern town. Not a virgin?" Caroline put in with the same quiet persistence. "Would your male pride have kept you from going to bed with me?"

Nick flung up his hands in a gesture of surrender. "Okay, okay. So maybe I'm more old-fashioned than I realized and just didn't want to be the first man." He hesitated. "I've never been with a virgin before. Maybe it was just male cowardice on my part. But, believe me, my holding back was no reflection upon you. It had—*has* to be obvious that I was—*am* very attracted to you."

"Yes, it was obvious, even to a virgin," Caroline acknowledged with quiet bitterness and then let her silence state more eloquently than words the impasse of understanding at which they had arrived. Now that everything had been explained, he still had his hang-ups about her, and she was still a virgin. So what now?

Temporarily at a loss as to how to respond to what seemed like some sort of ultimatum, Nick just sat there, feeling awkward as hell. Caroline, reaching her own conclusions about his silence, faced forward again and closed her eyes, leaving Nick to either stay there or leave, as he chose. He didn't actually choose to do either, and his own inconclusiveness bothered him. The sight of Caroline in that damned skimpy swimsuit also bothered him. With her breasts slightly flattened by her reclining position, he had a delectable view of the outside curve of the one nearest him. He would have liked to reach over and form it into a higher mound again. When his eyes left that temptation and drifted lower, there was the tender exposed flesh of her hip, almost up to her waist. The milk-white portion that was exposed to the sun for the first time was beginning to turn pink. The urge to reach over and touch her there was so compulsive he had to curl his fingers into fists.

"I'm afraid you may be getting sunburned in some places," he offered tentatively, feeling that he really should caution her even at the very likely risk of being told to mind his own business.

"Do you think so?" Caroline opened her eyes and looked down at herself concernedly. With one forefinger, she pressed against the same delicate swatch of white skin that had lured Nick, and they both observed the telltale impression that was left when she lifted her finger away.

"Looks like you flunk the sunburn test." Nick meant the remark to be light, but the huskiness in his voice made it intimate.

Caroline looked over at him uncertainly. "Or passed it. It depends on how you look at it."

"Either way, you'd better get some more clothes on, don't you think? You could put on another bathing suit, if you still want to sit in the sun."

Caroline's smile was ruefully confidential. "I've been dying to go put on one of my old bathing suits, anyway, so that I could go into the pool. I don't dare risk getting this one wet in full daylight in front of the whole world." She glanced away from Nick to note the approach of the college students, dripping wet and quite obviously triumphant that they had managed to add to their male numbers a couple of unattached girls about their own age. "Of course, these guys are going to be terribly disappointed. They've been hanging around, waiting to see what happened when I go into the water."

Nick found his reaction interesting. Thought of how she would look in the wet, clinging suit was unmistakably titillating, but that wasn't a sight he cared to share with the gaggle of college students or any other man there at the pool. With absolutely no justification for his feelings, he was quite possessive about the viewing of Caroline's body, to the extent that he resented the openly appreciative looks on the faces of the young men as they came abreast of Caroline's chair and greeted her as though they were old friends.

Managing to exude a lot of youthful energy, they wanted to know if Caroline wasn't about cooked in that hot sun. They'd finally gotten tired of waiting for her to come join them in the pool and were checking to see that she hadn't passed out from heat exposure.

If Caroline felt any fleeting temptation to flirt with her young admirers for Nick's benefit, she didn't succumb to it. Her smile was friendly, but casual.

"I have had about enough sun," she declared, sitting up and slipping into her beach robe under their avid gazes. She looked over at the two girls who were waiting in the background. "One of you is welcome to my chair."

The offer brought a flurry of enthusiastic replies to the effect that, like Caroline, they were bored with just sitting around. They thought they'd rent some mopeds and double up for some sightseeing around the island. Wouldn't Caroline like to come along with them?

"You can ride with me," offered Brian, the ringleader. "Don't worry. I've got a motorcycle at home that would make these little mopeds look like a tricycle in comparison."

Caroline heard a sound coming from Nick's direction and looked over at him curiously. She thought he might have the same expression on his face someday when he confronted suitors for a teenaged daughter. The stern shake of his head made him appear even more paternal.

"I rented one of those mopeds a couple of days ago myself," he told her in a tone as repressive as his expression. "It's tricky riding in the traffic when you're not used to driving on the left side of the road, especially at intersections. And the drivers here aren't any more considerate of two-wheel vehicles than drivers are in the States."

Caroline couldn't quite believe her eyes and ears. Nick's whole manner was that he was refusing her permission to go on the excursion! She found herself reacting much the same way his teenaged daughter was probably going to react in the future, resentful of the show of authority and rebellious.

"But I don't have anything else in particular to do," she pointed out to him crisply. "I would like to see more of Grand Bahama Island while I'm here." She turned her attention to a somewhat hesitant Brian, who wasn't sure how Nick fit into the picture. "Are you sure you're a safe driver?"

Nick sat there grim and silent during the chorus of jocular assurances from Brian and his buddies. When Caroline glanced over at him, still wavering, he let his silence speak for itself. He didn't approve, but he intended to do or say nothing further to deter her if she insisted upon being foolhardy. There was nothing in his manner to encourage Caroline to believe he had any intention of offering her an alternative proposal to pass the day enjoyably. In the end it was the knowledge that she owed it to herself to make as much of her brief vacation as possible that decided her.

"Okay, you've talked me into it," she told her new poolside acquaintances. "But you've got to promise me I won't get any broken arms or legs."

The promises were quickly forthcoming, and Caroline agreed to meet them in fifteen minutes at the thatched rental hut on the hotel grounds by the native straw market. They trooped off, joking and laughing, leaving Caroline to make what she assumed would be a cool parting with Nick. She stood up and tied her hip-length beach robe more securely around her waist as she stepped into her backless sandals.

"I suppose I'll see you again," she said, having to look up at him since he had stood up, too. When he didn't answer, she turned and started walking away. Realizing that he was following along behind her, she glanced over her shoulder at him in surprise. Once they were clear of the pool area, he continued to walk along beside her in frowning silence, leaving her to assume that he must be going to his room, too. His grave apology took her utterly by surprise.

"Look, I'm sorry I spoke out of turn back there. I know it's none of my business what you do. But if you're going along with those crazy kids just to make that point, I wish you'd reconsider."

Caroline was genuinely touched by his concern.

"I'm not. Honest. It just sounded kind of fun, and they seemed like nice kids."

"I'm sure they're fine as long as they stay sober, but don't think they're going to want to stop somewhere for a Coke when they get hot and thirsty. I remember what it was like to be with a bunch of guys that age. With a few Bahama Mammas inside them, I hate to think of you riding behind one of them on a moped. There's no telling what kind of stunts they'll egg one another into doing."

Caroline thought of the college pals' boastful conversation about the previous night's drinking and partying, carried on in loud tones for her benefit next to her at the pool. She was almost sure that it had been Brian who had claimed no memory of returning to the hotel.

"You're probably right," she mused. "I'd better go out there and tell them I've changed my mind."

She glanced over to catch Nick staring at her with a strange expression. His slow smile was unexpected and disconcertingly warm.

"Do you know you're a rarity. I didn't think, until I met you, that there was a woman in your age bracket living who would take advice from a man without putting up some argument about female liberation."

He sounded so admiring that Caroline was a little embarrassed. "I'm just not an extremely daring soul, that's all. I strictly leave skydiving and mountain climbing and all those other death-defying adventures to people who don't care about reaching a ripe old age."

"So do I. Would you believe I've never even gotten a speeding ticket?" Nick looked over his shoulder with pretended furtiveness. "That's not something I tell just anybody," he admitted with sheepish candor.

They smiled at each other companionably and felt the air magically cleared of the earlier tension. Suddenly Nick felt about as young and carefree as he'd felt when he was the age of the college kids.

"Tell you what," he said, opening the door to their hotel wing for Caroline. "Why don't I rent a moped and take you for a safe ride around the island." He elaborated on the suggestion as he followed her inside. "We could ride out to the western end of the island, very appropriately called West End." Catherine's quick smile at his drollness was encouraging. "There's a place on the way that sounds worth checking out for lunch, Harry's American Bar at Dead Man's Reef. Hopefully the name is purely reminiscent of some earlier mishap." He punched the elevator button. "Or, if you'd rather, we could rent a car and ride in more sedate style."

Caroline's reply was instant and enthusiastic.

"No, I think the moped sounds like fun!"

"The moped it is, then."

His little gesture for her to precede him into the elevator was unconsciously gallant, rising out of the old-fashioned code of courtesy ingrained into Nick by his background. There were times when he was made to feel awkward about his manners, that modern women could consider condescending, but never with Caroline. With her he enjoyed performing the little automatic niceties, knowing that she took them appreciatively for granted. She was stepping past him now, thinking it nothing but natural that a polite man would wait for his female companion to enter an elevator first.

Chapter Eleven

It was a day of fun and laughter and wonderful new openness. Several times Caroline shouted the lighthearted sentiment, "I don't think I've ever had so much fun!" from her perch behind Nick on the moped, her arms wrapped securely around his waist.

"Pretty exciting, huh?" he shouted back at her. "We must be going every bit of thirty-five miles an hour!" But his happiness in the moment was there in his voice. He liked the feel of her arms around his waist, liked her squeal of excitement when they would execute a turn at a busy intersection, liked the sun beating down on them and the wind tearing their hair. In truth, Nick didn't think he'd ever had any more fun himself.

Once they were on Eight-Mile Rock Highway, heading west, they seemed to leave all the traffic behind them back in the more populated Freeport-Lucaya area. Chugging along through small villages crowding right up to the edges of the highway and separated by stretches of uninhibited land, they carried on cheerful shouted exchanges.

"I never dreamed when I came on this trip that I'd be riding on a moped behind a CPA from New Orleans!"

"You didn't think you'd be so lucky, I take it!"

The wind created by their forward movement combined with the incessant trade breezes to snatch their laughter out of their mouths and send it over the arid countryside on either side of them, where away from the gardening staffs and sprinkling systems of the city, the trees were stunted and the vegetation sparse.

"I don't guess you came here expecting to team up with a third-grade schoolteacher from the boonies over in St. Tammany Parish, either."

"No, I can't say that I did. I'm revising my opinion of third-grade schoolteachers, though."

"And I'm having second thoughts about CPA's, too."

"Good. We're actually a very exciting group, especially around the time when the annual supplement to the federal tax code comes out. You should hear our conversations about the latest tax loopholes over lunch." Caroline's laughter rippled pleasantly in Nick's ear.

"If you want to hear stimulating conversation, you should drop by our teachers' lounge at lunchtime one day."

It was comfortable poking lighthearted fun at their chosen professions, viewed by society as staid ways to earn a living. Caroline was fairly sure she knew the answer even as she asked Nick, "Do you wish you'd gone into some other field besides accounting?"

"No, I like what I do. What about you? Do you wish you'd gone into something other than teaching?"

"No, I enjoy it. The kids are cute, and it's a very rewarding kind of work. I even like doing bulletin boards."

Perhaps it was the informality of the situation that allowed them to dispense with normal reticence and exchange such casual, but intimate insights. They were as companionable and easy in silence as they were in the spontaneous conversation that they carried on with raised voices over the steady putt-putting of the little moped motor. Caroline's cramped muscles told her she was ready for a break when they had located Harry's American Bar at the end of the rutted side road, but a part of her felt like chugging on forever, holding Nick around his lean, spare waist. In the sudden silence of the killed motor, she was embarrassed that Nick might be reading her feelings and resorted to clowning as a subterfuge.

"I may never walk normally again," she declared, heading for the rustic entrance on bowed legs. Her sense of awkwardness was swept aside by pleasure as they emerged onto an open terrace overlooking the sea. The individual tables were thick rough slabs of wood allowed to weather to a silver gray. Shading each one was a little cone-shaped thatched roof mounted on a pole in the center of the table. Serving as chairs were crude benches. "Isn't this delightful!" As she looked automatically to Nick for confirmation, she could see that he, too, was glad to slip past the stilted moment.

After they had been seated and were studying the simple lunch menu, Nick looked over at Caroline and was curious to know the reason for her secretive smile.

"What's funny?"

Before she even answered, he found himself responding warmly to the way the secretive smile turned confidential.

"I was just thinking of how different this would be if we were still pretending to be people we aren't. I'd be worried about what I should order to appear sophisticated."

Nick grinned broadly. "And I'd have to drink a beer or one of those potent rum concoctions. You know what I'd really like to have to drink if it were on the menu?"

"Iced tea!" They spoke in unison and then threw back their heads and laughed.

A few minutes later, when they were sipping Cokes and waiting for their order of conch fritters and hamburgers, Nick picked up on her thoughts.

"You have to admit it was fun while it lasted, pretending to be a different sort of person." The expression in his dark eyes and the little half smile on his lips as he looked her over made Caroline pleasurably self-conscious. She knew even before he continued that he was seeing her in her sophisticated guise. "You know you looked like a million dollars in that black dress with diamonds in your ears and that big diamond ring on your finger."

He picked up her hand and held it while he noted the rings she was wearing today, a gold filigree initial ring on her little finger and next to it on her ring finger an antique sapphire-and-diamond ring that was one of her favorites. Both were small and dainty and suited her taste in jewelry much better than Aunt Sarah's large diamond cluster, which weighed uncomfortably heavy on her finger. Caroline felt vaguely apologetic for her preference for the demure over the spectacular.

"And you looked very dashing and handsome," she mused. "You're right. It was fun while it lasted." Nick was keenly aware of the regret mixed with fond remembrance. He was uncomfortable with the thought that she was seeing him in his other appearance and comparing it to the way he looked now in his tailored short-sleeved shirt and shorts. He felt like apologizing for the difference, but then she smiled and turned her hand in his to give it a diffident squeeze. "But not any more fun than today, do you think?"

He squeezed her hand back hard. "No, not any more fun than today."

If Caroline had been bolder, she'd have told Nick in words what she had to rely upon her smile and the warmth in her eyes to convey. She thought he was appealingly masculine and attractive just as he looked now, with his neat dark hair ruffled by the wind, his clean-cut features kindled by a smile that lighted his dark eyes. When he toyed gently with her exquisite little sapphire-and-diamond ring and said, "This is very pretty," the words took on approving overtones that made her heart swell with happiness. The intuition that he might be experiencing a shyness similar to her own in voicing compliments only drew her to him more.

The arrival of their food served as a diversion, and conversation centered around it. They were in agreement that the conch fritters, shaped into small, irregular balls and crispy brown on the outside, reminded them of "hush puppies" the deep-fried corn-bread balls that were commonly served with fried seafood in Louisiana. After the initial cautious sampling, they both gave their enthusiastic approval. Nick dipped his in ketchup, and Caroline ate hers plain.

"I'm one of those people who likes ketchup on just about anything," he admitted wryly.

Caroline wrinkled her nose at him. "I figured as much when I saw you putting it on your scrambled eggs at breakfast yesterday."

"My business partner, Byron, accuses me of putting it on ice cream, but I don't go that far."

Several other times during the course of the meal, Nick made casual mention of his partner, causing Caroline at one point to comment, "It sounds as though you two are good friends and see a lot of each other."

"We are and we do." Nick explained that the friendship between the partners dated back to college. "He's one of the most generous people you'd ever meet. He'll literally give a friend the shirt off his back. It's just a little hard on the ego being out in company with him, that's all. Women fall all over each other trying to get his attention and totally ignore me.''

The frank envy in his voice made Caroline smile.

''I think you're exaggerating.'' She paused and added lightly what was actually a serious sentiment. ''Personally, I'm glad you came on this trip and not your partner, Byron. If he's as popular with women as you say, he wouldn't have noticed me, anyway.''

For Nick the two remarks side by side were like administering a stroke and following it up with a gentle kick. He knew she hadn't meant to be unkind, just honest.

''He'd have noticed you, especially when you were wearing that black dress cut down to the waist in front. You have the figure for that dress, you know, and Byron has a weakness for blondes, anyway.''

Caroline took the last sip of her Coke, unconvinced, but pleased nonetheless.

''I'm still glad that if only one of you could come, Byron stayed home.'' She smiled teasingly. ''I doubt if he's as good a driver as you are, for one thing.''

Nick made some light reply and gladly dropped the subject of Byron, leaving the rest of what he was thinking unsaid. There didn't seem any point in insisting that no matter what Caroline thought, he knew she'd be unlikely to notice him in Byron's company. She'd be like ninety-nine percent of the female population and drawn to Byron like a moth to a flame. In her case the description was all too apt. Nick shuddered to think of her and Byron coming together in Freeport. She wasn't in Byron's league and would have ended up getting hurt, for despite what she thought she wanted, Nick had learned enough about her in this short time to know that she wasn't psychologically or emotionally equipped to handle a sexual fling. She would give too freely of herself that first time and, afterward, when it was over, would feel guilt and emptiness and rejection that the deepest intimacy between herself and a man hadn't forged bonds of permanency. Nick was a man and had had enough one-night stands and affairs to have gotten used to that gut feeling of having been cheated, and yet he never had. He didn't like to think of Caroline having to cope with it.

Sitting next to him on the rough bench, she looked cute and feminine and fragile in her soft blue culotte outfit with her blond hair rumpled by the wind. As she drew in a deep, satisfied breath, lifting her breasts against the front of the modest, sleeveless, round-necked blouse, Nick was fully appreciative of the sight and glad for selfish, as well as for protective reasons, that he was sitting there beside her and not Byron or any other man.

The rest of the day passed as enjoyably. Back on the moped they felt like seasoned bike tourers as they turned onto the paved highway and kept heading west.

"Look at all those conch shells!" Caroline shouted in amazement as the open sea came into view upon their right and huge mounds of conch shells discarded by Bahamian fishermen formed a high continuous shoulder. "Why would anyone buy them in the markets when they could just come out here and get all they want for free?"

"Smell that fishy odor?" Nick shouted back. "The ones you buy from the natives in the markets have been cleaned out. You wouldn't want one of these in your yard, let alone your house. It would smell like our discarded oyster shells in Louisiana. Want to stop and see for yourself?"

Caroline's answer came back immediately. Nick smiled to himself at the distaste in her voice.

"No thanks, I'll take your word for it."

They stopped at the picturesque village at West End and shared a canned soft drink they purchased at the little general store. Caroline was tempted at the bargain prices of the conch shells offered for sale along the seawall, but her common sense prevailed. She'd do better to pay a dollar or two more in town and not have to hold on to a parcel on the moped.

On the return trip back to Freeport, they had to take Eight-Mile Rock Highway again and passed through the same little villages, but it was late enough in the afternoon that the school children were getting out of classes and walking home. Caroline was interested in the fact that each village seemed to have its own school uniform. She and Nick were regarded with curious stares as they chugged past, but there were friendly responses to her smile and her occasional wave.

At the juncture where a left turn would take them back toward Freeport, Nick brought the moped to a halt at the side of the highway and nodded over toward the hand-lettered sign that they'd both noticed earlier in the day announcing the location of the perfume factory that was mentioned in the Freeport guidebooks handed out free to tourists.

"Doesn't look like much of a road," Nick observed. "Want to give it a try?"

"Sure," Caroline agreed.

The road steadily deteriorated until Nick had to decrease their speed on the moped as low as possible to skirt the potholes and weather the bumps.

"This reminds me of a treasure hunt," Caroline said laughingly. "I can't believe there's really a factory of any kind back in here, can you?"

"Has all the markings of a tourist trap, doesn't it? There are probably lookouts all along the way, and they've already passed along the alert that a couple of suckers are on the way."

Despite their joking skepticism, neither of them suggested turning back. When they rounded a sharp curve that opened up a breathtaking view of open sea through a sparse grove of trees on their left, they'd never have guessed that they'd just reached their destination if it hadn't been for the neatly lettered sign out in front of three small buildings on the right declaring, Perfume Factory.

"You think maybe factory has a different meaning in the Bahamas?" Caroline ventured, giggling in disbelief. One of the buildings was about the size of a small house trailer with the same plain rectangular dimensions. The second one was larger and something about its somber exterior and steep-pitched roof made Caroline wonder if it hadn't once been a chapel. The third building was a tiny thatch-roofed hut, obviously the roadside shop where one could stop and pur-chase the perfumes ostensibly produced by the "factory."

"Well, let's check it out, shall we?"

Nick held the moped while she obediently climbed off. Fifteen minutes later he was wheeling it across the narrow street as, following the guided tour of the perfume factory, they were making their escape to the beach, trying to con-tain their mirth a few seconds longer.

"Can you *believe*?" Caroline choked out. "I thought I would *die* trying not to laugh!"

"The least you could have done was not look at me," Nick accused her in a voice vibrating with his barely sup-pressed laughter.

"I couldn't believe it when you actually bought a bottle of that strong-smelling stuff. And to think that they ac-tually wanted us to believe that they manufactured all those different scents in that one big stainless-steel vat in that lit-tle two-room building!"

Nick parked the moped in the thick sand on the beach side of the street and looped a long arm companionably around Caroline's shoulders as they headed by unspoken agree-ment toward the water's edge. Caroline's arm went natu-rally around his waist. It felt good there.

"I bought that for you," he told her, and grinned even broader when she groaned.

"Keep it and give it as a Christmas present to someone you really hate," she advised.

As they came to the edge of the grove of stunted, twisted trees, Nick topped her when their next steps would take them out into the brilliant sunshine. To release the pent-up hilarity inside him, he gave her shoulders a convulsive hug and drew her against his chest. What happened next wasn't premeditated. As he loosened his hold and smiled down into her face, he suddenly didn't want to laugh any more. He wanted to kiss her. And he could see in her startled eyes that she read his wish and wanted it, too.

Her lips felt as soft and tasted as sweet as he knew they would. The kiss was a most natural kind of continuation of the fun and companionship they'd shared all day. Nick wouldn't let it deepen into anything more, although the temptation was strong to let his suppressed sexual need take over. He was glad that he hadn't when he saw the dazed, vulnerable look on her face as he reluctantly raised his head. With a tender smile he gave her another brief, light kiss and released her.

To have her lips and her body separated from Nick was a physical pain for Caroline. She wanted to step back into his arms and feel herself enveloped by his warmth and gentle male strength. The depth of that need shocked her and yet it wasn't frightening. Nothing about Nick frightened her. She felt that she could trust him utterly.

"You know what," she said, arranging his collar for the excuse of touching him. "I think you're about the nicest guy I've ever known, Nick Denton."

It was Nick's urge to maintain her good opinion, not his male instincts, that made him grab her hands and take them quickly away from his neck. He knew she didn't have any inkling of the physical effect of her butterfly touches combined with the stroking softness of her voice, with all its innocent invitation. It took every ounce of his self-control not to think about lying down with her on the sand in the cool shade. He was deeply grateful for the presence of the perfume factory across the street.

"That's what the last girl who dumped me said," he declared with cheerful irony. When the look on Caroline's face didn't change, he took a long stride out into the sunshine, drawing her along with him. "Get a look at this beach, would you? I thought at first all that sculpted stuff was sand, but it isn't, is it? It's rock that's been carved out into all those shapes by the tide. That must be limestone."

"It's strange and beautiful," Caroline murmured, her steps dragging in the deep, hot sand. She wanted to protest against leaving the cool, shady spot. She wanted to protest against being pulled so unwillingly away from the brink of an intimacy she didn't perceive as anything to be avoided as Nick obviously did. But no equal to him in either physical or mental strength, she could only stumble out into the glare.

Restored to normalcy against her will, in the sunshine she talked and laughed with Nick, while one part of her carefully tucked away the memory of the kiss with all its sweet give and take and restrained yearning. She would keep it in a safe spot deep in her soul, a precious souvenir of a very special day in her life. There, the secret warm glow of gladness that the day had happened would live as long as she did. It didn't matter that nothing would ever come of it.

Nick noticed on the way back to Freeport that Caroline was quiet and rightly guessed the reason to be a quickly growing fatigue that matched his own. They'd covered a lot of miles on the moped since starting out that morning.

"Tired?" he inquired over his shoulder.

"Not tired—pooped," she called back cheerfully. "You must be exhausted."

"I won't be sorry to get back to the hotel and turn this thing in," he admitted readily. "Does a hot shower sound good, or not?"

"It sounds wonderful, but not as good as a soak in the tub."

Nick wasn't so tired that her completely innocent remark didn't cause him to have to banish a most alluring vision of a naked Caroline stepping into a steamy, full tub and sinking down into a sea of frothy bubbles. When the water had cooled and she stood up, languid and relaxed, she would be all pink and soft and fragrant with wisps of bubbles clinging here and there. Nick shouldn't allow himself to think about wrapping her in a big, fluffy towel and tenderly drying her off. Not unless he was prepared to forego the pleasures of a hot shower and take a cold one instead, he reminded himself. If only she weren't a *virgin*, for chrissakes, he silently added. But she was, *unless he wanted to change that fact*.

It was the first time the possibility had crept in, and Nick pulled back from it immediately, appalled at his male baseness. He would be no better than Byron and the other nameless men who would take advantage of her if they were in his place. But there was more than principle involved, especially after their day together. If Nick took her—and let her give herself to him—he wouldn't just be making love to a desirable woman, he knew. He'd be making some sort of a commitment, and as much fun as they'd had together and as physically attracted as he was to her, he still wasn't ready for that. His sense of caution told him that they were two people on a tropical holiday, soon to return to their regular lives, where they might look at each other differently.

Caroline was totally unaware of Nick's struggle with his conscience and thus relieved of any self-consciousness when the time came to make plans for the evening. Her ingenuousness left Nick without any defense but his own honor.

"I was only joking earlier about not ever walking normally again," she declared with a groan when they had turned the moped in at the hotel and were on their way to their wing. "Now I'm serious. This must be what it feels like when you've ridden a horse all day."

"Better be prepared for some stiff, sore muscles tomorrow," Nick advised sympathetically. "I know I'm going to have my share."

They walked on in easy silence until they had entered their wing and were standing by the elevator.

"How about dinner tonight?" Nick inquired, making the casual assumption that they would spend the evening together. "Feel up to getting dressed and going somewhere fancy?"

Caroline's groan was eloquent reply even before she spoke. "Right at this moment I don't feel like I'll want to leave my room tonight if I can make it there. You don't suppose they have pizza delivery here in Freeport? Wouldn't it just be heaven to settle down in front of the TV and munch pizza?"

Smiling at her fervor, Nick followed her inside the open elevator and punched the button for the second floor.

"No, I don't think you'll be able to have pizza delivered to your door here at the hotel," he told her with amused indulgence. "Not unless there's pizza on the room service menu."

Caroline's face lit up immediately. "Room service! Now that's an idea. We could have a nice meal and not have to go out. How about dinner in my room, my treat? We could even have a bottle of wine." She faltered a little in her enthusiasm when he didn't answer immediately. "If you'd rather go out, that would be fine, too. We could go somewhere informal.''

They reached her floor and the elevator door opened. Nick followed her out and accompanied her along the corridor, waging a brief losing battle with his better judgment. It sounded comfortable and snug eating a relaxed meal in her room with her in front of the TV set. As tired as they both were, he didn't foresee any serious problems with maintaining his restraint. They'd probably both wind up falling asleep.

''Don't try to get out of it after you've already offered to buy my dinner,'' he chided her teasingly. ''I was just wondering if there's something really expensive, like lobster, on the room service menu.''

Caroline was pleased and didn't give any more thought to his slight hesitation. ''You can have anything you want that's on the menu,'' she assured him generously. ''After all, you've been paying for everything, the snorkeling trip yesterday, dinner last night, renting the moped and lunch today. Of course, up until this morning I figured you could well afford it.'' Coming to a stop in front of her room door, she gazed up at Nick with an expression of growing dismay. ''Oh, my goodness, I lost all that money of yours in the casino! I didn't know a thing about betting, and I just put out stacks of your chips like I knew what I was doing. You must have been *sick* watching me!''

''I was,'' Nick admitted readily, grinning. He tapped her gently on the nose with a knuckle. ''But don't let it worry you. It was all money I'd won out of sheer beginner's luck. I was bound to lose it myself sooner or later. Once I'd run out of it, I hustled you right over to the bar, pose or no pose.''

Caroline laughed along with him and then shook her head. ''You certainly took me in. I was ready to believe you were right off the plane from Monte Carlo or one of those other ritzy gambling places.''

Nick's expression was dryly reminiscent. ''Remember our cagey conversation about jet lag. Neither one of us wanted to mention where we'd come from for fear that the other one knew all about the place. For the record, this is also my first time off the U.S. mainland, too,'' he added.

Caroline breathed out a tired, happy sigh.

''It's incredible the number of things we have in common, isn't it?'' she commented. ''But we can talk about all this later when you come to my room for dinner. Now I'd better go in and turn on that bath water while I can still make it to the tub. Thanks for a perfectly wonderful day.'' With only the briefest hesitation, she stood on tiptoe and offered Nick her lips for a friendly parting kiss.

Nick responded readily, in the same spirit of camaraderie. It was much like the kiss in the grove of trees by the sea, across from the perfume factory, sweet and simple and tormentingly not enough. Somehow Nick managed to keep from seeking her tongue out with his own, but the effort had his pulse racing and made his voice husky and strained as he freed his lips lingeringly of hers and stepped back.

''See you later.''

Caroline smiled after him dazedly as he strode away down the hall. It was only when she reached absentmindedly for the doorknob that she realized Nick hadn't taken her key from her and unlocked her door. *How odd,* she reflected in bemusement. His manners hadn't failed him before, even when he was taking his leave under the most stressful conditions, which certainly wasn't the case now. Somehow the oversight pleased Caroline. The chink in his chivalrous armor made him more accessible to her.

As she unlocked her door and went inside, Caroline was looking forward with yearning to her hot bath and with a more complacent anticipation to the relaxed evening ahead. As she lay soaking, lazily stretching first one muscle and then another, she smiled to herself to think that she'd invited a man to her room with such utter naturalness. Of course, it made all the difference that the man was Nick. Plus, this time there was no sense of preparing the stage for a culminating love scene—or sex scene, to be more accurate. The odds were that Nick would maintain his self control where she was concerned, but Caroline wasn't worrying about what would or would not happen. She simply looked forward to being with Nick, and if the situation led to intimacy, there was no reason for anxiety or fear. Making love with Nick would be beautiful and romantic and passionate, she mused contentedly.

Deliberately she let her thoughts drift to those two magic interludes with Nick in the hotel pool at midnight. Remembering in sensual detail the way he had caressed her body with the boldest intimacy and kissed her with hungry passion, she shivered involuntarily and felt her content replaced with restlessness. Closing her eyes, she imagined him stroking her breasts, hips and thighs in intimate detail. Her body's immediate, heated response to the fantasy shocked her. It was like a current running through her, burning away her fatigue and complacency and awaking her anew to the reality that she was a woman with a woman's mature physical needs.

Along with that realization came a sobering insight. All day she'd played along with Nick's "hands off" treatment of her because intuitively she wanted to be what he expected and please him, just as she'd always wanted to please everyone, especially people she cared about, and earn their approval. He wanted her to be sweet and innocent and pure, and that was what she had been. It wasn't fair of him, she concluded, no matter how decent his intentions, to deny her the right to be a total woman, especially when he had been the one, before he knew she was a virgin, to bring her to the full awareness of her sexuality.

With her eyes opened to this repetition of a pattern of behavior she was determined to break for her own good, Caroline got out of the tub and dried herself briskly. Her tiredness was all gone and in its place was a fine tension. She had to check the impulse to go to the phone and call Nick to tell him she'd changed her mind and would rather go out after all, since after her bath she felt fine. No, that would be avoiding the issue and taking the coward's way out. She would go along with the plans they'd made, but when Nick came to her room later on, he wasn't going to find his career virgin. He was going to find a woman, a late bloomer, to be sure, but a woman, nonetheless, and one in need of a man.

Caroline wanted Nick to be that man. She wanted it with all her heart, but the choice was his. Whatever he decided, he'd always be special, and she'd always be grateful to him for bringing her sensually alive. He was the man in her day-dream. It was ironic that he had made her into the woman she'd imagined herself to be and then couldn't accept his creation.

Chapter Twelve

Nick felt good after his shower and not at all tired. As he took the elevator from the third floor down to the second, he concentrated his thoughts upon dinner, an appetite he could hope to satisfy. Waiting for Caroline to respond to his tap on her door, he wondered what she'd be wearing and hoped to hell it wasn't anything sexy. The first sight of her in a pretty skirt and blouse in muted violets and pinks was reassuring, and when he sensed her nervousness, the need to come to her aid and put her at ease came as a relief.

He assumed that she was experiencing some self-consciousness at inviting a man into her bedroom. His best means of making her relaxed, he thought, would be to act as casual as possible himself.

"Mind if I make myself comfortable?" he asked, walking past her into the room. He made the question purely rhetorical as he strolled over to one of the full-size beds, kicked off his loafers and dropped down on it. "What's on the tube tonight, anyway?'' he inquired as he bunched both pillows behind his back and extended his long legs out in front of him.

"There doesn't seem to be any kind of listing," Caroline replied, unable to keep from staring at the sight of him lounging on her bed. He looked so clean and virile with his dark hair still damp from his shower, his deeply tanned skin glowing with health. Her response to his masculinity should have reinforced her resolve to declare her sexual emancipation, but the first impact of his genial, smiling presence had dealt her courage a killing blow and it showed no sign of returning. "We'll just have to flip the channel and see what's on, I guess. The reception isn't great."

"I guess you can't expect much when the stations are all out of Miami," Nick pointed out cheerfully. "My mind's more on food than entertainment, anyway. Let's go ahead and order dinner right away, since it'll probably be a while in coming. Have you made up your mind what you're having?"

"No, I thought I'd wait for you." Caroline's mind hadn't been much on food or the television reception. As she picked up the menu from where she'd placed it in readiness on the dresser and bore it over to him, she was as tense as he appeared relaxed.

"Hey, relax," Nick told her, taking the menu and tossing it aside while he squeezed her hand reassuringly. "This is just me, your old moped buddy who rode you around safely all day. I'm not going to attack you or rape you or anything cruel and sudden like that."

"I know," Caroline blurted out. "That's the whole problem." She could feel the shock travel through him and into her through their clasped hands. "I didn't mean to get into this until *after* we'd had dinner!" she wailed apologetically.

Nick felt awkward as hell sitting with her standing straight as a ramrod close beside him so that his eyes were right on a level with her breasts. "I guess we'd better talk about this," he said reluctantly, sitting up and patting the bed next to him.

Caroline dropped down and buried her face in her hands. "I'm so embarrassed," she murmured through them in a mortified tone, and then dropped her hands and faced him defiantly, determined to erase the impression of a distraught virgin that she knew she had unwittingly created.

"Would you like for me to go outside and come in again?" Nick asked with gentle teasing. "We could start all over again. I could even take the menu with me and look at it outside. Or why don't we go somewhere and eat? I don't think either one of us is as tired as we thought we'd be."

"Don't talk to me like that!" Caroline demanded. "I'm twenty-eight years old and a grown, mature woman, not a shy, blushing teenaged girl. Just because I haven't ever been to bed with a man before, that doesn't make me some delicate piece of porcelain that has to be handled with extreme care. I want you to talk to me and treat me the same way you'd treat any other woman my age! That's all I ask." Her last words were as conciliatory as she could allow herself to make them without sounding like a wimpering female. She could see that Nick was deeply offended.

"It's ridiculous, in the first place, to suggest that I would relate to all women in the same age category alike," he pointed out stiffly. "I'm sorry if my manners insult you. I've been accused of being 'too nice' before, as I mentioned this afternoon. Perhaps I could manage a loud belch at dinner or use some locker-room language to change my image."

His bitterness stripped Caroline of her mantle of self-righteousness. She hadn't meant to hurt his feelings.

"Your manners don't insult me, Nick! That's not what I meant at all!" She touched his arm tentatively as a healing overture and felt his reflex reaction.

"I think I know what you meant, Caroline," he countered grimly. The odd combination of his controlled tone and the angry fire in his eyes made Caroline's heart start to beat much faster. "You're no different from any other woman. Underneath all the game playing, what you women really want from a man is the cave-man treatment. What you want is *this*—"

Nick glared into her wide, startled eyes as he grabbed her roughly by the shoulders and pulled her toward him so that he could administer the kiss he meant solely as a harsh demonstration. He pressed his mouth hard against hers and deliberately bruised her softness, ignoring the little wimpering sound that came from her throat, but taking advantage of her parted lips. When he pushed his tongue into her mouth, it was harassment he intended, pure aggression. What he hadn't planned on was having his anger explode the pent-up sexual need inside him and turn punishment into a raging hunger.

Caroline felt the hard trembling of his body and the pounding of his heartbeat as he tore his mouth aside from her and crushed her close against him. "Nick?" she murmured, concerned and frightened for him as well as herself. She had wanted to shake his self-control and have him treat her like a woman, not unleash a primitive kind of behavior that could hurt both of them.

"Nick," she said again, a little more insistently. "Please, I'm sorry."

Nick's deeply indrawn breath was labored with his effort at control. His voice was bitterly proud and yet shamed.

"Don't sound so scared. A nice guy like me just doesn't have it in him to be a rapist." He put Caroline away from him and moved over from her on the bed, bending forward to rest his elbows on his knees and with his head dropped down. "Give me a minute and I'll be out of here," he said, taking deep breaths. "Are you all right?" he added with gruff concern, not looking at her.

"I'm fine." Her lips felt bruised and so did her heart as she looked at Nick longingly, wanting to move over close to him and touch him. The long line of his back was rigid, and the way he was hunkered over made her think that he was coping with pain. "Are *you* all right?" she asked worriedly.

"I'm wonderful, aside from the most incredible frustration I've ever experienced in my life," he said shortly, and then added in a bitterly exasperated tone, "Since you're obviously trying so damned hard to get into bed with me, I don't even know why I just don't go ahead. Believe me, some other guy is going to be glad to oblige."

Caroline felt her cheeks grow hot with embarrassment at his uncharacteristic coarseness, but the quickening of her heartbeat in her breast was nervous indecision as to how to respond. Feeling herself at an important crossroad, she swallowed, gathering up enough courage to make what felt like much more than a sexual proposal.

"Then why don't you make love to me, Nick? If you really want to, that is. It would be the first time for both of us, wouldn't it? Your first time with a virgin, and my first time with a man." She had to brace herself for what would be in his face and eyes as his head turned slowly sideways so that he could look at her. The suppressed desire mingled with all the other emotions was as daunting as it was encouraging. "If you're worried about any strings being attached, don't. I'm not so old-fashioned and naive that I'd expect you to marry me."

Between the sheer reasonableness of her argument, with its implication that he was making much ado over nothing, and the shy longing she was trying to hide, Nick suddenly didn't feel like fighting himself or her any longer. His whole resistance seemed like tilting at windmills, anyway. Who was he to decide what was right or best for her? As she'd pointed out to him, she was of an age and mind to make her own decisions.

Caroline felt as though it took Nick half a century to straighten up and twist sideways toward her on the bed. Her heart pounded so hard that the pulse beat in her ears was deafening. Her main concern was trying not to appear nervous and frightened and interfere with the transition she could sense taking place in him. He was about to become her lover!

"Are you sure this is what you want, Caroline?" It was more a final affirmation than a question. "Because this time I'm not going to stop. I don't think I'd be *able* to stop."

"I'm sure."

The reply was too emphatic and too simple, but the moment was too delicate for voicing the complex truth, that she was actually sure only of wanting to take all the risks of making love with him, not sure of the wisdom of her actions or of her ability to please him as a woman. As Nick reached for her and drew her into his arms, she was sorry that what was about to happen couldn't have evolved naturally out of their harmony and enjoyment of each other's company. Instead, it had grown out of confrontation. When he bent his head and kissed her neck, she closed her eyes, wishing that the light wasn't so bright. Even as she responded shiveringly to the heat of his breath on her skin and the touch of his hands as he ran them caressingly over her back, in the background hovered that vague knowledge that things weren't quite right. Everything wasn't perfect.

Nick's problem right from the beginning was keeping his arousal at a manageable level. The knowledge that it was Caroline's first time never left his mind. He knew he had to take things slow and make it pleasurable for her, and the

pace was agony for him because he had built up such a
powerful need for sexual release the past several days. Her
warm response did nothing to help him with his self-control.

As much as he wanted to undress her right away so that
he could see her naked and be naked with her, he stalled off
the urge in order to give her time to loosen her natural inhibitions while they kissed and touched at length. The feeling of her hands running shyly over his shoulders, back and
chest was delicious torture, especially when he thought of
coaxing them into bolder explorations.

Caroline was beginning to wonder if they would ever take
off their clothes when Nick started undoing the buttons on
her blouse. But even when he'd unbuttoned it all the way to
her waist and tugged it free of her skirt, he didn't take it off
at once, but slipped his hands inside to squeeze her breasts
and knead them gently. She could feel the hardness of her
nipples on his palms and arched her back in response.

At that point Nick gently removed her blouse, his eyes on
her breasts enclosed in the filmy lace of her bra. To have him
look at her in her undergarment was in itself incredibly intimate and stimulating for Caroline, but when he seemed
content to stroke the tender inner curves of her breasts with
his fingertips, her impatience overcame her reticence, and
she took matters into her own hands by reaching around to
her back and undoing the bra, lifting and thrusting her
breasts toward him in the process.

The sound that came from Nick's throat as he pulled the
bra straps down her arms and revealed her breasts to his
gaze made shivers ripple along her spine. She moaned her
pleasure when he cupped both breasts and bent to kiss each
hard pink tip. At first she clasped his head lightly and then
pressed it against her to signal her growing sense of urgency. When he responded by squeezing her breasts less
gently and sucking hard on the nipple he had been lapping
with his tongue, Caroline felt her warm, languid pleasure

sharpen and murmured his name aloud, only to be sorry when his fingers immediately relaxed and the demanding suction on her breast eased.

She started once or twice to tell him that he didn't have to be so gentle with her, but she stifled the words, fearing that they might sound critical, and yielded herself to his measured pace of lovemaking. Appreciation for his consideration canceled out regret for the absence of the abandoned passion that had made two such conservative people like themselves come to the brink of lovemaking in the hotel pool. It didn't really matter to Caroline that her first time making love wasn't the sublime, mindless experience extolled by film and fiction. She felt wonderfully tender toward Nick and concerned for his pleasure.

And then when they were finally both naked on the bed and had progressed to the most intimate possible fondling caresses, shy and tentative on Caroline's part at first, Nick's control gave way without warning. She had just clasped him in her hand when he groaned and grabbed her hand.

"God, I hope you're ready," he said, covering her with his body. "For me, I'm afraid it's now or never." Very carefully he poised himself between her legs and then seemed to brace himself for the pain she was going to feel. "I'm sorry this is going to hurt—" His thrust wasn't forceful enough the first time, but it hurt enough to bring a wincing expression to Caroline's face.

Nick closed his eyes against it, contorted his features and thrust hard, brutally hard, he thought with compassion as she cried out her pain at his penetration. The rush of stimulation at her velvety, encompassing warmth was almost more than he could handle. He went rigid in the effort to hold back his climax and kept his eyes closed and his teeth clenched as he muttered, "Oh, God, *no*."

Caroline didn't comprehend clearly the reason for his distress, but it roused her out of her total absorption in her own body's sensations. She wanted to reassure him that after the shaft of truly excruciating pain, which had been of short duration, it felt wonderful having him inside her.

"I'm fine," she told him softly, sliding her palms tenderly up his chest to his shoulders. "It feels so *warm*, doesn't it?" she added shyly, and moved her hips experimentally.

"Please, don't do that," Nick pleaded desperately, shocking Caroline into total submissiveness. After what seemed an eternity to her, he opened his eyes and took a deep breath. "If we take this nice and easy, it might last longer than five seconds," he apologized gruffly.

Slowly he moved inside her, arousing sensations that were so pleasurable that Caroline reached up again and grasped his shoulders because she had to make some physical response, and she wasn't sure whether it was all right to move her hips again.

"Am I hurting you?" Nick asked at once, with concern.

"No, you're not hurting me. It feels wonderful. Don't stop," she urged him softly and then had to follow her body's bidding as the tension that was a part of her pleasure made it imperative that she move her hips with his. When Nick didn't make any remonstrance and quickened the pace and depth of his thrusts, her movements became more abandoned and the urge for expression not to be denied.

"Nick, that feels so good, so wonderful," she murmured, and then cried out with the sharp pleasure of his penetration as he surged deeper and harder into her. When he went rigid and uttered a pained inarticulate sound, she didn't realize at once what was happening until she felt his explosion rock his body and knew that he had reached his climax. The selfish disappointment that their lovemaking was over was accompanied by pleasure in the knowledge of his satisfaction and acceptance that nature had simply taken its course. Certainly, she knew, Nick had done everything he could to prolong her pleasure.

She watched him anxiously for the moment when he would open his eyes, wanting to soothe any dissatisfactions he might be feeling with his performance. The tender male ego was a part of traditional romantic lore.

"I'm sorry. I couldn't hold off any longer," Nick muttered, drawing in a deep ragged breath. Making love to a woman had never been quite that kind of ordeal before, and his long-delayed orgasm had been shattering.

The apology was what she had been expecting, but not the abstracted tone in which it was spoken, which came across to Caroline as indifferent and made her feel silly to have wasted her sympathy lying there rehearsing reassurances. Suddenly she was awkwardly aware of being naked and lying with her body joined to a man's. What did they do now that it was over? What did they say to each other?

"It's okay. I doubt many women climax their first time."

Her polite, stilted offering brought Nick's eyes flying open with the comprehension that he had to come to his senses and deal with this new and delicate situation of conversing with a virgin just after he'd destroyed her maidenhead. Thinking that she might be lying there in physical discomfort, he eased his body carefully free of hers and lay sideways beside her, propped on his elbow. Her embarrassed glance down to his groin drew his own gaze to his flaccid male organ. He wondered sympathetically if she were viewing it as an unlikely instrument of torture. If only he'd had the courage to hear the answer, he'd like to ask her if she were glad or sorry now that the damage had been done and whether her pleasure had been worth the pain. If she was feeling frustrated, as she probably was, he could give her satisfaction with less conventional lovemaking techniques, but he didn't know what her reaction to them would be at this stage. A sense of delicacy and vague guilt made Nick unsure of how to broach any of the questions in his mind, but he knew he couldn't just lie there, feeling awkward and ineffectual.

"I guess it was pretty painful for you," he ventured, wanting to be casual in order to establish an easier atmosphere and yet not sound callous.

"Only at first, when you—you know, had to break through." If he'd been holding her in his arms or even touching her companionably, Caroline thought the conversation might not be so painfully embarrassing. She wished she were covered with the sheet or bedspread.

As her eyes met his and glanced away, Nick's male pride smarted at the thought that she was probably remembering his first unsuccessful attempt to penetrate. It had been his concern about hurting her that had caused him to be inept. He wanted to make sure she knew that.

"I was about to change my mind about the whole thing when I pushed into you the first time and saw how much it hurt. Frankly, it's not something I would look forward to doing again." Too late, Nick realized how tactless his words were. "Not that I'm sorry, now that it's done," he added hastily. "I just hope that you're not sorry." He reached over and placed his hand lightly on her thigh and felt her flinch in withdrawal.

"Why should I be sorry?" Caroline countered proudly. She sat up and with as much dignity as possible, considering her humiliation, edged herself over to the opposite side of the bed and swung her feet to the carpet, leaving Nick a view of bare buttocks and stiff spine. "I thought we went into this with the attitude that it was a first for both of us. Now you've deflowered a virgin, and I've been to bed with a man. As you've just pointed out, maybe once is enough."

Caroline held her breath, appalled at her own biting sarcasm, which was pure defense. She felt the movement of the bed as Nick sat up behind her and swung his legs to the floor on his side. She didn't look around, but she knew he was getting dressed while he made his own proud retaliation.

"Why don't you just come out and be honest about it? Go ahead and admit it. You were disappointed. You didn't hear music playing in the background. I didn't sweep you off your feet and make you feel like you were lying on a field of wildflowers. Well, like it or not, I gave it my best, lady, and I did the job you wanted done. Now you can sleep around to your heart's content." Nick heard her sharply indrawn breath and was more sorry than glad at the success of his barb. He knew he'd gone too far in his anger. "I apologize for that. I was out of line," he amended swiftly as she rose to her feet and turned around with the proud carriage of a queen to face him, too insulted and outraged to care that he was dressed and she was still naked.

"I don't accept your apology," she informed him scornfully. "Your big problem right from the start, Nick Denton, was that you didn't have enough confidence in yourself as a man! Now that you've done your good deed and made a trail for all the other men who'll come after you, you can take your Boy Scout kit somewhere else. Get out of here. This minute!"

"Gladly," he almost shouted back at her, and spun around to head for the door with long strides.

"I don't ever want to see you again!" Caroline called shrilly after him.

"Don't *worry*—" Nick shouted full volume from the hall, the doorknob in his hand. He slammed the door so hard behind him that the vibration seemed to shake the whole building.

"I don't ever want to see you again," Caroline whispered with pathetic defiance, and crumpled down on the bed where Nick had so painstakingly led her through the rites of womanhood. Tears welled, burning her eyes, and trickled down her cheeks, but they failed to relieve the anguish that spread through her like a cancer, pushing out all hope, all possibility that life would ever be fresh and wonderful again. At least there was only feeling and not thought, but the respite wasn't to last long.

When her mind started working again, Caroline's first thought was, *How am I going to bear the next two days?* It was only Thursday night, which meant she still had two more long days and additional nights to get through somehow before her return to New Orleans on Sunday. With Nick on the floor above her in the same wing, how could she possibly not run into him coming and going? The prospect of coming face-to-face with him and looking him in the eyes at first brought hot waves of shame and embarrassment until pride came to her rescue and she reminded herself that Nick couldn't look back upon what had happened between them that night with any male boastfulness. His performance had left something to be desired. He'd be as anxious to avoid her as she was him.

Oddly, that realization brought small consolation, and it led her unexpectedly to wonder what Nick was thinking and feeling that very moment. Since he was a man, he couldn't give in to his emotions as she was going, but Caroline knew that once his anger had cooled, he'd feel terrible—guilty for having made love to her, in the first place, and then sorry for losing his temper afterward. His pride wouldn't let him apologize, though, or ever again make a friendly overture. That remark of hers about his lack of confidence in himself as a man, following upon what he considered an unsuccessful performance on his part, had dealt a lethal blow to his manhood.

The more she thought about the remark, the more she regretted it and wished she could take it back, just as she wished that she could turn back the clock and redo the whole evening, which had gone wrong because of her. She had handled everything badly, bungled in her efforts to explain her feelings, forced the issue of sex upon Nick, despite his reservations, and then, when they both were disappointed, accused him of not being a man.

But words couldn't be unsaid, and actions couldn't be undone. Once the fragile material of a relationship had been torn, it couldn't be mended by regret or apologies. She doubted that Nick would ever want to have anything to do with her again.

Caroline's fatalistic perspective upon the evening didn't ease any of her guilt, sadness or deepening sense of loss, but it gave her the impetus she needed to haul herself up off the bed and get on with her life, empty as it seemed. She'd change into her nightgown and robe, she decided, and order a light meal from room service. She wasn't hungry, but she knew she should have something to eat.

On the way to the bathroom, it occurred to Caroline that her mental list hadn't included a thorough head-to-toe cleansing in the bath or shower. With the discovery that she didn't feel physically soiled by her lovemaking with Nick came the surprising realization that despite everything that had been wrong, despite everything that she would have liked to change, she still wasn't sorry over the loss of virginity itself. She just wished that the circumstances surrounding it hadn't been so tragically wrong.

If Nick had known, he would have felt a little better. His temper had already cooled by the time he found himself outside the wing on the hotel grounds, and he was appalled at his loss of control. He couldn't believe he'd actually shouted at Caroline and slammed her door with all his strength. The feeling of having bungled from start to finish made him keep on walking as though he could outdistance his shame and regret, but they easily kept pace with him, through the hotel and out the front entrance, over to International Bazaar where he roamed around the narrow alleyways past the closed shops, stopping finally at a noisy sidewalk café for a bite to eat.

It had been all wrong, from beginning to end. If only he'd been stronger and resisted her, Caroline's virginity would still be intact and he wouldn't be demoralized at his failure to make her first time good for her. Her disappointment was more than a blow to his ego. He hated to think what effect it was going to have on her future. She had waited so long to give herself to a man, and now she might never want to again. No man liked to carry that kind of burden around with him the rest of his life.

Not even the memory of her cutting attack upon his manhood, which had so enraged him at the time, helped Nick to feel much better. Looking back, he remembered not just the sarcasm in her voice and the words themselves, but the stricken pride in her eyes. She'd wanted to hurt him because she was so hurt inside. Still, whatever justification there was on her side or his for what had been said and done, the damage was deep and permanent. Given an opportunity during the next couple of days, Nick hoped he would be man enough to apologize for losing his temper, but beyond that, what was there left to say? *I'm sorry I wasn't man enough to please you* or *better luck the next time?* A man had his pride.

All the next day Nick was on edge expecting to encounter Caroline at any moment. She would probably look tense and unhappy and he would feel guilty and defensive as hell. But he didn't catch sight of her until that evening. Feeling bored and restless at the thought of two nights and another day to get through before his return to New Orleans, he walked over to the casino and decided, after drifting around and watching the gambling for a while, to eat the buffet dinner in the casino restaurant. He'd just finished heaping his plate, sat down and started to eat when Caroline walked in and not alone, Nick noted with instant resentment as he glanced up and then did a double take.

It was some small consolation that she was in the company of two other couples and didn't have a date, but he felt vaguely wronged that she didn't look unhappy at all, or lonely and bored, as he was feeling. At first he was relieved that she and her party didn't sit near him. He ate his dinner, irritated that he was allowing her to spoil his meal when she wasn't aware of his presence in the same room.

She was seated so that he could see her profile. He glanced over at her often, expecting at any moment that he might catch her sneaking a look at him. If she'd been more vivacious, he would have been suspicious that she knew he was there and was putting on a show for his benefit, but she smiled and joined in the conversation at her table in the most natural kind of way. Nick watched her more and more openly and felt lonelier and more excluded by the minute. If only they'd stayed friendly companions, she'd be sitting across from him instead, smiling at him, talking to him.

After he'd finished eating and had drunk his second cup of coffee, Nick picked up the check the waitress had left for him to pay at the cash register on his way out. As he stood up, he considered making a detour past Caroline's table and catching her attention, but then he vetoed the impulse as serving no good purpose. He should leave her alone with her friends and let her enjoy herself, he decided.

Caroline saw Nick on his way out and was jolted by the realization that he'd been there in the restaurant and she hadn't known it. Even from the back he was instantly familiar to her, the shape of his head and the short, neat cut of his dark hair, his tall narrow back and long arms and legs, his unhurried stride that covered so much territory that he'd always had to shorten it for her benefit. She was torn between her relief and her disappointment that they hadn't seen each other face-to-face and spoken.

After that, it required more effort on her part to pay attention to the conversation and take part in it. On the one hand she was glad that she'd accepted Lisa Preston's invitation to join her and her husband, Pat, and their close friends, Jane and Kyle Ellis, for dinner that night. The two couples were from Gretna, on the west bank of New Orleans, and were in Freeport on the same low-priced package trip as Caroline. On the beach that morning, where she'd gone to avoid Nick, she'd recognized them because Lisa and Pat had sat in the two seats next to her on the plane and Jane and Kyle had sat across the aisle. On the beach, when Jane discovered that she'd forgotten to bring along her sunglasses, Caroline had spoken up and offered to lend her an extra pair she had in her bag. The offer was promptly accepted and led to introductions and the eventual discovery that Lisa's great-aunt and Caroline's much revered dance teacher from the time she was four years old through high school were one and the same.

In the course of the informal beach conversation that passed back and forth, it came out that Caroline was alone in Freeport, that she was an elementary schoolteacher in Covington and that her aunt with whom she lived had just died. When Caroline began to gather up her beach things to return to the hotel, Jane had issued the invitation for dinner that night, and Caroline had gratefully accepted, not really minding that it was probably prompted by sympathy. They were pleasant people, and almost anything was preferable to being alone. She had known she wouldn't be so nervous at the prospect of running into Nick if she was in the company of other people and giving at least the appearance of having a good time.

But now with the realization that Nick had been there in the same restaurant, dining alone, she was struck with the fleeting, poignant wish that she'd been there alone, too.

Perhaps then he would have come over and spoken to her. Perhaps they might even have talked.

Caroline's common sense clamped down before conjecture could raise false hopes, but she still was deeply disappointed when Nick was nowhere to be seen in the casino after dinner. She stayed there with her friends until midnight, not playing or really even watching with any close attention, but keeping the constant alert that she'd kept all day. Only now it had subtly changed its character. Before, she'd been filled with dread at the thought that any moment she would see him. Now she searched the crowd in vain for the sight of a dark head and a pair of slender shoulders above the rest.

When she had to return to the hotel without having had another glimpse of him, she was filled with a sense of anticlimax that proved to be fertile soil for more aggressive emotions. By the time she'd finally managed to get to sleep, she had convinced herself that Nick's absence from the casino that night was proof that he'd seen her in the restaurant and had deliberately avoided her. Such behavior seemed cowardly and reprehensible in her eyes. It made her indignant to think she might have avoided him all day for nothing. She resolved not to take any such measures the next day, which would be her—and his—last day in Freeport. On Sunday they both would be returning to New Orleans.

Chapter Thirteen

Caroline awakened the next morning to discover with some annoyance that she'd overslept and thus wasn't likely to see Nick at breakfast. Sure enough, she didn't. Her vague sense of irritation at herself for the lost opportunity extended to Nick as the day passed and she didn't catch a single glimpse of him. He obviously intended to avoid her altogether. It was inconceivable to her that he didn't share her own feeling that the two of them had to have at least one last meaningful conversation before they parted ways and returned to their separate lives. Surely he sensed, too, the need for a caption on their holiday relationship. After all, they had meant something to each other.

By afternoon Caroline had worked up a strong case of indignation. Earlier in the day she had refused the invitation to join her Gretna acquaintances in a dinner excursion to a native restaurant, her reason being that she wanted to keep herself available should a chance encounter with Nick lead to truce and a dinner proposal from him. Facing the very likely probability of spending the whole evening alone, she grimly decided to change her mind. Jane had told her to meet them at the front entrance at eight o'clock if she decided she wanted to go with them after all, and she did.

She would wear the new sundress she'd bought in one of the boutiques in the International Bazaar, where she'd managed to kill the past two afternoons browsing, Caroline thought. If she hadn't had so much time on her hands, she'd never have tried on the dress. Its vivid stripe in primary colors wasn't really her style, but it was on a sales rack along with several others more to her liking. Once she saw it on and noted with amazement that in it she looked like a California Girl with her golden tan and blond hair, she couldn't resist buying it. Unlike the black dress, which she was certain she would never wear again, it would be a useful addition to her wardrobe and heralded a change. She was determined to work in some brighter colors and smarter styles.

Her only regret when she checked her appearance before going down to meet her friends that night was that Nick probably wouldn't see her looking as good as she'd ever looked in her life. Her blond hair was sleek and shining, her eyes more blue than gray in contrast to the smooth, golden hue of her bared shoulders and arms. Her jewelry was jaunty plastic, moderate-sized red hoops in her ears and on one arm several bracelets matching the primary colors in her dress.

Nick was on his way down to dinner at the Rib Room. It suited his mood to have a hearty but plain meat and potatoes meal in a quiet atmosphere even if it meant donning a jacket and tie. When the elevator stopped at the second floor, he barely had time to entertain the possibility that Caroline might be beyond the doors when they opened and there she was, like a flesh-and-blood mirage, looking unbelievably vibrant and lovely. He stared, his voice momentarily lost along with his presence of mind.

The sound of the doors starting to close again brought both of them out of their shocked paralysis. Nick hastily pressed the button to keep the door open, and Caroline walked inside the elevator with a cool "Hello, Nick." She stood with her eyes fixed on the lighted panel while the elevator made its slow descent, but her peripheral vision confirmed the vivid picture of Nick in her mind.

He looked simply marvelous, the white jacket contrasting with his black hair and eyes and darkly tanned skin. Tonight he'd teamed it with the dark green shirt, but he was wearing a plain silk tie and the effect was more dignified and sober than the open-throated look with the gaudy gold chain, but he was strikingly attractive just the same. Caroline was weak-kneed and tongue-tied with her physical awareness of his closeness.

"Here we are," Nick announced unnecessarily as the elevator doors slid open. He held his finger on the button to keep the doors open, but easily made up for his delay with long strides that brought him to the entrance of the wing in plenty of time to open the door for Caroline, who was in the process of rediscovering her voice.

"I'm going to dinner with some friends," she informed him. "We're going to some native restaurant."

"Are they the same ones I saw you out with last night and sitting with at the pool this morning?"

"Why, yes, they are." His open admission that he had seen her twice—the second time quite unbeknownst to her—and had made no effort to speak took Caroline aback and then brought her joltingly down to earth. This chance encounter wasn't going to lead to anything. She was shocked at the depth of her disappointment and talked simply to help herself regain her equilibrium. "They're very nice people. They're from Gretna, on the west bank. The husbands, Pat and Kyle, are both lawyers. They're partners in the same firm, Ellis, Preston and Davidson. Maybe you've heard of it?'' She glanced up at him guardedly while she spoke the name of the firm and steeled herself against the impact of his clean-cut handsomeness.

Nick shook his head in polite denial and made an effort to keep his voice clear of his resentment as he replied, ''No, I haven't heard of it.'' It was more than a little hard to take that his trip had been totally ruined, and she was having herself a good old time. Apparently the loss of her virginity had been much more a trauma for him than it was for her.

Caroline read a lack of interest in his expressionless tone and was stung at his whole attitude of indifference, which she thought extended to her, too. It was suddenly very important to impress upon him what a wonderful time she'd been having.

''They're loads of fun,'' she declared. ''I can't tell you how glad I am that I met them. Tonight after dinner we'll probably go back to the casino and close the place up again.''

The implication that she and her friends had stayed at the casino the night before until it had closed was enough of an exaggeration to qualify as a lie, since they'd actually left about midnight. She'd have been surprised and dismayed to know the interpretation Nick was giving to her gay defiance. He thought she was letting him know in advance her plans for the evening so that he would steer clear again and not spoil her fun. It irked him for her to think that she could declare the casino off limits for him. What did she expect him to do for entertainment his last night in Freeport?

''Maybe tonight will be the big night, and we'll both win our fortune in the casino and make this whole trip worthwhile,'' he said with an edge in his voice that sounded offensively like sarcasm to Caroline. Before she could recover her wits enough to decide what to say, he was stopping without warning at the entrance to the Rib Room, making her feel foolish when she took a step beyond him and then looked around in surprise that she'd passed him up.

"Here's where I leave you," Nick informed her stiffly. "I have dinner reservations inside. Have a good evening with your friends." *And save your sympathy. I don't mind dining alone,* he might have added, if pride hadn't prevented him.

"Thank you, I'm sure I will," Caroline retorted, and whirled around and marched off, furious at herself for her lack of possession in the face of his insulting cool.

It required enormous effort on her part to pretend to match the high spirits of her dinner companions, who were in a mood to make the most of the last evening in Freeport. She was secretly uneasy at going into the poor neighborhood where the taxi took them. The streets were narrow and just well lit enough to show the signs of poverty everywhere. The building housing the restaurant was a sagging, rundown structure. She couldn't help thinking what Nick's reaction to such a place would be. He'd take one look and order the taxi to drive away, a suggestion she was hoping one of the others would make.

Once they were inside, she relaxed a little at the sight of other tourists and tried not to show how distasteful the situation was for her. She would never have eaten in a comparable restaurant at home with oilcloth tablecloths and mismatched tables and chairs crowded together so that there was no privacy. Thought of what a glimpse of the kitchen might reveal turned her stomach.

"Relax, it's not as bad as you think," came a low amused voice, so close to her that she jumped.

Turning her head she met the smiling gaze of a sandy-haired bearded man sitting at an adjacent table, jammed so close to theirs that if Caroline and the man had raised their near elbows simultaneously, they would have touched. The portion of his face not covered by his beard was deeply tanned as were his throat and arms. He wore wrinkled, but expensive casual clothing, white slacks and a pale blue shirt with the sleeves rolled above his elbows and the front open almost to the waist. Around his neck was a heavy gold chain and medallion, nestled in thick tawny hair, and on the muscled forearm draped near Caroline a gold watch.

She smiled back at him sheepishly. "Was it that obvious? I take it you've been here before."

"So many times I've lost count. Would you believe that this dive is one of the attractions that keeps me coming in to port here on Grand Bahama Island any time I'm cruising this territory." His lazy, attractive smile broadened. "It's not just the food, but the company you can run into." He casually extended his hand, palm up. "Greg Norton. Can I buy you and your friends a drink?"

Introductions were made, and in a short time it was agreed by both parties to bring the two tables even closer together. Caroline and her friends were intrigued to learn that Greg and his four companions had come ashore from sailing yachts. They had sailed over from their home port in the Miami area and were cruising the Bahamas more or less in company. The three men appeared to be in the mid or late forties and all gave the impression of being successful and affluent. The two women were about Caroline's age and were introduced only by first names, leaving her to assume that they were girlfriends and not wives. Greg was the lone man of the group and didn't waste any time inviting Caroline to come aboard with him for a week or two. He did it so charmingly and openly, to the entertainment of the whole group, that she could only laugh and not be offended.

The situation was diverting, and she relaxed. By the time food was set on the table, she had had several daiquiris and was no longer repulsed by conjectures about the state of hygiene in the kitchen. She just wished that Nick could be somewhere in the room watching her have a wonderful time. When it was decided toward the last that they'd all go from the restaurant to the Royal International Casino, she was immediately delighted at the idea and made her feelings clear, though not the reason behind them. There was no doubt in her mind that Greg would be attentive at the casino, and she intended to give him every encouragement. Nick would be there and see for himself that she could hold her own with a truly confident, sophisticated man. Nick would be sorry then for the way he had treated her, sorry that he'd let her go.

It all went according to her plan and yet didn't give her the satisfaction she expected. Nick was there, and he did see her with Greg. Once or twice her gaze intersected his, but if she'd expected him to hover near, she was disappointed. He was apparently more interested in the gaming tables than in her. She'd have liked to do some reconnaissance and find out how he was faring with his betting, but Greg kept her at his side with his low-key but insistent generosity. He bought her drink after drink until she lost count of how many dai-quiris she'd had during the evening. He bought chips for her and only laughed and bought more when she lost them. As the hour grew late, he became more casually possessive in the way he touched her and called her "sweetheart" and "honey," so that she knew what impression they were giving to everybody around them, but she was too tipsy to care.

When Lisa came up to her to tell her that the rest of them were going back to the hotel, Caroline's common sense was not so drowned by alcohol that she didn't realize that she really should seize the opportunity to get away from Greg so that she wouldn't have to engineer a parting on her own. It was the sight of a dark head and a pair of white shoulders bent over the roulette table across the room that kept her from telling Lisa that she was ready to go, too.

"Remember, honey, the plane leaves fairly early in the morning," Lisa admonished, looking plainly reluctant to leave Caroline, whose effort at reassurance unfortunately came out a little slurred.

"Don't worry. I'll be on it."

A few minutes later she looked over at the same roulette table, and Nick wasn't there anymore.

"Who're you looking for, sweetheart?" Greg asked her as she searched the room in every direction and felt a rising sense of panic when she couldn't spot the dark head and white-jacketed shoulders anywhere. "Remember? Your friends have all gone back to the hotel. Don't worry about a thing, honey. I'll see that you make that plane in the morning. If you don't, it's no big tragedy. I'll just buy you another plane ticket. That is, if you don't change your mind and decide to come aboard with me and extend your vacation a week or two."

The honeyed caress in his voice and the glide of his palm across her back were in no way reassuring to Caroline. She now wished with all her heart that she'd returned to the hotel with the others. It seemed a betrayal of some kind on Nick's part that he'd disappeared like that, leaving her to her own devices.

"I think I'd really better go back to the hotel now, Greg. I'm dead tired, and I've had too much to drink. You don't have to leave. I'll take a taxi." As much as Caroline wanted to sound cool and forceful, she knew she came across as muddled and helpless.

"Don't be silly, honey," he chided her. "I'm ready to go."

In the taxi he tried to cajole her into going to the marina, where his sailboat was berthed. "Why not, honey? Wouldn't you like to see my sailboat? I've already told you not to worry about making that plane. If you really want to get back to New Orleans tomorrow, I'll see that you get there." He pulled her into the circle of his arms with a gentle insistence that let Caroline feel his superior strength.

"Please, Greg," she begged, going limp against him with her desperation. "I want to go to the hotel."

"Okay, honey, the hotel it is," he agreed, his tone making her out as a silly child he was willing to indulge. "My, my, your little heart is pounding away," he teased, casually fondling her breast. He bent his head and kissed her neck. When she shrank away, he chuckled and rubbed his bearded cheek against her sensitive skin. "My beard tickles? Wait until you feel it all over you, honey. You're going to think it feels great."

Caroline's reaction to his words and his casually possessive touch was violent disgust. She wanted to shove against him with all her strength and shrink over in the far corner of the taxi seat, but fear and a sense of helplessness prevented her. If she resisted him openly, he might order the taxi driver to take them to the marina. She thought it would be better for her to remain passive until they'd arrived at her hotel. There she would be safe and could get rid of him.

"Your skin is so pretty, such a delicate color," Greg complimented silkily, taking his hand away from her breast when he noted the way she had stiffened and caressed her bare shoulder and arm instead. Her sudden turnabout was of no serious concern to him, but seemed rather a challenge.

"I have a hard time tanning," Caroline told him nervously. "My skin is so pale."

"I can't wait to see," Greg murmured, giving her words a provocative interpretation. He ran exploratory fingers up her inner thigh and felt her stiffen again.

"Please, you don't have to see me to my room," she begged him when the taxi stopped at the hotel entrance and Greg got out with her. "It's not necessary. You can take this same taxi to the marina."

"Come on, sweetheart, we're wasting time." His voice was smooth silk, but his grip on her arm was steel. Caroline walked along next to him, feeling as though she were being propelled by his strength and will and not by her own legs. Passing the entrance of the Rib Room, which was long closed at this late hour, she thought despairingly of Nick and wished with all her heart that he would appear suddenly out of nowhere to rescue her.

Emerging onto the walkway circling the inner grounds of the hotel, Caroline made an effort to balk and succeeded only in slowing their steps.

"Greg, I know I've probably given you the wrong impression," she began. "I'm not really the sort of woman you think I am."

He laughed softly. "You know the kind of woman I think you are, honey? I think you're cute and sweet and sexy."

"Greg, please—you've got to listen to me!"

"Sure, I'll listen to you, sweetheart, but not out here where anybody passing by can hear what we say to each other. Come on, honey, it's late."

Nick had to contain a savage anger to keep from stepping out from the shadows and taking a swing at the guy, like some jealous ass of a boyfriend. He'd been standing there, trying to talk himself into going on to his room, calling himself every kind of fool for being worried about her, but with the first sound of her voice, he knew she was scared silly. She'd gotten herself into more than she could handle, just as he'd been afraid when he first spotted the bearded smoothie she was hanging all over in the casino.

Nick had been able to size up the guy from across the room. He was older than Byron, but cut out of the same cloth, used to having his way with women. The honeyed steel in his voice as he talked to Caroline and called her "sweetheart" and "honey" told Nick that the guy had no intention of being turned away at Caroline's door. He'd use charm and every other trick in the book, and if none of those worked, he wouldn't be averse to forcing his way inside.

It was really no business of Nick's. He knew that, even as he headed with long strides in the opposite direction around the circular walkway, arriving at his and Caroline's wing ahead of her and "Greg." Ducking into the stairwell, he held the door slightly ajar and waited long enough to hear Caroline make another unsuccessful effort to turn her determined escort away at the elevator. Then he sped up the stairs to the second floor and took up vigil just inside the door. When the elevator arrived, clanging open and then closing again, and there were no voices, Nick peered out and saw them walking down the corridor in silence. The sight of Greg's hand placed possessively at Caroline's back made him clench his fists as savage anger rose up in him again.

If she let the guy talk his way into her room, that was one thing, he told himself, but if he thought he was going to use muscle, that was something else again. He'd have to walk over Nick first.

If Caroline had had any inkling that Nick was within sound of her voice, pride wouldn't have held her back. She'd have called out for his help. But she thought she had no one to rely upon except herself.

"This is my room," she announced coming to a stop in front of her door. "Good night and thank you for a wonderful time—"

"Give me the key, honey," Greg ordered gently, holding out his hand. "I'll unlock the door for you."

"No!" Caroline held her little handbag behind her. "I'll open the door myself *after* you've gone. Because you *are* leaving, you know. I'm *not* inviting you in my room." She backed away from him as he stepped closer and reached around behind her for her purse. "I'm warning you, Greg, I'm going to scream—"

He laughed and clamped a hand across her mouth. "Come on, sweetheart, you know you don't really want to make a scene." He pressed her up against the wall and moved his hips against hers. "Feel that, honey. I'm going to make you feel so good you'll want to scream for a different reason. Now give me that key."

He pried the purse forcibly out of her hand and then stood there, still keeping her pinned to the wall, while he opened it and searched for the key. He glanced unconcernedly at Nick approaching with long strides, apparently assuming that the tall, dark fellow was just some other guest with a room on that floor. By the time he saw the expression on Caroline's face and realized what was happening when she called out, *"Nick!* Thank *God!"* it was too late for him to protect himself. Nick's arcing fist caught him hard on the jaw and sent him staggering sideways.

"What the *hell*!" Greg muttered, finally recovering his balance. He stood there uncertainly, rubbing his jaw and sizing up the situation. Caroline was still slumped against the wall, but she was looking at her rescuer as though he'd come right down from heaven. The tall dark fellow who packed an unbelievable punch was standing there with murder in his face, obviously prepared to do more battle. In Greg's opinion, it was silly for two men to fight over the same woman. There were too many women in the world, enough to go around and then some. But now was the time to act on that philosophy, not discuss it, he decided sagely.

"Sorry, fellow," he told Nick, with an apologetic shrug. "Nobody including her mentioned she had a boyfriend." He edged around Nick cautiously and headed off down the hall to the elevator, not looking back. His instincts told him Nick wasn't a pugilist at heart.

Nick and Caroline both watched him all the way. Only when he'd stepped inside the elevator and was gone did Nick unclench his fists and Caroline straighten away from the wall, where she'd been experiencing to the fullest extent the feeling of being weak with relief.

"Nick, I just can't thank you enough—"

"Don't bother," he cut in harshly. "I'm the one who ought to be apologizing to that guy, not vice versa. The way you were acting in the casino, he had good reason to think what he did."

"But I tried to tell him—"

"You tried to tell him, all right, after you'd led him on all night!" Nick cut in angrily, reaching down to pick up her purse, lying open on the carpeted floor, where Greg had dropped it. "For God's sake, grow up, Caroline," he advised her bitterly, finding the key among the purse's contents and inserting it into the lock. "A man doesn't pay attention to a woman's saying no when she's been telling him yes all night in a hundred different ways." He opened the door with a savage twist of the knob, pushed it open and thrust the purse out at her.

Caroline was too battered and too grateful to defend herself. She took the purse from Nick and kept her eyes trained on it as she admitted shamefully. "You're right, Nick, it was all my fault." She looked up at him and then away from the harsh disapproval she saw in his face. "I wanted to show you that I could attract other men. Tonight I wouldn't have stayed so late with him in the casino, after the others were leaving, but you were still there." She lifted her shoulders in a little shrug. "I know it's silly, but I felt safe. Then I looked around and you were gone. It was the loneliest, scariest feeling I've ever had in my life. And then in the taxi—"

"For God's sake, Caroline, I don't want to hear all this!" Nick burst out. He looked down and saw that his fists were clenched again and made an abrupt production of jerking his left arm up, shoving aside his jacket sleeve and consulting his wristwatch. "Do you see what time it is? In about six hours we've both got to be up and packed and checked out of our rooms. Instead of standing here talking, you need to be getting some sleep.'' He shoved his hands into his pockets and then immediately took them out again.

Caroline submitted without resistance as he took her by the shoulders, turned her and gave her the gentlest possible push before he strode away down the hall, almost as quickly as he had come to her rescue minutes earlier. She turned and watched him, feeling the imprint of his hands on her bare shoulders and marveling that one man's touch could be so different from another's.

The morning was a rushed nightmare. Caroline turned off her little travel clock when it went off, fell back into her drugged sleep and awoke over an hour later, so that there was no time for breakfast. Not that food appealed to her with her throbbing head and queasy stomach, reminding her of all the daiquiris she had drunk the night before. She was sure she'd never drink another one the rest of her life.

Packing was a trial. Making no effort at neatness or organization, she jammed everything into her suitcase and hanging wardrobe and tried not to think about how she was going to have to manage to carry them herself in her shaky condition. She hadn't been able to get a response from the bell captain's number, the obvious reason being that everybody in her wing was checking out at the same time.

When a knock came to her door, her first thought was that it had to be Nick coming to her rescue again. She gave her appearance a hurried, despairing check in the mirror on her way to answer it, confirming what she already knew, that she looked as bad as she felt. Her disappointment was overwhelming and ridiculous, under the circumstances, when she saw not Nick outside her door, but a bellman.

''A gentleman downstairs sent me to get your bags, ma'am. He said you're supposed to be going to the airport in one of those limousines loading up right this minute.''

"And I still have to check out!" Caroline wailed.

"Don't worry. There's time," he soothed. "There's a mountain of luggage piled up down there and a long line ahead of you. You'll make it on that plane."

She was in the last limousine. Nick had obviously already gone on to the airport, but she didn't see him there, either. Most of the passengers had already gone through customs. By the time she got to the gate, the plane was boarding. The seat assignments were the same, and her Gretna friends were already seated at the front of the plane. They greeted her with noisy, teasing comments about how they were beginning to wonder whether she'd decided to take Greg up on his invitation to cruise with him on his sailboat.

Caroline glanced toward the back of the plane, searching for some sight of Nick, hoping that he wasn't able to hear the good-natured gibes from wherever he was sitting. She saw him in an aisle seat, his dark head bent forward, as though he was reading. He didn't look up in response to the silent, soulful message she sent back to him.

"Hurry up, Caroline, and sit down," Lisa was urging her. "Let's get this plane off the ground as soon as possible so that the hostess can start serving drinks. I'm dying for a Bloody Mary!"

The whole day was going to rank forever as one of the worst in her life. Waves of nausea hit her as the plane took off and left her weak and spent for most of the flight afterward. She dozed and kept her eyes closed when she wasn't sleeping just to avoid the sympathetic overtures from the Gretna party. Landing affected her the same way that taking off had. Her legs felt like jelly as she debarked from the plane.

"Gosh, honey, you look awful," Lisa commented sympathetically when they came out of the tunnel into the waiting area, which was crowded with friends and relatives awaiting the arrivals. "Are you sure you're feeling up to driving all the way across that causeway? Why not come on home with Pat and me. I'll bring you back over here to-morrow, and you can pick up your car, or, better still, one of us can drive it now."

"That's okay. I'm fine," Caroline demurred. "I'm just going to sit here a minute. There's a friend on the plane I want to say goodbye to."

She found an empty chair beyond the milling crowd and sank down in it gratefully while she waited for Nick. She wanted to thank him for sending the bellman that morning, thank him for the past night, thank him for everything. It didn't once occur to her as she watched for Nick's tall fig-ure to emerge from the tunnel that someone else might be watching for him, too. She hadn't considered the possibil-ity that he might have someone meeting him. The sound of his name being called out in a confident, masculine voice came as a paralyzing shock.

"Nick! Over here, you tanned son of a gun!"

Nick didn't even glance in her direction. He looked over the heads and shoulders of shorter people and headed out beyond the waiting room into the open concourse. Caro-line came to her feet and stretched and craned her neck to catch sight of him walking away beside a shorter sandy-haired man about his age. He was clapping Nick on the back and doing most of the talking. It was obvious from his manner that he was a good friend of Nick's.

Byron, his partner, Caroline concluded dully, taking a few steps out toward the concourse so that she could watch Nick walk away from her, watch his tall, lean figure grow smaller and smaller in the distance until the tears welling in her eyes made him and all the other hurrying people a watery blur. Unmindful of curious or incurious eyes, Caroline stood there and wept her heart out. It just wasn't right, she thought sadly, it wasn't fair, for things to end like this, for Nick to walk away from her without some word or gesture or even an expression on his face to give significance to what had happened between them. If she weren't so weak and tired and sick at heart, she'd go after him. Instead, she stood there and leaned on a cold plaster pillar until her legs felt strong enough for her to walk.

"Who're you looking for?" Byron wanted to know when Nick had picked his luggage off the moving track and stood there, frowning, while he searched the crowd for some sight of Caroline. He hadn't caught a glimpse of her since he'd gotten off the plane, and he'd been looking. He could tell at a glance when she got on the plane that she was suffering a terrific hangover. Her loud-mouthed friends' teasing hullabaloo, identifying the bearded fellow as some rich yachtsman, had served to squelch his sympathy. Now he was a little worried that she might be in a rest room, sick. He didn't know whether she had had someone meet her or had left her car at the airport on Monday. She was certainly in no condition to drive herself across the causeway.

"Oh, just a girl who was on the plane," he told Byron, not wanting to get into a discussion of Caroline. Byron would want to know right off whether Nick had taken her to bed, and that was a whole sensitive subject he didn't intend ever discussing with anyone, not even his best friend. It was more than a matter of protecting his own ego. He felt honor-bound to protect Caroline's privacy.

Byron pretended an exaggerated interest. "Blond, brunette or redhead? I'll help you look if you promise to introduce us."

"Not a chance."

The clipped reply made Byron raise his eyebrows a notch in surprise. "Sounds serious."

"You wouldn't be interested. She's a third-grade schoolteacher from across the lake over in Covington and not your type at all. But I don't see her around."

Ignoring Byron's openly curious expression, which accused him of being suspiciously closemouthed and defensive, Nick headed toward the checkout gate with his luggage, leaving his friend and partner to follow along. He wished like hell now that he hadn't been so protective of his new BMW, which he hadn't wanted to leave in an airport parking lot. His misguided forethought in arranging for Byron to be there at the airport to give him a ride seemed just one more evidence of bungling on his part.

Chapter Fourteen

A week later to the day, Caroline attended morning church services as usual and afterward sat out on the shady front veranda browsing through the Sunday paper with an empty feeling of leisure. Being alone was her own choice, since she'd declined an invitation from a fellow church member and friend to go home with her and her family for lunch. She still felt tired and listless after her Bahama vacation. It was too much of an effort to pretend to be cheerful and up.

The sound of a car on the street in front of her aunt's house drew an automatic, but incurious glance. The dark blue BMW moving at a sedate pace didn't excite any surprise or interest. Smart imports were more the rule than the exception on the affluent north shore.

Caroline sighed, gave herself another little push in the swing, and turned another page of the newspaper section she was thumbing through and then looked up again, this time with both surprise and interest, as the car turned into her driveway. She identified the driver with anything but equanimity as he opened the car door and stepped out, rising to his lanky height.

"Nick!"

She threw down the newspaper and was across the veranda and down the steps in a surge of gladness before her natural reticence took hold. "What a surprise," she called ahead of her, advancing along the bricked walk to the driveway at a more dignified pace.

Nick's stride covered the usual two-to-one ratio, so that he met her halfway between the steps and the driveway. She was every bit as softly feminine as Nick remembered, but the reality of her presence carried more impact than his memory. The gladness in her eyes that she was trying cautiously to restrain so matched what he was feeling that he was tempted to rush things and take her into his arms, right there in her front yard, in full sight of any neighbors who were peeking from behind lace curtains and window shades. But this was one time in his life he definitely didn't want to bungle things with a woman. Just because he'd thought everything out in the past week didn't mean that she had. He knew he needed to take it slow and easy and not get off on the wrong foot.

"It was such a nice day I decided to drive over here and see what Covington was like," he told her casually. "Once I was here, I figured I might as well try to look you up."

"Well, I'm certainly glad you did. Won't you come in? I was just sitting here reading the paper, working up enough energy to fix myself a glass of iced tea." She smiled at him, inviting him to share one of the pleasant, safe memories of their time together in Freeport, their lunch at Harry's American Bar when they'd both admitted their Southerner's passion for iced tea. "Would you like to join me?"

"I can't think of anything I'd like better."

They paused again on the veranda, where Nick gave Caroline the delicious opportunity to look at him while he glanced around, taking a closer look at the house and well-kept spacious grounds to reinforce his first impressions of solid, old-fashioned grace and dignity.

"This is really a nice old house. Nice neighborhood, too," he said approvingly. "It reminds me a lot of my parents' house in Natchez and the neighborhood I grew up in."

"It's awfully big for one person, as you'll see." She led him inside, her heart pounding with an unreasoning happiness that he looked so natural and right in her home surroundings. "As you know, these old houses usually have this big central hallway down the middle. Back here is the kitchen and sun porch, where my aunt and I practically lived. We almost never used the living room and dining room."

In the huge old-fashioned kitchen she took two tall iced-tea glasses from a glass-fronted cabinet, self-conscious that Nick was watching her every movement. Slowly the reality was sinking in that he was actually there, in Covington, on New Hampshire Street, in her house, and for no other reason than to see her!

"Why don't we sit out here on the sun porch?" she suggested, handing him his glass of iced tea and then exclaiming happily as she led the way, "You don't know how nice it is to see you."

Nick did know, and he had to stifle his impatience with the slow, polite pace. He took the wicker chair she designated, set at a comfortable conversational angle next to hers, and sipped his glass of tea.

"This is very good," he complimented, and glanced around at the cheerful wicker-furnished room with its profusion of plants. "I can see why you and your aunt preferred this room."

"Isn't it nice?" Caroline sighed and her expression saddened. "I hate to think of selling this house. I've thought of renting it and using the income to pay for something much smaller for myself, but that seems silly. I'd just have the worry and the upkeep."

"But then you'd also have the house to use as your home when you married and had children." Nick made a careful production of looking around the room again. "This would be a great house for raising kids."

They looked at each other in the silence. Nick made an impatient sound and set his iced tea down on the wicker-based glass table. Then he leaned forward and relieved Caroline of her glass so that he could take her hands in his.

"From the way we're both acting, you'd think I drove up outside in a horse and buggy instead of an automobile," he said dryly. "Sooner or later we're going to have to come out from behind our perfect Southern manners and say something, you know." He squeezed her hands and smiled when she returned the pressure. "What happened to you at the airport last Sunday, anyway? I looked for you and you'd just disappeared into thin air. I'd have gone back looking for you, but—" He paused as though having second thoughts about what he was going to say.

"But your partner Byron met you at the airport," Caroline finished softly for him. "And you probably didn't want to introduce me to him." She made a little rueful face. "The way I looked Sunday morning, I can't say I blame you."

Nick was staring at her. "How did you know? That Byron met me, I mean."

"I was waiting for you to come off the plane."

"Then why didn't I see you?"

"Because I was feeling so rotten I had to sit down, and there were people between us. Byron called to you as soon as you stepped out of the tunnel, and you went right over to him and walked on off." Caroline bit her bottom lip and dropped her eyelashes while she considered whether she was going to tell him the rest, about the way she had cried her eyes out.

"I wish you'd said something—no, I'm just as glad you didn't," Nick amended honestly, bringing Caroline's eyelashes flying up. "Of course, sooner or later I'm going to have to take my chances and introduce you to Byron."

Caroline's smile was tender. "I'm sure he won't be any more impressed with me than I was with him. You know—" A startled, considering expression came over her face and then was joined by caution. "Not to bring up painful subjects, but you know who he reminded me of?" she said hesitantly, and then wished that she'd kept the fleeting similarity to herself when she saw the grim line of Nick's jaw.

"Your bearded friend I had to take a swing at."

"It's probably just the hair color and the build," she said hastily, knowing that the likeness had had more to do with the male confidence Byron had exuded in his voice and laugh and manner. "And I wasn't meaning to insult your partner's character. Greg Norton was actually a very pleasant man. You said yourself that what happened was my fault."

Nick knew that what he was feeling was a combination of envy and jealousy, the first general and the second specific. He envied men like Byron and the Norton fellow their charisma and he was jealous at the idea of Caroline falling prey to their fatal charm.

"There're just some men, Caroline, who have what it takes with women, and it spoils them to the point that they really can't accept 'no' from a woman. Byron's one of those men, and—as much as I hate to admit it—so is that Greg Norton guy." He spoke the last three words as though they left a bitter taste in his mouth.

"And you don't think you are one of those men, do you, Nick?"

Nick met her gaze and melted at its softness, even if the tender emotion was motivated by pity.

"I know I'm not," he said with bleak honesty. He gave her hands another squeeze. "But look on the positive side of it. You can't expect a guy like that to be faithful to any one woman. There's too much temptation. It's the ordinary guys like me that made the good husbands and fathers. We're not exciting, but we're dependable. We earn a good living for our families, and we're there when we're needed."

Caroline's eyes had gradually widened with her surprise when she was able to detect no note of irony in Nick's voice. As incredible as it was, he seemed to be presenting a sincere case for his suitability as a husband and family man! She was temporarily at a loss as to what to say, but then Nick wasn't finished yet.

"As for sexual compatibility, that's something that a man and a woman can work on together. If the spark of attraction is there in the first place, that's the main thing that matters. Every time is not going to be earthshaking. It takes getting used to a person, finding out what he or she likes—" Nick moved restlessly, finding the going awkward. He hadn't meant just to plow in like this.

Caroline gently disentangled her hands and used them to frame his face. "Do you think that you and I have that spark of attraction, Nick?" she asked him with frank wistfulness.

Nick went down on his knees in front of her and put his arms around her waist. "In my opinion, we do," he replied soberly. "What do you think?" He closed his eyes with the sudden intensity of his pleasure as she caressed his face with tender fingertips.

"I think we do, too, Nick, but then I'm not sure you should put much account into my opinion." The shy teasing note in her voice brought his eyes open. "You're the only man I've never been able to say 'no' to. I guess I just didn't have the experience to know you weren't in the irresistible class of men. Greg Norton made my skin crawl when he touched me. And last Sunday, as sick as I was, I could still see that Byron isn't nearly as handsome as you are. He isn't as tall or dark or—"

Nick cut off the list of Byron's deficiencies with his lips and rediscovered the sweetness that didn't satisfy but only whetted his hunger for more of her.

"It'll be different when we make love the next time," he promised her unsteadily when he pulled back to take a breath. "But it'll be up to you when that happens. I'm not rushing you." Her stifled giggle plainly took him aback.

"May I remind you that you didn't exactly rush me into anything the first time," she pointed out teasingly, and kissed him lingeringly on the mouth, thrilled with her freedom and her budding confidence. "I was wondering if you'd like to see the rest of the house," she murmured against his lips, and felt his smile.

"On a Sunday afternoon? Won't the neighbors be shocked?"

"Very."

There was some shyness on her part as she led him up the stairs to her room. Nick's reaction was that of any normal man as he looked into her single woman's citadel with its chaste colors and feminine ruffles. When he paused at the door, she tugged at his hand and pulled him inside.

In the middle of the room he put his arms around her and held her carefully, gently, as though she were as breakable as one of her pretty porcelain figurines.

"This isn't the reason I came over here today, Caroline," he began hesitantly. "I want you to know that what happens—or doesn't happen, for that matter—won't make a whole lot of difference with my feelings.'' He stopped with an impatient sound as dismay crept across her face. ''As usual, I'm making a mess of explaining the way I feel. What I meant to say is that my feelings about you are more of a serious nature.''

''Nick!'' Caroline breathed, a smile of purest relief lighting her face. ''You had me really scared for a second or two there.''

His arms tightened around her, drawing her closer. He smiled a rueful, tender smile. ''You were thinking I just dropped over for iced tea? It was a good thing I didn't decide to be a courtroom attorney, wasn't it? I guess I'm a lot more comfortable with numbers than words.''

''It's not always necessary to say things.'' Caroline touched the clean, angular planes of his face with loving fingers.

Nick's mental resistance to the butterfly caresses was of short duration. He gave in to the temptation to postpone important explanations that would have to be made. Perhaps, he thought absently, he would be more eloquent after they made love.

''This time it will be different,'' he promised her, kissing her with restrained passion.

''Don't think about this time or last time or next time,'' Caroline begged him softly. ''Just make love to me, Nick.''

He followed her bidding and was that same passionate man who'd awakened the sensuous woman in her with his midnight lovemaking in the exotic setting of the hotel pool. Only now there was an added tenderness, a new intensity to the black fire in his eyes as he looked into hers, a thrilling note in his voice. Caroline was transported to a plane of joyous sensation that went far beyond physical pleasure. And for her, the intimacy afterward was a rare and precious delight all in itself.

"I think I felt the world move this time," she told Nick dazedly, lying close in his arms with her cheek against his bare, warm chest, so that she could feel the gradual slowing of his heartbeat. "You're a wonderful lover, Nick."

He hugged her hard in a spasm of tender gratitude. "I take that as the compliment it was intended, even though the lady has little basis for comparison. A fact that I find extremely pleasing, I might add."

She raised up her head and looked into his face searchingly. "Do you really?"

He nodded. "I do, really. And it's more than not having to give any thought to whether I'm measuring up to my competition. Although that's probably a factor. A man doesn't like the feeling of being rated on a scale of one to ten," he added with rueful honesty. "Sex is entirely different with you than it's ever been for me with any other woman. It's special. It has meaning other than pleasure."

"But couldn't that be true even if I had been to bed with another man before you?"

Nick gave her question careful thought. He wanted to be perfectly honest with her and with himself.

"I actually don't know. Maybe the fact that you were a virgin, and I was the first man, isn't responsible for the way I feel. All I can tell you is that I wanted to kill that guy Norton. When I saw you with him in the casino, it drove me out of my mind to think of him touching you."

Caroline touched his jaw with a tender forefinger to ease away the sudden grimness. "I've never been so happy to see anyone in my life as I was to see you that night. I'd been praying that by some miracle you would show up. Afterward, I wondered—"

"You wondered how I managed to come right out of the woodwork. When I left the casino, I was so mad at you and the Norton fellow that I told myself you deserved whatever happened to you. But then when I got back to the hotel, I

hid around in the shrubbery until you came along. I eaves-
dropped on your conversation, took the other direction
around to our wing and laid in wait for the two of you in the
stairwells. Just like the jealous boyfriend in some bad flick."
The account was humorous, but underlaid with flint that
matched the hardness in his face. Nothing about the memory provided Nick with amusement.

He changed their positions, easing Caroline back on the
pillow and turning and raising up on his elbow so that he
could look into her face. Feeling the gentleness of his touch
as he stroked her hair back from her face and shaped the
delicate curve of her cheek and jawline, she recalled the dull
thud of that same hand balled into a fist and connecting
with Greg Norton's jaw, recalled Nick's barely controlled
violence that had pulsed like a tangible presence in the hallway, the savagery in his face. The thought that jealousy of
her had raised that kind of powerful emotion in him was
awesome, but brought her no egotistical pleasure, only the
deepest apology.

"I'm really sorry, Nick, that I caused you to go through
those horrible feelings. But if you hadn't been there, I hate
to think what would have happened."

"Let's don't talk about it any more," he said brusquely.
"I don't even want to think about it. I was there and nothing happened."

Caroline responded to his hard, possessive kiss, thinking
that it was his way of placing a period at the end of an unpleasant chapter. But when he raised his head and she saw
the look in his eyes, she knew even before he said anything
else that it was also the opening of a new wonderful chapter he'd already worked out in his mind.

"And if I have anything to say about it, nothing is ever
going to happen between you and another man," he stated
firmly. "I'm not rushing you into anything. We can take our
time, get to know each other better, make sure that we're

really suited. You'll want to meet my family. My mother's going to be crazy about you, and you're going to get along fine with her. I already know that. I can warn you in advance she likes big weddings and lots of showers and parties—'' He broke off, puzzled and not sure whether he should be offended when Caroline burst into peals of laughter. He relaxed and grinned when she rubbed her nose against his.

"How many children do you think we ought to have, Nick?'' she asked him teasingly. "Surely you've worked all that out, too. Do you think I should continue teaching school after we start having a family? Or should I stay home and take care of the chil—''

Nick cut her off with a kiss. "I think one boy and one girl will be perfectly adequate, don't you?'' He sobered and met her gaze with earnest apology. "I know I'm approaching this all the wrong way, not saying the right things, being too serious and not romantic enough.''

"You're being you, Nick,'' she told him with love shining in her eyes. "I wouldn't have you any other way. You're exactly right for me. Somehow I knew that right from the first, but I didn't think I'd ever be lucky enough for you to want me.'' She blinked at the mist of tears in her eyes and added in a husky voice, "And I think one boy and one girl would be perfect.'' Her smile was secretive and shy. "After what just happened, one of them may even be on the way. Had you thought of that?''

Nick studied her bemused face, reading in it total lack of concern. "Aren't you worried?''

She shook her head slowly side to side on the pillow. "With any other man, I might be worried, but not with you. I trust you completely. I know that whatever happens, you'll take care of me.''

Those were precisely the words Nick wanted to hear. The fact that they came straight from her heart and she didn't

feel in the least diminished for saying them was only further proof that she was uncannily the perfect woman for
him. He wanted to take care of her on a permanent basis.
He wanted his ring on her finger, marking her as his own.
He wanted to share his life with her. He wanted to see her
grow large with his child when they both were ready to have
a family. But all in good time, he reminded himself. They'd
known each other such a short while.

"How's the time of the month?" Nick inquired, drawing back from her reluctantly.

Caroline looked thoughtful as she did the necessary calculation. "I suppose it's about perfect for making babies."

The soft complacency of her tone caused Nick to raise his
eyebrows with a hint of reproof. Caroline watched with a
secretive smile while he went through some mental process
of decision. His sudden rakish smile took her delightfully by
surprise. It transformed his sensitive, sober features. She'd
seen the same light in his eyes before in another entirely
different setting, when he was about to lay down a stack of
chips on a numbered square on a roulette table.

"I guess it's a little late to worry about it now," he said,
leaning over her, the fire of passion kindled in his dark eyes.
"I might just have to make an honest woman of you in a
hurry."

Caroline didn't offer any argument on either point. She
opened her arms and drew her reckless gambler down to her,
thrilled by his impetuousness as well as by the solid commitment behind it. A man like Nick didn't lightly throw
caution and good sense to the winds. It made Caroline
deeply happy to know that she was more than a considered
choice, although she was glad that she was that, too.

Silhouette Special Edition

COMING NEXT MONTH

THE ARISTOCRAT—Catherine Coulter
An arranged marriage in this day and age? There was no way Lord Brant Asher was going to marry Daphne, the ugly duckling. Until he found that the ugly duckling had grown into a beautiful swan.

A SLICE OF HEAVEN—Carole McElhaney
Lamont Cosmetics *had* to have Dr. Alex Harrison launch their new line. So Cass Mulcahy went to Texas to reason with him—and instead found herself losing all reason.

LINDSEY'S RAINBOW—Curtiss Ann Matlock
The Ingraham heiress suddenly found herself fighting for control of the family business. How dared Michael Garrity try to take it from her! Then Lindsey and Michael came face-to-face—and heart to heart.

FOREVER AND A DAY—Pamela Wallace
Stephen Kramer didn't want novelist Marina Turner to write her own screenplay. But she refused to let him turn her novel into a trashy teen flick. How could she prove to him that a collaboration would be profitable to both of them?

RETURN TO SUMMER—Barbara Faith
Fifteen years earlier Sarah had fled Mexico in shame. Now she was back, and history threatened to repeat itself. Was their future doomed by the past, or would it survive the dark secret she kept hidden from the man she loved?

YESTERDAY'S TOMORROW—Maggi Charles
Just one ride aboard *Alligator Annie* convinced Susan Bannister to stay in the alligator-infested backwater that was Florida State Park. She needed a distraction—and *Annie*'s silver-eyed captain filled the bill.

AVAILABLE NOW:

SOMETHING ABOUT SUMMER
Linda Shaw

EQUAL SHARES
Sondra Stanford

ALMOST FOREVER
Linda Howard

MATCHED PAIR
Carole Halston

SILVER THAW
Natalie Bishop

EMERALD LOVE, SAPPHIRE DREAMS
Monica Barrie

The Silhouette Cameo Tote Bag Now available for just $6.99

Handsomely designed in blue and bright pink, its stylish good looks make the Cameo Tote Bag an attractive accessory. The Cameo Tote Bag is big and roomy (13″ square), with reinforced handles and a snap-shut top. You can buy the Cameo Tote Bag for $6.99, plus $1.50 for postage and handling.

Send your name and address with check or money order for $6.99 (plus $1.50 postage and handling), a total of $8.49 to:

**Silhouette Books
120 Brighton Road
P.O. Box 5084
Clifton, NJ 07015-5084
ATTN: Tote Bag**

SIL—T–1R

The Silhouette Cameo Tote Bag can be purchased pre-paid only. No charges will be accepted. Please allow 4 to 6 weeks for delivery.

N.Y. State Residents Please Add Sales Tax

Silhouette ❤ Romance

**Enchanting love stories
that warm the hearts
of women everywhere.**

Silhouette ❤ Romance

FOUR UNIQUE SERIES
FOR EVERY WOMAN YOU ARE . . .

Silhouette Romance

Heartwarming romances that will make you
laugh and cry as they bring you all the wonder
and magic of falling in love.

6 titles per month

Silhouette Special Edition

Expanded romances written with emotion and
heightened romantic tension to ensure
powerful stories. A rare blend of passion and
dramatic realism.

6 titles per month

Silhouette Desire

Believable, sensuous, compelling—and
above all, romantic—these stories deliver
the promise of love, the guarantee
of satisfaction.

6 titles per month

Silhouette Intimate Moments

Love stories that entice; longer, more
sensuous romances filled with adventure,
suspense, glamour and melodrama.

4 titles per month

SIL-GEN-1RR